PENGUIN

The Little Man fro
AND
Monsieur Monde

Georges Simenon was born at Liège in Belgium in 1903. At six-teen he began work as a journalist on the *Gazette de Liège*. He has published over 212 novels in his own name, many of which be-long to the Inspector Maigret series, and his work has been pub-lished in thirty-two countries. He has had a great influence upon French cinema, and more than forty of his novels have been filmed.

Simenon's novels are largely psychological. He describes hidden fears, tensions and alliances beneath the surface of life's ordinary routine which suddenly explode into violence and crime. André Gide wrote to him: 'You are living on a false reputation – just like Baudelaire or Chopin. But nothing is more difficult than making the public go back on a too hasty first impression. You are still the slave of your first successes and the reader's idleness would like to put a stop to your triumphs there . . . You are much more important than is commonly supposed'; and François Mauriac wrote, 'I am afraid I may not have the courage to descend right to the depths of this nightmare which Simenon describes with such unendurable art.'

Simenon has travelled a great deal and once lived on a cutter, making long journeys of exploration round the the coasts of Northern Europe. A book of reminiscences, *Letter to My Mother*, was published in England in 1976. He is married and lives near Lausanne in Switzerland.

GEORGES SIMENON

The Little Man from Archangel

Translated by Nigel Ryan

AND

Monsieur Monde Vanishes

Translated by Jean Stewart

Penguin Books
in association with
Hamish Hamilton

Penguin Books Ltd, Harmondsworth, Middlesex, England
Viking Penguin Inc., 40 West 23rd Street, New York, New York 10010, U.S.A.
Penguin Books Australia Ltd, Ringwood, Victoria, Australia
Penguin Books Canada Limited, 2801 John Street, Markham, Ontario, Canada L3R 1B4
Penguin Books (N.Z.) Ltd, 182–190 Wairau Road, Auckland 10, New Zealand

Le petit homme d'Arkhangelsk first published 1957
This translation first published by Hamish Hamilton 1957
Published in Penguin Books 1964
Copyright © Georges Simenon, 1957

La fuite de Monsieur Monde first published 1952
This translation first published by Hamish Hamilton 1967
Published in Penguin Books 1970
Copyright 1952 by Georges Simenon
Translation copyright © Hamish Hamilton Ltd, 1967
All rights reserved

This edition in Penguin Books 1986

Made and printed in Great Britain by
Richard Clay (The Chaucer Press) Ltd,
Bungay, Suffolk

CONTENTS

The Little Man from Archangel

ONE

HE made the mistake of telling a lie. He felt it intuitively the moment he opened his mouth to reply to Fernand Le Bouc, and it was actually from timidity, lack of sangfroid, that he did not alter the words which came to his lips.

What he said was:

'She's gone to Bourges.'

Le Bouc asked, as he rinsed a glass behind his counter:

'Is La Loute still there?'

He replied without looking at him:

'I suppose so.'

It was ten o'clock in the morning, and as it was Thursday the market was in full swing. In Fernand's small bistro, almost entirely enclosed in glass, on the corner of the Impasse des Trois-Rois, five or six men were standing at the bar. At that moment it didn't matter who was there, but this was to become important, and Jonas Milk was later to try to identify each face.

Near him was Gaston Ancel, the red-faced butcher, in his blood-stained apron, who came in three or four times a morning for a quick glass of white wine and who had a particular way of wiping his mouth afterwards. He was constantly cracking jokes in his loud voice and, in his butcher's shop, used to tease the customers, while at the cash desk Madame Ancel apologized for her husband's bad language.

With Ancel, a cup of coffee in his hand, stood Benaiche, the policeman on duty at the market, known to everybody as Julien.

The little old man with the greenish coat and trembling hands must have spent the night outside, as he did most of the time. Nobody knew who he was, nor where he came from, but they had got used to him and he had ended up by becoming part of the surroundings.

Who were the others? An electrician whom Jonas didn't know, with someone whose pocket was stuffed with pencils, a foreman or the boss of some small business.

He never recalled the sixth, but he could have sworn that there was a figure between himself and the window.

At the tables behind the men, three or four women vegetable vendors dressed in black were eating sandwiches.

It was the same atmosphere as on any market morning, that is to say, on Tuesdays, Thursdays, and Saturdays. That Thursday a clear and warm June sun beat down full on the fronts of the houses, while under the huge roof of the covered-in market the people were bustling round the hampers and stalls in a bluish half-light.

Jonas had been anxious to avoid any hitch in his routine. As ten o'clock approached, his shop being free of customers, he had walked the five yards of pavement which separated him from Fernand's bistro, and from there, through the windows, he could watch the boxes of second-hand books arrayed against his shop front.

He could quite well not have opened his mouth. Some of them, at Fernand's, used to go up to the bar without a word, for it was known in advance what they were going to have. For him, it was invariably an espresso coffee.

Even so he said, possibly out of humility, or from a need to be precise : 'An espresso coffee.'

Practically everyone knew everyone else, and sometimes they didn't say good morning to each other, thinking they had already met earlier in the day.

Fernand Le Bouc, for example, was on his feet from three o'clock in the morning for the arrival of the lorries, and Ancel, the butcher, who awoke at five, had already been in at least twice to the bar.

The shops were clustered round the slate roof of the market, which had no walls and was bordered by a gutter littered with broken crates and packing-cases, rotting oranges, and trampled wood shavings.

The housewives who trod in this debris had no idea that the square, before their arrival, long before they were awake, had already seen, amidst the noise of heavy lorries and the smell of diesel oil, several hours of feverish existence.

Jonas was watching the coffee falling drop by drop from the

tiny chromium tap into the brown cup. He had another habit :
before being handed his coffee he would unwrap the transparent
paper containing his two pieces of sugar.

'Is Gina all right?' Le Bouc had asked him.

He had at first replied :

'She's all right.'

It was only because of what Fernand said next that he felt
obliged to tell a lie.

'I was wondering if she was ill. I haven't seen her this
morning.'

The butcher interrupted his conversation with the policeman
to remark :

'That's funny ! I haven't seen her either.'

Normally Gina did her shopping early, in bedroom slippers,
often without combing her hair, sometimes in a sort of flowered
dressing-gown affair, before the arrival of the crowds.

Jonas opened his mouth, and it was then that, despite his
instinct which told him it was unwise, he could not bring himself to change the words he had prepared :

'She's gone to Bourges.'

From time to time his wife did happen to go to Bourges to see
La Loute, as she was called, the daughter of the grain merchant
over the way, who had been living there for the past two years.
But almost invariably, as everyone must have known, she took
the half past eleven bus.

He was annoyed by his reply, not only because it was a lie
and he did not like telling lies, but because something told him
it was a mistake. Yet he couldn't reveal the truth, still less so
because at any moment Palestri, Gina's father, would be climbing out of his carrier-tricycle to come and have a drink.

It was the butcher who asked, addressing no one in particular :

'Does anybody really know what La Loute does in Bourges?'

And Fernand, indifferently :

'Whoring, probably.'

It was strange that the butcher should have been present just
then and taken part in the conversation, because his own
daughter Clémence, the eldest, the one who was married, had
been more or less mixed up in the affair.

11

Jonas was drinking his piping hot coffee in little sips, and the steam was misting over his glasses, which made him look different from the way he usually looked.

'See you later,' he said, placing the money on the linoleum of the counter.

Nobody had touched the books in the two boxes. It was rare for him to sell any during the market, and in the morning he hardly ever did more than a few exchanges. Mechanically he straightened the books, glanced at the window display and went into his shop where there was a sweet smell of dust and mildewed paper.

He hadn't dared to visit Clémence, the butcher's daughter, that night, but he had seen her a short time before, doing her shopping while she pushed the baby in its pram. He had gone up to her, deliberately.

'Good morning, Clémence.'

'Good morning, Monsieur Jonas.'

If she called him 'Monsieur', it was because she was twenty-two years old while he was forty. She had been at school with Gina. Both of them were born in the Place du Vieux-Marché. Gina was the daughter of Palestri, the greengrocer who, while his wife kept shop, delivered the orders in his three-wheeler.

'Nice day!' he had called out again, peering at Clémence through his thick lenses.

'Yes. It looks as if it's going to be a hot one.'

He bent over to look at the baby, Poupou, who was enormous.

'He's growing!' he observed gravely.

'I think he's cutting his first tooth. Give my love to Gina!'

All this was at about nine o'clock. As she uttered her last remark, Clémence had glanced into the back of the shop as if she were expecting to catch sight of her friend in the kitchen.

She hadn't seemed embarrassed. Pushing Poupou's pram before her, she had moved off towards Chaigne's, the grocer's, and gone into the shop.

That meant that Gina had lied, and Jonas had been almost sure of it since the evening before. He had shut the shop as usual at seven o'clock, or rather he had closed the door without removing the handle, for as long as he stayed up there was no point in missing a customer, and some of them used to come fairly late, to exchange their books from the lending library department. From the kitchen it was possible to hear the bell which the door operated when it opened. The house was narrow, one of the oldest in the Place du Vieux-Marché, with a coat-of-arms still carved on one of the stones and the date 1596.

'Dinner's ready!' Gina had called out, while at the same time he could hear a sizzling sound from the oven.

'I'm coming.'

She was wearing a tight-fitting red cotton dress. He had never dared to say a word to her on that subject. She had large breasts and ample haunches and she always made her dressmaker give her close-fitting dresses, beneath which she wore only a slip and a brassière, so that when she moved even the contour of her navel was outlined.

It was fish that she was cooking, and before it there was sorrel soup. They did not lay a tablecloth, but ate on the oil-cloth, and often Gina did not take the trouble to use dishes, merely putting the pans straight on the table.

Outside, with strangers, she was gay, with a naughty sparkle in her eye, a smile at her lips, and she laughed all the more for having dazzling white teeth.

She was the most beautiful girl in the Market, everyone was agreed, even if some of them made certain reservations or put on a disapproving expression when she came into the conversation.

Alone with Jonas her face would darken. Sometimes the transformation was noticeable the moment she crossed the doorway of the shop. Gaily she would throw out some last jest to a passer-by, and in the time it took her to turn round to enter the house, her face would lose all expression, her walk was no longer the same, and if she still swayed her hips it was with a sudden lassitude.

They sometimes ate without uttering a word, as quickly as possible, as if to have done with a chore, and he would still be at table when she began, behind his back, to wash up the dishes at the sink.

Had they spoken that evening? As he hadn't known then

what was afoot, he had not noticed, but he could not recall a single remark being said.

The old market-place, so teeming with life in the morning, was becoming very calm as the evening drew on, and there was only the sound of the cars passing in the rue de Bourges, more than a hundred yards away, a mother calling from time to time from her doorway to her children who had lingered on under the great slate roof.

While she was washing up she had announced:

'I'm going to see Clémence.'

The butcher's eldest daughter had married an employee at the waterworks two years before and it had been a fine wedding at which everyone from the square had been present. She was called Reverdi now and the young family lived in a flat in the rue des Deux-Ponts.

As he did not press his wife for an explanation she had added, turning her back to him:

'There's a film they want to see.'

On those occasions Gina would sometimes go and sit with the baby, which was only eight months old. She would take a book with her, and the key, and would not be back until midnight, for the Reverdis went to the second house.

The lights hadn't been turned on yet. There was enough daylight from the window and the door into the back yard. The air was bluish, of an extraordinary stillness, as it often is at the end of very long summer days. Some birds were twittering in the lime tree belonging to Chaigne the grocer, the only tree in the whole cluster of houses, in the middle of an enormous yard cluttered with barrels and crates.

Gina had gone upstairs. The staircase rose not from the kitchen, but from the little room separating it from the shop, which Jonas called his office.

When she came down again, she had neither hat nor coat on. Actually she only wore a hat for going to Mass on Sundays. On other days she went about bareheaded, her brown hair all untidy and, when it fell on her cheek, she would flick it back with a toss of her head.

'See you later!'

14

He had noticed that she was clutching close to her the large rectangular patent-leather bag which he had given her for her last birthday. He had almost called her back to say :

'You're forgetting your book.'

But she was already away down the pavement, walking briskly, almost running in the direction of rue des Prémontrés. He had remained a little while on the doorstep, following her with his eyes, then just breathing in the still warm air of the evening and watching the lamps which were beginning to light up, to the left, in the rue de Bourges.

What had he done until midnight? The boxes of books which he used to put on the pavement in the morning had been brought in. He had changed the places of a few volumes for no particular reason except to arrange them by the colour of their covers. He had switched on the light. There were books everywhere, on the shelves up to the ceiling and in piles on the counter, on the floor in the corners. They were second-hand books, nearly all of them worn, dirty, held together with sticking-paper, and he lent out more of them than he sold.

On one side of the room could be seen only old bindings, seventeenth- and eighteenth-century editions, an old La Fontaine published in Belgium, a Latin bible with curious engravings, some Bourdaloue sermons, five copies in different formats of *Télémaque*, then below, more recent collections such as *The History of the Consulate and the Empire* bound in dark green.

Jonas didn't smoke. Apart from coffee, he did not drink either. He only went to the cinema once in a while to please Gina. Did it really please Gina? He wasn't sure. She insisted on it, however, as she insisted on taking a *loge*, which to her way of thinking, showed that she was a married woman.

He didn't hold it against her. He didn't hold anything against her, even now. By what right could he have expected anything from her?

His little office-room, between the shop and the kitchen, had no window, received no air except through the two doors, and here, too, there were books up to the ceiling. But most important of all, in the desk at which he never sat down without a sigh of satisfaction, were his books on philately and his stamps.

For he wasn't just a second-hand bookseller. He was a stamp dealer. And if his shop, squeezed between the food shops of the Vieux-Marché, was not much to look at, the local shopkeepers would have been surprised to learn that the name of Jonas Milk was known by dealers and collectors the world over.

In a drawer within arm's reach were arranged precision instruments for counting and measuring perforations on stamps, studying the texture of the paper, the water-mark, discovering the defects of an issue or a surcharge, checking on the colours.

Unlike the majority of his colleagues, he bought everything that came to hand, sent abroad for those packets of five hundred, a thousand, and ten thousand stamps which are sold to beginners and are theoretically of no value.

These stamps, despite the fact that they had passed through the hands of experienced dealers, he studied one by one, rejecting nothing out of hand, and every now and then he would make a find.

A certain issue, for example, unremarkable in its ordinary form, became a rarity when the vignette was printed from a defective block; another had been printed in the experimental stage in a colour different from the one finally selected, and the specimens of it were great rarities.

Most dealers, like most collectors, confine themselves to one period, one type of stamp.

Jonas Milk had specialized in freaks, in stamps which, for one reason or another, were out of the ordinary.

That night, magnifying glass in hand, he had worked until half past eleven. At one moment he had made up his mind to shut up the house and go and fetch his wife. Clémence and her husband lived only ten minutes away, in a quiet street leading to the canal.

He would have enjoyed walking slowly back with Gina along the deserted pavements, even if they had found nothing to say to one another.

From fear of displeasing her, he did not carry out his project. She was quite capable of believing that he had gone out to watch over her, to make sure that she really had gone to Clémence's, or that she was coming home alone.

He went into the kitchen and lit the gas to make himself a cup of coffee, for coffee didn't prevent him from sleeping. He took the opportunity to tidy up, as his wife hadn't even put the pans away.

He didn't hold that against her either. Since his marriage the house had been dirtier than when he had lived in it alone and had managed for himself almost entirely. He did not dare tidy up or do any polishing in his wife's presence, for fear that she might take it as a reproach, but when she was not there, he always found something that needed attention.

That day for example, it was the oven, which she had not found time to clean and which smelt of herring.

Midnight sounded from St Cecilia's Church, at the far end of the Market, on the corner of the rue de Bourges. He calculated, as he had done on other occasions, that the cinema had finished at half past eleven, that it took the Reverdis barely twenty minutes to reach the rue des Deux-Ponts, that they would probably stop for a few minutes to chat with Gina.

She would not be home before half past twelve, and so, leaving one light on downstairs, he went up to the first floor, wondering whether his wife had taken a key with her. He did not remember seeing one in her hand. Usually it was almost a ritual act to slip it into her bag at the last moment.

It would only be a matter of going downstairs to open the door for her, since he wouldn't go to sleep yet. Their room had a low ceiling, with a large white-painted beam in the middle and a walnut bed, a double-fronted wardrobe with mirrors, which he had bought at the sale-room.

Even here the smell of old books came up from below mixed with the smells of the kitchen, that evening the smell of herrings.

He undressed, put on his pyjamas, and cleaned his teeth. There were two windows, and from the one giving on to the yard he could see, beyond the Chaignes' yard, the windows of the Palestris, Gina's family. They had gone to bed. Like the rest of the Market people they rose before daybreak and there was no light except in the window of Gina's brother Frédo's room. Had he, perhaps, just returned from the cinema? He was a strange fellow, with his hair growing low over his forehead, his

17

thick eyebrows, his way of looking at Jonas as if he could not forgive him for marrying his sister.

At half past twelve she hadn't come back and Milk, in bed but still wearing his glasses, was staring at the ceiling with melancholy patience.

He was not anxious yet. He might have been, for it had happened before that she did not come in, and once she had stayed away for three whole days.

On her return she had not given him any explanation. She could not have been very proud of herself, at heart. Her face was drawn, her eyes tired, she had seemed to carry an alien smell about her, but as she passed in front of him she had none the less drawn herself up to toss him a look of defiance.

He had said nothing to her. What was the use? What could he have said? On the contrary, he had been softer, more attentive than usual, and two evenings later it was she who had suggested a walk along the canal, where she had slipped her hand into his arm.

She was not a bad girl. She did not hate him, like her brother Frédo. He was convinced that she was doing her best to be a good wife, and that she was grateful to him for having married her.

Twice or three times he gave a start on hearing noises, but it was the mice downstairs, of which he had given up trying to rid himself. All round the Market, where hung such delicious smells, where so many appetizing victuals were piled, the walls were riddled with warrens forming a secret city for the rodents.

Fortunately both rats and mice found sufficient to eat outside not to be tempted to set on the books, so that Jonas no longer bothered with them. Occasionally the mice ran about the bedroom while he and Gina were in bed, they came right up to the foot of the bed as if curious to see human beings sleeping, and they had lost their fear of the human voice.

A motor-bike belonging to the young Chenu, from the fishmonger's, came to a halt on the far side of the square, then the silence returned and the church clock struck the quarter, then one o'clock, and only then did Jonas get up and go over to the straw-bottomed chair where he had laid his clothes.

The first time it had happened, he had run about the town, ashamed, searching in the dark corners, looking into the window of the only bar still open in the neighbourhood of the factory.

Today there was a possible explanation. Perhaps Poupou, Clémence's baby, was ill and Gina had stayed on to help out?

He dressed, still hoping, went downstairs, glanced into the kitchen which was empty and smelt of cold herring. He picked up his hat on his way through his office, walked out of the house locking the door behind him.

And what if Gina hadn't got a key? If she came back while he was away? If she was returning from Clémence's by another route?

He decided to turn the key in the lock once more, so that she could let herself in again. The sky was clear above the vast slate roof, with a few clouds gleaming in the moonlight. Some way off a couple were walking along the rue de Bourges and the air was so still that in spite of the distance, he could hear each remark they exchanged.

As far as the rue des Deux-Ponts he met nobody, saw only one lighted window, possibly someone waiting like him, or an invalid, someone in pain?

He was disturbed by the noise of his shoes on the pavings and it gave him the feeling of an intruder.

He knew the Reverdis' house, the second on the left after the corner, and he could see at once that there was no light on the floor the young couple occupied.

What was the use of ringing, starting a disturbance, giving rise to questions which no one could answer?

Perhaps Gina had gone back home after all. It was more than likely that she had lied, that she had not been to Clémence's, that the young couple had not been to the cinema at all.

He remembered that she had not taken a book with her as she used to do when she went to look after Poupou and it had also struck him that she took her black patent-leather bag.

For no particular reason he stood for a good five minutes on the edge of the pavement, gazing at the windows behind which there were people sleeping, then he moved off almost on tip-toe.

When he reached the Place du Vieux-Marché an enormous lorry from Moulins, the first of the day, was almost blocking the rue des Prémontrés and the driver was asleep in the cab with his mouth wide open.

In his doorway he called:

'Gina!'

As if to conjure fate, he tried to speak in a natural voice, without betraying anxiety.

'Are you there, Gina?'

He locked the door again and bolted it, hesitated whether to make a fresh cup of coffee, decided against it, and went up to his room and got back into bed.

If he slept, he was not conscious of doing so. He had left the light on for no reason and an hour went by before he removed his spectacles, without which he could see only a vague, misty world. He heard some other lorries arriving, the slamming of doors, crates and boxes being stacked on the ground.

He also heard Fernand Le Bouc opening his bar, then the first vans of the retailers.

Gina hadn't come back. Gina wouldn't be coming back.

He must have dropped off to sleep, because he didn't notice the transition from night to day. At one moment there was still a darkness pierced by the lights of the Market, then suddenly there had been sunshine in the bedroom and on the bed.

With a hesitant hand he felt the place beside him, and, of course, it was empty. Usually Gina was warm, lying like a gun dog, and she had a strong feminine smell. Sometimes in her sleep she would turn over sharply and, one thigh over Jonas's thigh, press on it hard, breathing more and more heavily as she did so.

He decided not to go down, nor to get up before the right time, to follow the same routine as every other day. He did not go to sleep again and, to keep his mind occupied, he listened to the noises of the market, which he tried to identify with the same meticulousness as he applied to the scrutiny of a postage stamp.

He, too, had practically been born here. Not quite. Not like the others. But they talked to him in the mornings as they talked to one another, with the same familiar friendliness, and he had his place, so to speak, at Le Bouc's counter.

Twice he heard Ancel the butcher's voice on the pavement arguing with a man delivering some quarters of beef, and there was a row about some mutton which was fairly infuriating him. Chaigne's grocery opposite opened later, and the next house belonged to the Palestris where Angèle, Gina's mother, was already at work.

It was she who attended to the business. Louis, her husband, was a pleasant fellow, but he could not stop himself from drinking. So to keep him occupied they had bought him a three-wheeler and he delivered the orders, not only for his own shop, but for the market people who had no means of transport.

It used to humiliate him. He didn't admit it. On the one hand he was content to spend the whole day out of his house, free to drink at his leisure. But on the other hand he was no dupe, and realized that he didn't count, that he was no longer the real head of the family, and this made him drink all the more.

What ought Angèle to have done? Jonas had wondered to himself and had not found the answer.

Gina had no respect for her father. When he came to see her between errands, she would put the bottle of wine and a glass down on the table, with the words:

'There! Is that what you want?'

He would pretend to laugh, to take it as a joke. He knew it was meant seriously and yet he did not resist the need to fill his glass, though he might call out on leaving:

'You're a proper bitch!'

Jonas tried not to be present when that happened. In front of him, Palestri felt even more humiliated, and that was perhaps one of the reasons why he had nearly as big a grudge against him as his son had.

He rose at six, went down to make his coffee. He was always the first one down and in summer his first action was to open the door into the yard. Often Gina wasn't to be seen downstairs until about half past seven or eight when the shop was already open.

She liked to hang about in dressing-gown and slippers, her

face glistening after her night's sleep, and it did not disturb her to be seen thus by strangers; she would go and stand on the doorstep, walk past the Chaignes' on her way to say good morning to her mother, return with vegetables or fruit.

' 'Morning, Gina!'

' 'Morning, Pierrot!'

She knew everybody, the wholesalers, the retailers, the heavy-lorry drivers as well as the country women who came to sell the produce from their gardens or their backyards. As a little girl she used to run about with bare behind between the crates and baskets.

She was no longer a little girl now. She was a woman of twenty-four and her friend Clémence had a child, while others had two or three.

She had not come home and Jonas, with careful movements, was setting down his boxes in front of the shop window, re-arranging the price tickets and going over to the baker opposite to buy some *croissants*. He always bought five, three for himself, two for his wife, and when they automatically wrapped them up for him in brown tissue paper he did not protest.

He could easily throw away the two extra *croissants*, and this gave him the idea of saying nothing, which, to him, meant not admitting that Gina had gone off without telling him.

Besides, had she really gone off? When she left in the evening she was only wearing her red cotton dress, only had with her her patent-leather bag.

She might come back in the course of the day, at any moment. Perhaps she was already there?

Once again he tried to conjure the fates.

'Gina!' he called, going inside, a note almost of delight in his voice.

Then he ate alone, on a corner of the kitchen table, washed up his cup, his plate, and swept up the crumbs from the *croissants*. To set his mind at rest he went upstairs to make sure that his wife's suitcase was still in the cupboard. She only possessed that one. The day before, when he was having his coffee at Le Bouc's, for example, she could have taken her case out of the house and left it somewhere.

22

The postman called and it whiled away a little time reading the post, glancing cursorily over the stamps he had ordered from Cairo.

Then all of a sudden it was ten o'clock and he went round to Fernand Le Bouc's, as he did every other morning.

'How's Gina?'

'She's all right.'

'I was wondering if she was ill. I haven't seen her this morning.'

Why hadn't he answered anything else rather than:

'*She's gone to Bourges.*'

He was angry with himself for this clumsy mistake. She might come back in half an hour, in an hour, and how would his reply be interpreted then?

A girl who sold flowers not far from the shop came rushing in to change her book, as she did every morning, for she read a novel a day.

'Is this a good one?'

He said it was. She always chose the same kind of book whose gaudy covers were a guarantee of the contents.

'Gina not here?'

'Not at the moment.'

'Is she all right?'

'Yes.'

An idea suddenly occurred to him, which made him blush, for he was ashamed of distrusting other people, of what he called evil thoughts about them. As soon as the little florist departed he went up to his room, opened the wardrobe with the mirrors, at the back of which, under his and Gina's clothes which were hanging there, he kept a steel strong-box bought at Viroulet's.

The safe was in its place and Jonas had to make an effort to go any further, take the key from his pocket, and insert it in the lock.

If Gina had returned at that moment he would have fainted for shame.

But Gina did not return and no doubt she would not be returning so soon.

The transparent envelopes containing his rarest stamps, among others the Trinidad five cents blue of 1847, with the picture of the steamer *Lady McLeod*, had vanished.

TWO

HE was still standing in front of the wardrobe with the mirrors, with beads of sweat on his upper lip, when he heard footsteps in the shop, then in the little room. It was rare for him to close the outside door in summer, for the house, built in depth, was ill-ventilated. Standing stock still, he waited for the male or female voice of a customer to call:

'Anyone there?'

But the steps went on into the kitchen, where the visitor waited before returning to the foot of the stairway. It was a man's step, heavy, dragging slightly, and Jonas, rooted to the spot, wondering whether the stranger was going to climb the stairs, when the harsh voice of his father-in-law grated up the staircase:

'You there, Gina?'

Why was he seized with panic, as if he had been caught out? Without shutting the steel box, he pushed the wardrobe doors to, hesitating whether to go down or let it be thought that there was nobody at home. A footstep sounded on the bottom stair. The voice called again:

'Gina!'

Only then did he stammer out:

'I'll be down in a moment.'

Before leaving the room he had time to see in the mirror that his face had reddened.

By that hour, however, Palestri was not yet drunk. Even in the evenings he never reached the point of reeling. Early in the morning his eyes would be slightly red and bleary, and he had a tumbledown look, but after a glass or two of *marc*, or rather *grappa*, its Italian version, he was no longer entirely steady.

He did not only drink *grappa*, which Le Bouc bought especially for him, but everything he was offered or whatever he could find in the other bars where he dropped in.

When Jonas came down, his pupils were beginning to lose their lustre and his face was flushed.

'Where's Gina?' he asked, looking in the direction of the kitchen where he had expected to find her.

It surprised him as well to see his son-in-law coming down from the first floor when there was nobody downstairs, and he seemed to be waiting for some explanation. Jonas had not had the time to reflect. Just as a short while before at Fernand's, he had been caught on the wrong foot. And since he had mentioned Bourges once already, was it not better to continue?

He felt a need to defend himself, even though he had done nothing. Palestri over-awed him with roughness, his great desiccated, gnarled body standing there.

He stammered :

'She's gone to Bourges.'

He realized that he was not convincing, that his eyes, behind the thick lenses, must appear to be avoiding the other's gaze.

'To see La Loute?'

'That's what she said.'

'Did she say good-bye to her mother?'

'I don't know. ...'

Like a coward, he was retreating towards the kitchen, and as Gina used to do, took the bottle of red wine from the cupboard, put it on the wax tablecloth with a glass beside it.

'When did she go?'

Later he was to ask himself why, from that moment onwards, he acted as if he were guilty. He remembered, for example, his wife's suitcase in the cupboard. If she had gone the day before to see her friend, she would have taken the case with her. So she must have left the house that same day.

That is why he replied :

'This morning.'

Louis had stretched out his hand to the glass he had poured himself, but seemed to be hesitating suspiciously before drinking from it.

'By the 7.10 bus?'

There was only that one before the half past eleven bus, which had not yet gone through. So Jonas was forced to answer yes.

It was stupid. He was becoming caught up in a web of lies, which were bound to lead to others, and from which he would never be able to extricate himself. At seven in the morning the market was almost deserted. It was the time of the lull between the wholesalers and the ordinary customers. Gina's mother would certainly have seen her daughter passing, and in any case the girl would have gone into the shop to say good morning to her.

Other people would have seen her as well. There are some streets where people stay in their houses as if in water-tight compartments and each scarcely knows his neighbour. The Place du Vieux-Marché was different, it was rather like a barracks where the doors remained open and people knew from hour to hour what was going on in the family next door.

Why did Palestri eye his son-in-law suspiciously? Wasn't it because he looked as if he were lying? At all events he emptied his glass, in a gulp, wiped his mouth with his usual gesture, similar to that of the butcher, but did not go away immediately: he was gazing round him at the kitchen and Jonas thought he understood the reason for the contraction of his eyebrows.

There was something unnatural, that morning, in the atmosphere of the house. It was too tidy. There was nothing lying about, there was no sense of the disarray that Gina always left behind her.

' 'Bye!' he finally mumbled, heading for the door of the shop. He added, as if for his own benefit:

'I'll tell her mother she's gone. When's she coming back?'

'I don't know.'

Would it have been better for Jonas to have called him back and confessed the truth, told him that his daughter had gone off, taking his valuable stamps with her?

The ones downstairs, in the drawers of the desk, were only the common or garden stamps he bought by the packet, and the ones he had already sorted, which he was swapping or selling to schoolboys.

The strong-box, on the other hand, contained till the day before a veritable fortune, the rare stamps which he had discovered, by dint of patience and flair, over more than twenty-five years, for he had first taken an interest in stamps while at school.

One specimen alone, the pearl of his collection, a French stamp of 1849 with the head of Ceres on a bright vermilion ground, was worth, at the catalogue valuation, six hundred thousand francs.

The Trinidad stamp, with the steamer *Lady McLeod,* was assessed at three hundred thousand francs, and he possessed others of considerable value, such as the Puerto Rican two peseta pink with the overprinted surcharge, for which he was being offered thirty-five thousand francs.

He had never calculated the total value of his collection, but it could not have been much less than ten million francs.

The people of the Old Market had no suspicion of this wealth. He never spoke of it to anyone and he did not mind being thought a crank.

One evening, however, when one of the catalogues was lying about on the desk, Gina had begun idly turning over its pages.

'What does that mean, *double surcharge*?'

He had explained it to her.

'And *sep-ol*?'

'Sepia and olive colour.'

'And 2 *p*?'

'Two pesetas.'

The abbreviations intrigued her.

'It's very complicated!' she had sighed.

She was on the point of shutting the catalogue when she had asked one last question.

'And the figure 4,000 in this column?'

'The value of the stamp.'

'You mean that stamp is worth four thousand francs?'

He had smiled.

'Certainly.'

'Do all the figures in this column stand for the value of the stamps?'

'Yes.'

She had turned over the pages of the catalogue with renewed interest.

'Here it says 700,000. Are there really stamps worth seven hundred thousand francs?'

'Yes.'

'Have you got one?'

'I haven't got that one, no.'

'Have you other ones as valuable?'

'Not quite.'

'Some very valuable ones?'

'Some fairly valuable.'

'Is that what you bought a steel safe for?'

This happened the previous winter and he remembered that it was snowing outside, that he could see a white rim round the window panes. The stove was roaring in the little room. It must have been about eight o'clock in the evening.

'Goodness!'

'What?'

'Nothing. I'd never have thought it.'

In the Place du Vieux-Marché he had the reputation of having money and it would have been difficult to trace the origin of this rumour. Perhaps it was due to the fact that he had remained a bachelor for a long time? Ordinary folk naturally imagine that a bachelor puts money to one side. Apart from that, before marrying Gina, he used to eat in the restaurant, at Pepito's, another Italian, in the first house in the rue Haute, past the Grimoux-Marmion grocery, which stood on the corner of the square.

Probably for these tradespeople who were in and out of his shop all day, he seemed something of an amateur. Could anyone really make a living buying, selling, and hiring out old books? Weren't there times when an hour or even two went by without any customer going into his shop?

So, since he was alive, and since, moreover, he had a woman in two hours a day and for the whole morning on Saturdays, he must have had money.

Had Gina been disappointed that he didn't change any of his

habits after marrying her? Had she been expecting a new existence?

He hadn't asked himself the question, and only now did he realize that he had been living without noticing what was happening around him.

If he looked in the drawer of the till, where he kept the money in a big wallet grey with use, would he find the right amount there? He was almost sure he would not. Gina had sometimes pilfered small amounts, rather in the manner of a child wanting to buy sweets. At first she contented herself with a few hundred franc pieces, which she took from the drawer with the compartments where he kept the change.

Later on she had ventured opening the wallet and he had sometimes noticed that a thousand franc note would be missing.

Yet he gave her plenty of money for housekeeping, never refused her a new dress, underclothing, or shoes.

Perhaps at first she acted merely on a private whim, and he suspected that she had taken money in the same way from her parents' till when she lived with them. Only it must have been more difficult then, for Angèle, despite her jolly, motherly air, had a sharp eye for money. He had never mentioned it to Gina. He had thought a lot about it, and had finally come to the conclusion that it was for her brother that she stole in this way. She was five years older than he and yet people could sense an affinity between them of the kind that is normally only found between twins. There were times when one might have thought Frédo was in love with his sister, and that she reciprocated it.

It was enough for them, wherever they were, to exchange a glance to understand one another, and if Gina frowned her brother became as anxious as a lover.

Was that why he disliked Jonas? At the wedding he had been the only one not to congratulate him, and he had left right in the middle of the reception. Gina had run after him. They had whispered together a long time in the corridor of the Hôtel du Commerce where the banquet had taken place. When she came back, still dressed in white satin, it was obvious that she had been crying, and she had at once poured herself out a glass of champagne.

At the time Frédo was only seventeen. Their marriage had taken place two weeks before Clémence Ancel, their bridesmaid, had hers.

Resigned, he opened the drawer with his key, picked up the wallet and discovered to his surprise that there was not a single note missing.

It was explicable. He hadn't thought. The day before Gina had not left until after dinner and, up till the last moment, he might have had to open the cash drawer. With the stamps it was another matter, as sometimes he went a whole week without touching the steel box.

There were still some details which he did not understand, but they were material details of no great importance. For example, he always carried his keys in his trouser pocket, attached to a silver chain. When had his wife managed to get hold of them without his knowing? Not at night, because he slept more lightly than she did, and besides he was the first down in the morning. Ocassionally, it was true, in order not to wake her, he would go downstairs in pyjamas and dressing-gown to make his coffee. It had not happened the day before, but the day before that, and he hadn't touched the safe since then.

'Have you got a book about bee-keeping, please?'

It was a boy about twelve years old, who had just come in, and spoken in an assured voice, his face covered in freckles, his copper-coloured hair streaked with sunlight.

'Are you thinking of keeping bees?'

'I found a swarm in a tree in the vegetable garden and my parents are going to let me make a hive, provided I do it with my own money.'

Jonas had fair ginger hair too, with freckles on the bridge of his nose. But at this child's age he must have already worn glasses as thick as the ones he was wearing now.

He had wondered to himself sometimes whether on account of his short-sightedness he saw things and people differently from others. The question intrigued him. He had read, for example, that the various species of animals do not see us as we really are, but as their eyes show us to them, and that for some we are ten times as tall, which is what makes them so timid when we approach them.

Does the same phenomenon occur with a short-sighted person, even though his sight is more or less corrected by spectacles? Without glasses the world was to him only a more or less luminous cloud in which floated shapes so insubstantial that he could not be sure of being able to touch them.

His spectacles, on the other hand, revealed to him the details of objects and faces as if he had been looking at them through a magnifying glass or as if they had been engraved.

Did this cause him to live in a separate sphere? Were these spectacles, without which he had to grope his way, a barrier between himself and the world outside?

In a shelf of books about animals he finally found one on bees and bee-hives.

'How about that one?'

'Is it expensive?'

He consulted, on the back cover, the pencilled price.

'A hundred francs.'

'Would you let me have it if I paid half next week?'

Jonas didn't know him. He was not from the neighbourhood. He was a country boy whose mother had probably come into the market with vegetables or poultry.

'You can take it.'

'Thank you. I will be in again next Thursday without fail.'

Outside in the sun of the street and the shade of the covered market the clientèle had changed insensibly. Early in the morning there was a preponderance of working-class women doing their shopping after taking their children to school. It was also the time for the vans from the hotels and restaurants.

As early as nine o'clock, and especially around ten o'clock the shoppers were better dressed, and at eleven some of them brought their maids with them to carry the parcels.

The shavings in the gutter, trampled underfoot, were losing their golden hue to turn brown and sticky, and were now becoming mixed with outer leaves of leeks, carrots, and fish heads.

Gina had taken no change of clothes with her, no underclothes, not even a coat, though the nights were still cool.

If she had been intending to stay in the town, on the other hand, would she have had the nerve to take his most valuable stamps?

After seven o'clock in the evening, there were no more buses to Bourges, nor for anywhere else, only a train at 8.52 which connected with the Paris train, and, at 9.40, the slow train from Moulins.

The station employees knew her, but he didn't dare go and question them. It was too late. He had twice spoken of Bourges and he was obliged to stick to it.

Why had he behaved in this way? He could not account for it. It was not from fear of ridicule, because everyone, not only in the Place·du Vieux-Marchè, but throughout the town, knew that Gina had had many lovers before marrying him. It could not have passed unnoticed, either, that since her marriage she had had several adventures.

Was it a sort of shame that had prompted him to reply, first to Le Bouc, then to Palestri:

'She has gone to Bourges'?

Shame which was born of shyness? What happened between him and Gina did not concern anybody else, and he believed himself to be the last person to have any right to discuss it.

But for the disappearance of the stamps he would have waited all day, then all night, hoping from one moment to the next to see her return like a dog which has run away.

The room upstairs had not been done, and the strong box had not been closed, so he went up, made his bed as meticulously as when he was a bachelor and the maid was away.

It was as a maid that Gina had come into the house. Before her there had been another, old Léonie, who at the age of seventy still put in her eight or nine hours a day with different employers. In the end her legs had swollen up. Latterly she could hardly manage to climb the stairs, and as her children, who lived in Paris, did not care to look after her, Dr Joublin had put her in a home.

For a month Jonas had been without anyone, and it didn't worry him unduly. He knew Gina, like everyone else, through having seen her pass by, or from selling her an occasional book.

At that time she had behaved in a provocative manner with him as she used to with all men, and he blushed every time she came into his shop, especially in summer, when it seemed to him that she left behind her a trace of the smell of her armpits.

'Haven't you got anyone yet?' Le Bouc had asked him one morning when he was having his coffee in the little bar.

He had never understood why Le Bouc and the others from the Square did not use the familiar '*tu*' with him, for they nearly all used it among themselves, calling one another by their Christian names.

They didn't call him Milk, however, almost as if it were not his name, nor Monsieur Milk, but, nearly always, Monsieur Jonas.

And yet at the age of two he was living in the Square, just next door to Ancel's, the butcher's, and it was his father who had converted the fishmonger's, '*À La Marée*', now kept by the Chenus.

It was not because he had not been to the communal school either, like most of them, but to a private school, then to the *lycée*. The proof was that they were already addressing his father before him as Monsieur Constantin.

Fernand had asked him:

'Haven't you got anybody yet?'

He had replied no, and Le Bouc had leant over his counter.

'You ought to have a word or two with Angèle.'

He had been so surprised that he had asked, as if there could have been two Angèles:

'The greengrocer?'

'Yes. She's having trouble with Gina. She can't do anything with her. I think she wouldn't be sorry to see her working outside so that someone else could break her in.'

Up till then Gina had been more or less helping her mother in the shop, and slipping off at every opportunity.

'You wouldn't like to talk to her yourself?' Jonas had suggested.

It seemed to him incongruous, indecent almost, on his part, as a bachelor, although he had no ulterior motives, to go and ask a woman like Angèle to let him have her daughter for three hours a day.

'I'll have a word with her father. No! I'd better see Angèle. I'll give you her reply tomorrow.'

To his great surprise, the reply next day was yes, or as good as yes, and he was almost frightened by it. Angèle had told Le Bouc, to be precise :

'*Tell that Jonas I'll come round and see him.*'

She had come, late one afternoon during a slack period, had insisted on seeing over the house, and had discussed wages.

That meant changing his habits, and it was not without reluctance that he gave up going at half past twelve and sitting in Pepito's little restaurant, where he had his own pigeon-hole for his table-napkin and his bottle of mineral water.

'After all, if she's going to work at all, it might as well be worth her while. It's high time she got down to some cooking, and we hardly have time in our place at midday to eat more than a piece of sausage or some cheese.'

Didn't Gina resent his having engaged her, at first? Anyone would have thought she was doing everything possible to make herself unbearable so that he would throw her out.

After a week with him she was working from nine o'clock in the morning until one. Then Angèle had decided :

'It's absurd to cook for one person alone. It costs no more to do it for two. She might just as well have lunch with you and do the washing-up before leaving.'

Suddenly his life had changed. He didn't know everything, because he didn't hear the gossip, perhaps also because people didn't speak freely in front of him. He didn't understand, at first, why Gina was always in low spirits and why she would suddenly turn aggressive only, soon afterwards, to burst into tears in the middle of her housework.

It was then three months since Marcel Jenot had been arrested and Jonas hardly ever read the papers. He had heard his name mentioned at Le Bouc's, for it had created quite a sensation. Marcel Jenot, the son of a dressmaker who worked for most of the women of the Market, including the Palestris, was under-cook at the Commercial Hotel, the best and most expensive in town. Jonas must have seen him at some time or other without paying any attention. His photograph, in the papers, showed a young man with a high forehead and a serious expression with, however, a rather disquieting curl to his lip.

At twenty-one he had just finished his military service in Indo-China and was once more living with his mother in the rue des Belles-Feuilles, the street beyond Pepito's restaurant.

Like most young men of his age he owned a motor-cycle. One evening on the Saint-Amand road, a large car-load of Parisians had been stopped by a motor-cyclist who seemed to be asking for help and then, brandishing an automatic, had demanded money from the occupants, after which he had punctured the four tyres of the car and made off.

The motor-cycle's number plate, at the time of the hold-up, was covered with a layer of black paint. How had the police managed to trace it to Marcel? The papers must have explained it, but Jonas didn't know.

The investigation was under way when Gina had gone into service with him, and a month later the trial had taken place at Montluçon.

It was Le Bouc who had told the bookseller about it.

'How is Gina?'

'She does her best.'

'Not too upset?'

'Why?'

'Marcel is being tried next week.'

'Which Marcel?'

'The one in the hold-up. It's her boy friend.'

She actually had to stay away for a few days and when she came back to resume work, it was a long time before she opened her mouth.

That had been nearly three years ago now. A year after she had joined him as a housemaid Jonas married her, surprised at what was happening to him. He was thirty-eight and she twenty-two. Even when, in the sunlight, her body almost naked under her dress, she used to move to and fro around him and he breathed her smell, he had never made a single ambiguous gesture.

35

At Le Bouc's they had adopted the habit of asking him, with a smile at the corner of the mouth:

'Well, well! And how's Gina?'

He would reply, naïvely:

'She's very well.'

Some of them went so far as to give him a wink, which he would pretend not to see, and others seemed to suspect him of keeping something up his sleeve.

By keeping his ears pricked and asking a few questions here and there, he could easily have found out the names of all the lovers Gina had had since she had begun to knock about with men at the age of thirteen. He could also have found out about what had happened between her and Marcel. He was not unaware that she had been questioned several times by the police in the course of the inquiry and that Angèle had been summoned by the magistrate.

What would be the use? It was not in his character. He had always lived alone, without imagining that he would one day be able to live otherwise.

Gina did not keep house as well as old Léonie. Her tablecloths, when she took the trouble to use them, were seldom clean and, if she sometimes sang as she worked, there were days when her face remained set, her mouth truculent.

Often, in the middle of the morning, she would disappear on the pretext of doing some shopping up the road and come back, with no apology, two hours later.

Even so, hadn't her presence in the house become essential to Jonas? Had there been a conspiracy, as some people claimed, to force his hand?

One afternoon Angèle had called in the clothes she always wore during the day in her shop, for she only really dressed up on Sundays.

'Well now, Jonas!'

She was one of the few people not to call him Monsieur Jonas. True, she addressed most of the customers in the most familiar manner.

'Don't touch those pears, love!' she would shout at Dr Martroux's wife, one of the most prim and proper women in the town. 'When I go to see your husband I don't play with his instruments.'

That day she strode into the kitchen and sat down on a chair.

'I've come to tell you I've had an offer for my daughter.'

Her gaze made an inventory of the room, where nothing can have escaped her attention.

'Some people from Paris who have just settled in the town. The husband, an engineer, has been appointed assistant manager of the factory and they are looking for someone. It's a good post, and Gina would get board and lodging. I promised them a reply the day after tomorrow. You can think it over.'

He had had twenty-four hours of panic and had turned the question over in his mind in all its aspects again and again. ... As a bachelor he couldn't have a living-in maid. Besides, there was only one bedroom in the house. That Angèle knew. So why had she come to offer him a sort of first refusal?

It was difficult enough to keep Gina in the house all day for she would have nothing to do for hours on end.

Had Angèle thought of all this?

During this time Gina seemed to be unaware of what was going on and behaved in her normal way.

They always had lunch together, in the kitchen, opposite one another, she with her back to the oven, from where she reached for the pots as she needed them, without having to get up.

'Gina!'

'Yes.'

'There's something I want to ask you.'

'What?'

'You promise to answer me frankly?'

He could still see her clearly as he pronounced these words, but the next moment she was nothing more than a wraith before his eyes, for his spectacles had suddenly misted over.

'Aren't I always frank?'

'Yes.'

'Usually I get criticized for being too frank.'

'Not by me.'

'What do you want to ask?'

'Do you like the house?'

37

She looked round her with what seemed to him like indifference.

'I mean,' he persisted, 'would you like to live here altogether?'

'Why do you ask me that?'

'Because I should be happy if you would accept.'

'Accept what?'

'Becoming my wife.'

If there had been a plot, Gina was not in it, for she exclaimed with a nervous laugh:

'Don't be silly!'

'I'm serious.'

'You'd marry me?'

'That's what I am suggesting.'

'*Me?*'

'You.'

'You realize what sort of a girl I am?'

'I think I know you as well as anybody else.'

'In that case you're a brave man.'

'What's your answer?'

'My answer's that you're very kind, but that it's impossible.'

There was a splash of sunlight on the table and it was on this that Jonas fastened his gaze, rather than on the young girl's face.

'Why?'

'Because.'

'You don't want me?'

'I didn't say that, Monsieur Jonas. You are certainly very decent. In fact you're the only man who never tried to take advantage of the situation. Even Ancel himself, though he's the father of one of my friends, took me into the shed in his backyard when I was only fifteen. I could name nearly all of them, one by one, and you would be amazed. To start with I wondered when you were going to pluck up courage.'

'Do you think you couldn't be happy here?'

Then she made her frankest reply:

'It would be peaceful, at any rate.'

'Well, that's something, isn't it?'

'Yes, of course. Only supposing we didn't get on together? Better not say any more about it. I'm not the kind of girl to make a man like you happy.'

'It's not me that counts.'

'Who does then?'

'You.'

He was sincere. He was so overcome with tenderness while he was talking about this subject, that he didn't dare move from fear of allowing his emotion to break out.

'Me and happiness . . .' she said bitterly, between her clenched teeth.

'Let's say peace, as you called it yourself.'

She had glanced at him sharply.

'Was it my mother who suggested it to you? I knew she'd been to see you, but . . .'

'No. She only told me you were being offered a better job.'

'My mother has always wanted to get me out of the way.'

'Won't you think it over?'

'What's the point?'

'Wait at any rate until tomorrow before giving me a definite answer, will you?'

'If you insist!'

That day she had broken a plate while she was doing the washing up, and as had happened now, two years later, she had gone off forgetting to clean the stove.

At about four o'clock in the afternoon, as usual, Jonas had gone for his cup of coffee at Le Bouc's and Fernand had watched him closely.

'Is it true, what they're saying?'

'What are they saying?'

'That you are going to marry Gina.'

'Who told you that?'

'Louis, just now. He had a quarrel with Angèle over it.'

'Why?'

Le Bouc had looked uncomfortable.

'They don't have the same ideas.'

'He's against it?'

'I'll say!'

'Why?'

Louis had certainly given a reason, but Le Bouc did not pass it on.

'You never can tell just what's going on in his head,' he replied evasively.

'Is he angry?'

'He talked about going and knocking your block off. That won't stop him doing what Angèle decides. It makes no difference him protesting, he's got no say in his house.'

'And Gina?'

'You must know what she said to you better than I do. The most difficult of all will be her brother.'

'Why?'

'I don't know. It's just a hunch. He's a strange lad, with ideas all his own.'

'He doesn't like me?'

'Apart from his sister he probably likes nobody. She's the only one who can stop him making a fool of himself. A month ago he wanted to join up in Indo-China.'

'She didn't want him to?'

'He's only a boy. He's never been anywhere. As soon as he got there he would be even more unhappy than he is here.'

A customer was going into the shop, near by, and Jonas made for the door.

'See you soon.'

'Good luck!'

He had slept badly, that night. At eight o'clock Gina had come in to start work without speaking, without looking at him, and he had waited a long quarter of an hour before questioning her.

'Have you got the answer?'

'Do you really mean it?'

'Yes.'

'You won't hold it against me later?'

'I promise.'

She had shrugged her shoulders.

'In that case it's as you wish.'

It was so unexpected that it made him empty of all emotion.

He looked at her dumbfounded, without daring to approach, without taking her hand, and even less did it occur to him to kiss her.

Afraid of having misunderstood her, he insisted:

'You are consenting to marry me?'

She was sixteen years younger than he and yet it was she who had looked at him as if he were a child, a protective smile at her lips.

'Yes.'

So as not to betray himself in front of her, he had gone up to his room and, before leaning out of the window, had stood for a long while in a trance in front of one of the wardrobe mirrors. It was in May. A shower had just fallen but the sun was shining again and making great bright patches on the wet tiles of the immense roof. There was a market, like today, and he had gone out to buy strawberries, the first of the season.

A big, strong woman, dressed in black, a blue apron round her middle, was entering his shop in an authoritative manner and casting a great shadow. It was Angèle, whose hand always smelt of leeks.

'Is it true what Louis tells me? What's she gone to Bourges for?'

He was smaller than she was and a great deal less powerful. He stammered:

'I don't know.'

'Did she take the bus this morning?'

'Yes.'

'Without coming to see me?'

She, too, was looking at him suspiciously.

'Was there a quarrel between the two of you?'

'No.'

'Answer me like a man, for God's sake! What's gone wrong?'

'Nothing ...'

She had begun to address him familiarly the day of the engagement, but Louis had never been willing to follow her example.

'*Nothing! Nothing! ...*' she mimicked. 'You ought at least

41

to be capable of preventing your wife from running away. When did she promise to come back?'

'She didn't say.'

'That's better than ever!'

She seemed to flatten him with a look, with all her vigorous bulk, and then, turning sharply on her heel to leave, she ground out:

'Little rat!'

THREE

His first impulse had been to go and buy a slice of ham, or some cold meat from Pascal, the butcher on the other side of the market, just at the beginning of the rue du Canal, or even not to eat at all, or perhaps to make do with the two extra *croissants* he had been given that morning. He ought not to have taken them. That did not fit in with the supposed departure of Gina for Bourges. Strictly he would only have needed to buy three *croissants*.

It was not on his own account that he was so distraught, out of self-respect or fear of what people would say.

It was on her account. Her theft of his stamps, which were all he cared about in the world apart from her, made no difference: he considered it his duty to defend her.

He did not know yet what against. He had been a prey, particularly since that morning, to a vague uneasiness which almost prevented him from thinking about his own distress. In time, every one of his feelings would doubtless detach themselves more clearly and he would be able to single them out. For the moment, stunned, he was dealing with the immediate problems first, in the belief that by acting in this way it was Gina he was protecting.

On the rare occasions when she had visited La Loute and had spent the whole day at Bourges, he had returned to his bachelor habits and eaten at Pepito's. This, then, was what he had to do today, and when, at noon, the bell announcing the end of the market pealed out into the sunlight, vibrating like a convent bell, he began to bring the boxes of books indoors.

Already the refuse lorry was advancing yard by yard round the square, while five men loaded on to it everything they could shovel up out of the gutter. Many of the market women, especially the ones from the country, had already left, and some, before taking their bus, were eating the snacks they had brought with them, at Le Bouc's or the Trianon Bar.

It went against the grain to leave the house, rather as if he were betraying something, and, against all evidence, he told himself that Gina would perhaps return while he was away.

The rue Haute was a narrow, gently sloping street, despite its name, and formed the main artery of the most densely populated neighbourhood. The shops in it were more varied than elsewhere. American surplus stores and cheap jewellery were sold in it, and there were at least three junk shops and old-clothes stores.

Since the chemical products factory had been installed a kilometre away, it had become a sort of Italian quarter at the far end, which some people actually called Little Italy. As the factory grew in importance, workers had come from elsewhere, first of all Poles, who had installed themselves a little farther up, then at the end, almost outside the factory gates, a few families of Algerians.

Pepito's restaurant with the olive-coloured walls and the crinkled paper cloths, had nevertheless preserved its peaceful character and, at midday, the same habitués were to be found there, who, as Jonas had done for such a long time, took their meals there year in year out.

Marie, the *patron*'s wife, did the cooking while her husband ran the bar and their niece waited at table.

'Why, Monsieur Jonas!' the little Italian cried out on catching sight of him. 'What a pleasant surprise to see you!'

Then, afraid suddenly that he had committed a gaffe to appear so pleased:

'Gina's not ill, I trust?'

And he had to repeat his old refrain:

'She's gone to Bourges.'

'Well, we all have to change our routine now and again. There, your old table's free. Julia! Lay a place for Monsieur Jonas.'

It was probably here that Jonas became most aware of the vacuum which had just been created in his life. For years Pepito's restaurant, where nothing had changed, had been a second home for him. Yet, here he was, feeling out of place, seized with panic at the idea that he might have to return every day.

The Widower was in his place, and seemed almost to be on the point of welcoming Jonas with the batting of his eyelids which in the old days had served as a greeting.

They had never spoken to one another. For years, they had occupied two tables opposite one another by the window, and they used to arrive at more or less the same time.

Jonas knew his name, through Pepito. He was Monsieur Métras, chief clerk at the Town Hall, but in his mind he always labelled him The Widower.

He had never known Madame Métras, who had died fifteen years before. As there were no children in the family, the husband, left to his own devices, had taken to having his meals at Pepito's.

He must have been fifty-five years old, perhaps more. He was a tall man, very broadly built, thick and hard, with iron grey hair, bushy eyebrows and darker hair sprouting from his nostrils and ears. His complexion was greyish as well, and Jonas had never seen him smile. He didn't read the paper as he ate, like most single diners, never joined in a conversation with anybody, and chewed his food carefully, gazing straight to his front.

Many months had passed before they batted eyelids at one another in greeting, and Jonas was the only person to whom The Widower had ever made this concession.

A diminutive, asthmatic dog, fat and almost impotent, used to sit under the table; it could not have been far off twenty years old, for it had once been Madame Métras's dog.

The Widower used to go and fetch it from his flat on coming out of his office, and take it to the restaurant where they gave it its food. Then he led it off again, slowly, waiting while it relieved itself before returning to the Town Hall, and in the evening the performance was repeated.

Why, while Jonas was eating, did The Widower watch him today more closely than before? It wasn't possible that he already knew. Yet anyone would have sworn that he was thinking to himself, restraining a snigger:

'Ah! So, you're back again!'

Rather as if the two of them had been members of the same club, as if Jonas had left it for a time and finally come back, repentant, to the fold.

All this existed only in his imagination, but what was not imagination was his terror at the idea of once again sitting opposite the chief clerk every day.

'What will you have for dessert, Monsieur Jonas? There's éclairs and apple tart.'

He had always liked pudding, particularly apple tart, which he chose, and he felt guilty at yielding to his greed at such a moment.

'What's your news, Monsieur Jonas?'

Pepito was tall like Palestri, dry and lean, but unlike his compatriot he was always smiling and affable. Anyone would have thought running a restaurant was all a game for him, he did it with such good humour. Maria, his wife, had become enormous as a result of living in a kitchen six yards square, but that did not prevent her remaining young and alluring. She, too, was jolly and would burst into laughter over nothing.

As they had no children, they had adopted a nephew whom they had had sent over from their country and who could be seen doing his homework in the evening at one of the restaurant tables.

'How's Gina?'

'She's all right.'

'The other day my wife met her in the market and, I don't know why, she got the impression that she was expecting a baby. Is that true?'

He said no, almost ashamed, for he was sure it was his fault if Gina was not pregnant.

What had misled Maria was that recently Gina had taken

45

to eating more than usual, with a sort of frenzy, and from being plump as she was before, had become fat to the extent of needing to alter her clothes.

At first he had rejoiced at her appetite, for in the early days of their marriage she hardly ate at all. He used to encourage her, seeing it as a sign of contentment, thinking that she was acclimatizing herself to their life, and that she might end by actually feeling happy.

He had said so to her and she had replied with a vague, rather protective smile, which she turned on him increasingly often now. She had not her mother's authoritative personality, quite the opposite. She did not concern herself with business, or money, or the decisions that had to be taken in household matters.

Yet, despite the difference in age, it was she who adopted an indulgent manner now and then towards Jonas.

He was her husband and she treated him as such. But in her eyes, perhaps, he was not quite a man, a real male, and she seemed to look on him as a backward child.

Had he been wrong not to have been more severe with her? Ought he to have taken her in hand? Would that have changed matters?

He had no desire to think about it. The Widower, opposite, was hypnotizing him and he finished up his apple tart faster than he would have wished, in order to escape his gaze.

'So soon?' exclaimed Pepito when he asked for the bill. 'Aren't you going to have your coffee?'

He would take it at Le Bouc's, with the possibility in the back of his mind of hearing some news there. In the old days he used to eat as slowly as Monsieur Métras, and the majority of single men who lunched in the restaurant and who, for the most part, chatted with the *patron* afterwards.

'Julia! Monsieur Jonas's bill.'

And, addressing him:

'Shall we be seeing you this evening?'

'Perhaps.'

'She hasn't gone for long?'

'I don't know yet.'

It was starting all over again. He was floundering, no longer knowing what to reply to the questions that were being put to him, realizing that it would be worse tomorrow and worse still in the days to follow.

What would happen, for example, if La Loute came to see her family and disclosed that Gina had not been to Bourges? It was unlikely, but he was envisaging everything. The woman everyone called La Loute was really Louise Hariel, and her parents kept the grain store in the market, just opposite Jonas, on the other side of the great roof.

He had seen her, in the same way as he had seen Gina, running about among the crates when she was not yet ten. At that time, with her round face, her blue eyes with long lashes and her curly hair, she looked like a doll. It was odd, for her father was a thin, plain little man and her mother in the drab background of the grain store, which faced north and never got the sun, looked like a dried-up old spinster.

The two Hariels, man and wife, wore the same grey smock and, from living together, each behind their own counter, making the same movements, they had ended by resembling one another.

La Loute had been the only one of the girls of the Square to be educated in a convent, which she had not left until the age of seventeen. She was also the best-dressed and her clothes were very lady-like. On Sundays when she went to High Mass with her parents, everyone used to turn round, and the mothers held up her deportment as an example to their daughters.

For about two years she had worked as a secretary to the Privas Press, a business which had been flourishing for three generations, then, all of a sudden, it had been put about that she had found a better job in Bourges.

Her parents didn't mention the subject. The two of them were the most cantankerous shopkeepers in the Old Market and many customers preferred to go all the way to the rue de la Gare for their purchases.

La Loute and Gina were good friends. With Clémence, the butcher's daughter, they had for long been an inseparable trio.

At first people had said that La Loute was working with an

47

architect in Bourges, then with a bachelor doctor with whom she had lived on marital terms.

Various people had met her there, and there was talk of her expensive tastes, her fur coat. The latest news was that she had a baby Citroën, which had been seen outside her parents' door one evening.

La Loute had not spent the night with them. The neighbours claimed to have heard raised voices, which was strange, for the Hariels hardly ever opened their mouths and someone had actually called them the two fish.

To Jonas, Gina had contented herself with saying, on one of her returns from Bourges :

'She leads her life as best she can and it's not easy for anyone.'

After a moment's reflection she had added :

'Poor girl. She's too kind.'

Why too kind? Jonas had not inquired. He recognized that it was none of his business, that it was women's and even girls' gossip, that friends like Clémence, La Loute and Gina, when they got together, became schoolgirls again and had a right to their own secrets.

Another time, Gina had said :

'It's all plain sailing for some people.'

Was she referring to Clémence, who had a young husband, a good-looking fellow, and who had had the finest wedding in the Old Market ?

He himself wasn't young, nor a good-looking fellow, and all he had been able to offer was security. Had Gina really wanted security, *peace*, as he had said the first day ?

Where was she at that moment, with the stamps which she imagined she could sell without difficulty? Surely she could have had hardly any money on her, even if, without Jonas's knowledge, she had put some aside for the occasion ? Her brother could not have given her anything either, because it was she who slipped him money from time to time.

Because she had seen the prices in the catalogue she had told herself that she had only to call at any stamp dealer, in Paris or anywhere else, to sell them. It was true of certain of them, the ones only comparatively rare, but it was not the case for the valuable ones, like the 1849 Ceres.

Stamp dealers, like diamond merchants, form a sort of confraternity throughout the world, and are more or less known to one another. They know, usually, in whose hands such and such a rare stamp is, and watch for a chance to acquire it for their customers.

At least five of the stamps she had taken were known in this way. If she were to offer them for sale at any reputable dealers there was a good chance that the assistant would detain her on some pretext and telephone the police.

She was in no danger of being put into prison, because she was his wife and theft is not recognized between married people. Even so they would start an inquiry and they would get in touch with him.

Would it be in this way, on account of her ignorance, that her escapade would come to an end?

He was not sure he would wish that. He didn't wish it. It hurt him to think of Gina's shame, her discomfiture, her rage.

Wouldn't it be still worse if she were to entrust the sale to someone else? By now she was no longer alone, on that score he had no illusions. And this time it was not a question of some young male from the town whom she had not been able to resist following for a night or two.

She had set off deliberately and her departure had been premeditated, organized at least twenty-four hours in advance. In other words he had lived with her for twenty-four hours without realizing that it was probably the last day they would spend together.

He was walking along the street now, with slow steps, and the bare space under the tile roof seemed immense, given over to a few men who were hosing it down and scrubbing the cement flooring with brooms. Most of the shops were shut until two o'clock.

He was shrinking from the moment of going into Le Bouc's to drink his coffee, for he didn't feel like speaking to anybody, least of all to answer any more questions. He was devoid of hatred, or bitterness. What was filling his heart was a sad, anxious, and almost serene tenderness, and he stopped for a good minute watching two puppies, one of them lying on its back in the sun, with its four paws waving in the air, playing at biting each other.

He remembered the smell of herrings, in the kitchen, the oven which Gina in her haste had not washed and to which bits of fish were sticking. He tried to remember what they had found to talk about at that last meal, but could not do so. Then he tried to recall the minute details of the day before, which he had spent like an ordinary day, when it was really the most important one in his life.

One image came back to him: he was behind his counter, serving an old gentleman who didn't know exactly what he wanted when Gina, who had gone up a little earlier than usual to do her face, had come down in her red dress. It was one of last year's dresses, and this was the first time he had seen it this season; because Gina had put on weight it clung more closely than ever to her body.

She had gone over to the doorway and into the triangle of sunlight, and he could never remember having seen her looking so lovely.

He hadn't told her so because, when he paid her a compliment, she would shrug her shoulders irritably and sometimes her face would cloud over.

Once she had countered, almost dryly:

'Forget it! I'll be an old woman soon enough, for God's sake!'

He thought he understood. He had no wish to analyse the matter any further. Obviously she meant that she was losing her youth in this old house which smelt of mouldering paper. It was doubtless an ironic way of reassuring him, of letting him know that they would soon be on equal terms and that he would no longer need to be afraid.

'I'm going to go and say good morning to Mama,' she had told him.

Usually, at that hour, her visits to her mother's shop didn't last for long, for Angèle, harassed with customers, had no time to waste. But Gina had been absent for nearly an hour. When she had come back, she didn't come from the right, but from the left, in other words from the opposite direction to the house of her parents, and yet she was not carrying any parcels.

She never received any letters, it suddenly struck him. Not counting La Loute, she had several married friends who no longer lived in the town. Oughtn't she to have received at least a postcard from them now and again?

The Post Office was in the rue Haute, five minutes from Pepito's. Did she have her mail sent there poste restante? Or had she been to make a telephone call from the box?

During the two years they had been married she had never mentioned Marcel, who had been sentenced to five years in prison. When she had gone off on her escapades, it was perforce with other men, which had led Jonas to suppose that she had forgotten about Jenot.

It was at least six months since she had gone out in the evening on her own, except to look after Clémence's baby, and each time she had returned punctually. Besides, if she had seen a man, he would have noticed, for she was not a woman on whom love left no mark. He knew the look on her face when she had been with a man, her slack, shifty manner, and even the smell of her body which was not the same.

Madame Hariel, the grain seller, stood behind her shop door with the handle removed, her pale face pressed to the glass panel, watching him as he wandered along the pavement like a man who does not know where he is going, and he finally headed in the direction of Le Bouc's bar. The latter was still at lunch with his wife at the back of the café, and they were finishing their black pudding.

'Don't move,' he said. 'I've plenty of time.'

It was the slack time of the day. Fernand, before having his lunch, had swept up the dirty sawdust and the red floor stones shone brightly, the house smelt of cleanliness.

'Did you have lunch at Pepito's?'

He nodded. Le Bouc had a bony face, and used to wear a blue apron. Except on Sundays and two or three times at the cinema, Jonas had never seen him in a coat.

With his mouth full, he said as he went over to the percolator :

'Louis asked me just now if I had seen Gina go past and I said I hadn't. He was having one of his bad bouts. It's a pity that a fine chap like him can't stop himself from drinking.'

Jonas unwrapped his two lumps of sugar and held them in his hand, while waiting for his cup of coffee. He liked the smell of Le Bouc's bar, even though it was loaded with alcohol, just as he liked the smell of old books which reigned in his own house. He liked the smell of the market as well, especially during the fresh fruit season, and he sometimes strolled about among the stalls to breathe it in, at the same time keeping an eye on his bookshop from afar.

Le Bouc had just said, referring to Louis :

'A fine chap . . .'

And Jonas noticed for the first time that it was an expression he often used. Ancel was a fine chap as well, and Benaiche the police constable, for whom the retailers filled a crate of provisions every morning, which his wife came to fetch at nine o'clock.

Angèle, too, despite her shrewish temperament, was a fine woman.

Everybody, around the Market, except perhaps for the Hariels, who shut themselves up in their own house as if to avoid God knows what contagion, greeted one another each morning with good humour and cordiality. Everybody also worked hard and respected hard work in others.

Of Marcel, when the hold-up affair had come to light, they had said pityingly :

'It's funny. Such a nice lad . . .'

Then they had added :

'It must be Indo-China that did it to him. That's no place for young lads.'

If they spoke of La Loute and the mysterious life she led at Bourges, they didn't hold that against her either.

'Girls today aren't what they used to be. Education's changed too.'

As for Gina, she remained one of the most popular figures in the Market, and when she passed by with a sway of her hips, a smile on her lips, her teeth sparkling, their faces would light up. They all followed her latest adventures. She had been seen one evening, when she was hardly seventeen, lying with a lorry driver on the back of a lorry.

'Hullo there, Gina!' they used to call out to her.

And no doubt they envied the good fortune of the men who had slept with her. Many of them had tried. Some had succeeded. Nobody held it against her for being what she was. They were nearer to being grateful, for without her the Vieux-Marché would not have been quite what it was.

'Is it true that she took the morning bus?' asked Le Bouc, returning to his place at the table.

As Jonas made no reply, he took his silence to mean that he was correct and went on :

'In that case, she will have been with my niece, Gaston's daughter, who's gone to see a new specialist.'

Jonas knew her. She was a young girl with a pretty but anaemic face who had a deformed hip and in order to walk had to thrust the right-hand side of her body forward. She was seventeen years old.

Since the age of twelve, she had been in the hands of specialists, who had made her undergo various courses of treatment. She had been operated on two or three times without any appreciable success and, at about the age of fifteen, she had spent an entire year in plaster.

She remained sweet and cheerful and her mother came several times a week to change books for her, sentimental novels which she chose carefully herself, out of fear that one of the characters might have been crippled as she was.

'Is her mother with her?'

'No. She went by herself. Gina will have kept her company.'

'Is she coming back this evening?'

'On the five o'clock bus.'

So, then, they would know that Gina had not gone to Bourges. What would he say to Louis when he came to demand an explanation?

For the Palestri family would certainly want explanations

from him. They had entrusted their daughter to him, and considered him henceforth responsible for her.

Incapable of looking after her, living in fear of a scandal which might at any moment break out, Angèle had thrust her into his arms. It was that, to put it bluntly, that she had come to do when she had talked to him about a place for her daughter with the assistant manager of the factory. The story may have been true, but she had taken advantage of it.

Even now he was grateful to her for it, for his life without Gina had had no flavour; it was a little as if he had not lived before.

What intrigued him was what had happened in the Palestri family during that period. That there had been discussions there was no question. Frédo's attitude was not in any doubt either, and he must have argued with his parents that they were pushing his sister into the arms of an old man.

But Louis? Did he, too, prefer to see his daughter chasing men than married to Jonas?

'It looks as if we're in for a hot summer. That's what the almanack says, anyway. Storms next week.'

He wiped his spectacles which the steam of his coffee had misted over, and stood there for a moment like an owl in the sun, blinking his pink eyelids. It was rare for him to take off his glasses in public; he didn't know exactly why he had done so, for he had never found himself in this position before. It gave him a sense of inferiority, rather as when one dreams that one is stark naked or trouserless in the middle of a crowd.

Gina used to see him like this every day and perhaps that was why she treated him differently from the others. His thick lenses, not rimmed with metal or tortoise-shell, worked both ways. While they enabled him to observe the minutest details of the world outside, they enlarged his pupils for other people and gave them a fixed look, a hardness which in reality they did not possess.

Once, standing in his doorway, he had heard a small boy who was passing say to his mother:

'Hasn't that man got large eyes!'

Actually his eyes weren't large. It was the glasses which gave them a globular appearance.

'See you later,' he sighed, after counting out his coins and putting them on the counter.

'See you later. Good afternoon.'

At around five o'clock Le Bouc would close his bar, for in the afternoon few customers came. If he stayed open it was mainly for the convenience of his neighbours. The day before a market he would go to bed at eight in the evening so as to be up at three next morning.

Tomorrow, Friday, there was no market. Every other day, four days in the week to be precise, the space beneath the tiled roof stood empty and served as a parking place for cars and a playground for children.

For the last two or three weeks, the children were to be seen charging about on roller skates which made a screeching sound for miles around, then, as if they had been given the word, they changed their game and took up skittles, spinning-tops, or yo-yos. It followed a rhythm, like the seasons, only more ·mysterious, for it was impossible to tell where the decision came from and the vendor at the bazaar in the rue Haute was taken by surprise every time.

'I want a kite, please.'

He would sell ten, twenty, in the space of two days, order others and then only sell one for the rest of the year.

Taking his keys from his pocket reminded Jonas of the steel strong-box and Gina's departure. He encountered the smell of the house again, and the atmosphere was stale, now that the sun no longer fell on its front. He took out the two book-boxes, mounted on legs with castors, then stood in the middle of the shop, not knowing what to do with himself.

Yet he had spent many years like this, alone, and had never suffered from it. Had not even noticed that there was something missing.

What did he do in the old days, at this time? He sometimes would read, behind the counter. He had read a great deal, not only novels, but works on the most varied subjects, sometimes the most unexpected ones, ranging from political economy to the report of an archaeological excavation. Everything interested him. He would pick out at random a book on mechanics, for example, thinking only to glance over a couple of pages, and then read it from cover to cover. He had read in this way, from the first page to the last, *The History of the Consulate and the Empire*, as he had read, before selling them to a lawyer, twenty-one odd volumes of nineteenth-century trials.

He particularly liked works on geography, ones following a region from its geological formation right up to its economic and cultural expansion.

His stamps acted as reference marks. The names of countries, sovereigns, and dictators, did not evoke in his mind a brightly coloured map or photograph, but a delicate vignette enclosed in a transparent packet.

It was in this way, rather than through literature, that he came to know Russia, where he had been born forty years before.

His parents were living in Archangel at the time, right at the top of the map, on the White Sea, where five sisters and a brother had been born before him.

Of the entire family he was the only one not to know Russia, which he had left at the age of one. Maybe this was why at school he had begun to collect stamps. He must have been thirteen when one of his classmates had shown him his album.

'Look!' he had said to him. 'There's a picture of your country.'

It was, he could remember all the better now that he possessed the stamp along with many other Russian ones, a 1905 blue and pink with a picture of the Kremlin.

'I've got some other ones, you know, but they're portraits.'

The stamps, issued in 1913 for the third centenary of the Romanovs, depicted Peter I, Alexander II, Alexis Michaelovitch, Paul I.

Later he was to make a complete collection of them, including the Winter Palace and the wooden palace of the Boyar Romanovs.

His eldest sister Alyosha, who was sixteen when he was born, would now be fifty-six – if she were still alive. Nastasia would be fifty-four and Daniel, his only brother, who died in infancy, would have been just fifty.

The other three sisters, Stéphanie, Sonia, and Doussia, were forty-eight, forty-five, and forty-two and, because he was the nearest to her in age, also because of her name, it was of Doussia that he thought most often.

He had never seen their faces. He didn't know anything about them, whether they were dead or alive, if they had rallied to the party or been massacred.

The manner of his departure from Russia had been typical of his mother, Natalie, typical of the Oudonovs, as his father would say, for the Oudonovs had always passed as eccentrics.

When he was born in their house at Archangel, where there had been eight servants, his father, who owned an important fishing fleet, had just left as an administrative officer for the army, and was somewhere behind the front line.

In order to be nearer to him his mother – a regular carrier-pigeon, as his father kept saying – had left with all her family in the train for Moscow and they had descended on Aunt Zina.

Her real name was Zinaida Oudonova, but he had always heard her called Aunt Zina.

She lived, according to his parents, in a house so big that you could lose yourself in the corridors, and she was very rich. It was in her house that Jonas fell ill at the age of six months. He had contracted an infectious form of pneumonia which he did not seem to be able to throw off, and the doctors had recommended the gentler climate of the South.

They had some friends in the Crimea, at Yalta, the Shepilovs, and without a word of warning, his mother had decided one morning to go to them with the baby.

'I leave the girls in your care, Zina,' she had said to the aunt. 'We shall be back in a few weeks, as soon as we've got the colour back into this lad's cheeks."

It was not easy, in the middle of a war, to travel across Russia, but nothing was impossible for an Oudonov. Fortunately her mother had found the Shepilovs at Yalta. She had lingered, as was to be expected with her, and it was there that the Revolution had taken her by surprise.

There was no further news of the father. The daughters were still with Zina in Moscow, and Natalie talked about leaving the baby at Yalta to go and fetch them.

The Shepilovs had dissuaded her. Shepilov was a pessimist. The exodus was starting. Lenin and Trotsky were taking over power. The Wrangel army was being formed.

Why not go to Constantinople to let the storm pass, and return in a few months?

The Shepilovs had taken his mother and they had become part of the Russian colony which invaded the hotels of Turkey, some of them with money, others in search of any sort of employment to keep themselves alive.

The Shepilovs had managed to bring out some gold and jewellery. Natalie had a few diamonds with her.

Why had they gone on to Paris from Constantinople? And how, from Paris, had they finished up in a little town in the Berry?

It was not altogether a mystery. Shepilov, before the war, used to entertain lavishly on his estates in the Ukraine and thus he had entertained a certain number of French people, in particular, for several weeks at a time, the Comte de Coubert whose château and farms were some eight miles from Louvant.

They had met after the exodus, which they still thought of as purely temporary, and Coubert had suggested to Shepilov that he should install himself in his château. Natalie had followed, and with her Jonas, who had still no comprehensive grasp of the world across which he was being dragged in this way.

During this time Constantin Milk, who had been taken prisoner by the Germans, had been released at Aix-la-Chapelle following on the armistice. He was given neither provisions nor money, nor any means of transport, and there was no question of returning under these circumstances to the distant soil of Russia.

Stage by stage, begging his way with others like himself, Milk had reached Paris and one day the Comte de Coubert had seen his name in a list of Russian prisoners recently arrived.

Nothing was known of Aunt Zina, nor the girls, who probably had not had time to cross the frontier.

Constantin Milk wore thick spectacles, as his son was soon to do, and, being short in the leg, had the build of a Siberian bear. He had quickly tired of the life of inaction in the château and, one evening, had announced that he had bought a fish-mongery in the town with Natalie's jewels.

'It may be a little hard for an Oudonov,' he had said with his enigmatic smile, 'but she'll jolly well have to get down to it.'

From his door Jonas could see the shop '*À la Marée*', with its two white marble counters and its big copper scales. He had lived for years on the first floor, in the room with the sky-light now occupied by Chenu's daughter.

Until the time he went to school he had spoken hardly anything but Russian and then had almost completely forgotten it.

Russia was for him a mysterious and bloody country where his five sisters, including Doussia, had very probably been massacred with Aunt Zina, like the Imperial family.

His father, like the Oudonovs whom he used to taunt, had also been a man of sudden decisions, or at any rate, if they matured slowly he never mentioned them to anyone.

In 1930, when Jonas was fourteen years old and going to the local *lycée*, Constantin Milk had announced that he was leaving for Moscow. As Natalie insisted that they should all go together, he had looked at his son and declared :

'*Better make sure that at least one of us is left!*'

Nobody knew what fate was in store for him out there. He had promised to send news somehow or other, but at the end of a year they had still heard nothing.

The Shepilovs had set up house in Paris where they had opened a bookshop in the rue Jacob, and Natalie had written to ask them whether they would look after Jonas, whom she had sent to a *lycée* in Paris, while she in her turn would undertake the journey to Russia.

That was how he came to enter Condorcet.

In the meantime another war had broken out, in which his eyesight had prevented him from taking part, whole populations had been disturbed once more, there had been new exoduses, new waves of refugees.

Jonas had applied to all the authorities imaginable, Russian as well as French, without obtaining any news of his family.

Could he hope that his father, at eighty-two years old, and his mother, at seventy-six, were still alive?

What had happened to Aunt Zina, in whose house people lost themselves, and his sisters, whose faces were unknown to him?

Did Doussia even know that she had a brother somewhere in the world.

All around him the walls were covered with old books. In his little room was a large stove which he kept roaring hot in winter as a luxury, and today he would have sworn that the smell of herrings still hung in the air in the kitchen.

The huge roof of the market was streaked with sunlight opposite his window and all around there were shops hardly larger than his own, except on the side of the rue de Bourges where St Cecilia's Church stood.

He could put a name to every face, recognize everyone's voice, and, when people saw him in his doorway or when he went into Le Bouc's, they used to call out:

'Hullo, Monsieur Jonas!'

It was a world in which he had shut himself up, and Gina had walked in one fine day with a sway of her hips, bringing a warm smell of armpits with her into this world of his.

She had just walked out again, and he was overcome with a fit of giddiness.

FOUR

IT was not that day that the complications were to begin, but he still had the feeling of a person who is incubating an illness.

In the afternoon, fortunately, the customers were fairly numerous in the shop and he received, among others, a visit from Monsieur Legendre, a retired railway guard, who used to read a book a day, sometimes two, changed them by the half-dozen and always sat down in a chair for a chat. He used to smoke a meerschaum pipe which made a spluttering noise each time he sucked at it, and as he had a habit of pressing down the burning tobacco, the entire top joint of his index finger was a golden brown colour.

He was not a widower nor a bachelor. His wife, small and thin, used to shop at the market, a black hat on her head, three times a week, and stop in front of all the stalls, disputing the price before buying a bunch of leeks.

Monsieur Legendre stayed for nearly an hour. The door was open. In the shadow of the covered market the cement, after being washed down, was drying slowly, leaving damp patches and, as it was Thursday, a crowd of children had taken possession of it and this time were playing at cowboys.

Two or three customers had interrupted the ex-railwayman's discourse and he waited, quite used to it, for the bookseller to finish serving them before carrying on the conversation at the exact point where he had left off.

'As I was saying . . .'

At seven o'clock, Jonas hesitated whether to lock up and go and have dinner at Pepito's as it seemed to him he ought to do, but finally he hadn't the heart. Instead he decided to walk across the Square and buy some eggs at Coutelle's, the dairy, where, as he expected, Madame Coutelle asked him:

'Isn't Gina there?'

It was without conviction, this time, that he replied:

'She's gone to Bourges.'

He made himself an omelette. It was good for him to keep himself occupied. His movements were meticulous. Just before pouring the whipped-up eggs into the pan he yielded once more to gluttony, as he had done at midday with the apple tart, and went into the yard to pick a few chives which were growing in a box.

Oughtn't he to have been indifferent to what he ate, seeing that Gina had gone? He arranged the butter, bread and coffee on the table, unfolded his napkin and ate his meal slowly, to all appearances thinking of nothing.

He had read in some book or other, probably war memoirs, that a certain time nearly always elapses before the most seriously wounded feel any pain, that sometimes they do not even realize at once that they have been hit.

In his case it was a little different. He felt no violent pain, nor despair. It was more that a void had been created inside him. He was no longer in a state of equilibrium. The kitchen, which had not changed, seemed to him not so much strange as lifeless, without any definite shape, as if he had been looking at it without his glasses.

He did not weep, did not sigh, that evening, any more than the day before. After eating a banana which had been bought by Gina, he did the washing up, swept out the kitchen, then went over to the doorway to watch the sun setting.

He did not stay where he was because the Chaignes, the grocers from next door, had brought their chairs out onto the pavement and were chatting in low voices with the butcher, who had come to keep them company.

If he no longer had his valuable stamps at least he still had his collection of Russian ones, for this, which was purely of sentimental value, he had stuck into an album rather in the way that in other houses family portraits are pasted in.

Yet he did not feel himself to be particularly Russian, witness the fact that he only felt at home in the Vieux-Marché.

The shopkeepers had been friendly when the Milks had set themselves up there, and, although to start with Milk's father did not speak one word of French, he had soon made great headway. It sometimes provoked his great laugh, devoid of bitterness, to be selling fish by the pound when, a few years earlier, he owned the most important fishing fleet in Archangel, and his boats went as far as Spitzbergen and Novaya Zembla. A little while before the war he had even equipped his ships as whalers, and it was perhaps a sort of sense of humour all his own that prompted him to call his son Jonas.

Natalie was slower to adapt herself to their new life and her husband used to tease her in Russian in front of the customers, who did not understand a word.

'Come on, Ignatievna Oudonova, dip your pretty little hands into that tub and serve this fat lady with half a dozen whiting.'

Jonas knew practically nothing about the Oudonovs, his mother's family, except that they were merchants who provisioned boats. While Constantin Milk, whose grandfather was a shipowner before him, had kept some of his rough plebian habits, the Oudonovs liked good manners and mixed in high society.

When he was in a good mood, Milk did not call his wife Natalie, but Ignatievna Oudonova, or simply Oudonova, and she would pout as if it were a reproach.

Her chief despair was that there were no synagogues in the town, for the Milks, like the Oudonovs, were Jews. There were other Jews in the district, especially among the second-hand shops and small stores in the rue Haute, but because the Milks were red-haired, with fair skin and blue eyes, the local people did not seem to be aware of their race.

To the world at large they were Russians, and in a sense it was true.

At school, at first, when he had hardly been able to speak French and often used comical expressions, Jonas had been the butt of many gibes, but it had not lasted long.

'They are very nice,' he would say to his parents when they asked him how his schoolmates treated him.

It was perfectly true. Everyone was nice to them. After his father's departure, nobody went into the shop without asking Natalie:

'Still no news?'

Jonas was rather proud at heart that his mother had abandoned him to go and join her husband. It had upset him more to leave the Old Market to go to Condorcet, and above all to meet the Shepilovs again.

Serge Sergeevitch Shepilov was an intellectual, and it could be seen in the attitudes he struck, in his way of speaking, of looking at the person he was talking to with a certain air of condescension. After eleven years of living in France he still regarded himself as an exile and went to all the White Russian meetings, worked for their newspaper and their reviews.

When Jonas used to go and see them on holidays, in the bookshop in the rue Jacob, at the back of which they lived in a minute studio, Shepilov liked to address him in Russian then, stopping short, would remark bitterly :

'Ah, but then you've forgotten the language of your country !'

Shepilov was still alive. So, too, was his wife, Nina Ignatievna. Both old now, they had eventually installed themselves in Nice where the odd article which Shepilov sold to a newspaper from time to time enabled them to vegetate. Around the samovar they spent their declining years in the cult of the past and the denigration of the present.

'If your father hasn't been shot or sent to Siberia, then it's because he's rallied to the party cause, in which case I prefer never to see him again.'

Jonas hated nobody, not even the Bolsheviks, whose rise had scattered his family. If he ever thought of Doussia, it was less as a real person than as a sort of fairy. In his imagination Doussia resembled nobody he knew; she had become the symbol of fragile, tender femininity which brought tears to his eyes every time he thought of it.

So as not to be left with nothing to do for the whole evening, he turned over the pages of Russian stamps, and in the little room where he had turned on the light, the history of his country unfolded itself before his eyes.

This collection, almost complete, had taken him a long time to build up, and it had required a great deal of patience, letters and exchanges with hundreds of philatelists, even though the entire album was worth less commercially than four or five of the stamps Gina had taken away.

The first stamp, which was also the first issued in Russia, dating from 1857, depicted an eagle in relief, and although Jonas possessed the ten and twenty kopeks, he had never managed to get hold of the thirty kopeks.

For years, the same symbol had been used with minor variations until the tercentenary in 1905, which the school friend from Condorcet had shown him.

Then with the 1914 war there came the charity stamps with the portrait of Murometz and the Cossack of the Don. He particularly liked, for its style and engraving, a St George and the Dragon which, however, was only catalogued at forty francs.

He thought to himself as he fondled them :

'When this stamp was issued my father was twenty years old. ... He was twenty-five. ... He was meeting my mother. ... That one dates from Alyosha's birth. ...'

In 1917 it was the Phrygian cap of the Democratic Republic, with the two crossed sabres, then the stamps of Kerensky, on which a powerful hand was breaking a chain.

1921, 1922 saw the advent of illustrations with harder, coarser lines, and from 1923 onwards the commemorations started once again, no longer of the Romanovs, but of the fourth anniversary of the October Revolution, the fifth anniversary of the Soviet Republic.

Some more charity stamps at the time of the famine, then, with the U.S.S.R. pictures of workers, ploughmen, soldiers, the portrait of Lenin, in red and black for the first time in 1924.

He did not soften or feel touched with nostalgia. It was more curiosity which had impelled him to assemble this collection of pictures of a far-off world and place them side by side.

A Samoyed village, or a group of Tajiks beside a cornfield plunged him into the same dreamland as a child with a book of holy pictures.

The idea of going back there had never occurred to him, and it was not due to fear of the fate which might await him, nor, as with Shepilov, hatred for the Party.

From the moment he had come of age, on the contrary, two years before the war, he had renounced his 'Nansen' passport and become a naturalized Frenchman.

France itself was too big for him. After school he had worked for several months in a bookshop in the Boulevard Saint-Michel and the Shepilovs had ben unable to believe their ears when he had told them that he preferred to return to the Berry.

He had gone back alone, had taken a furnished room with old Mademoiselle Buttereau, who had died during the war, and had gone to work as a clerk in Duret's bookshop, in the rue du Bourges.

It was still in existence. Old Duret had retired, almost gaga, but the two sons continued the business. It was the chief newsagent-bookshop in town and one of its windows was devoted to devotional objects.

He had not yet taken to eating at Pepito's at that time, because it was too expensive. When the bookseller's shop, where he now lived, had become vacant, he had moved in there as if the rue de Bourges, only a stone's throw away, had been too far.

He was back once again in the heart of the Old Market of his childhood and everyone had recognized him.

Gina's departure had suddenly destroyed this equilibrium, acquired by perseverance, with the same brutality as the Revolution, earlier on, had scattered his own family.

He did not peruse the album to the end. He made himself a cup of coffee, went and removed the handle from the door, turned the key in the lock, shot the bolt, and a little while later went up to his room.

It was, as always when there was no market, a quiet night, without any noise except for the occasional distant motor horn, and the even more distant rumble of a goods train.

Alone in his bed, without the spectacles which made him look like a man, he huddled up like a frightened child and finally went to sleep, with a sad twist to his lips, one hand in the place where Gina ought to have been.

When the sun woke him, coming into his room, the air was still as calm as ever and the bells of St Cecilia's were sounding out the first Mass. All of a sudden he felt the void of his loneliness again, and he almost dressed without washing as sometimes happened before Gina's day. But he was intent at all costs on following the same routine as every other day, so that he even hesitated when he was being served his *croissants* at the baker's opposite.

'Only three,' he finally murmured regretfully.

'Isn't Gina there?'

These people didn't know yet. True, they were almost new to the Square, where they had bought the business only five years before.

'No. She's not there.'

He was surprised not to be pressed, that the news was received with indifference.

It was half past seven. He hadn't closed the door to go across the Square. He never did. When he came back he had a shock, for a man rose before him and as he was walking with his eyes cast down, plunged in thought, he had not recognized him immediately.

'Where is my sister?' Frédo's hard voice was demanding.

He stood in the middle of the shop, in a leather jerkin, his black hair still damp, showing the track of his comb.

Since the day before, Jonas had been expecting something to happen, but he was taken by surprise, and still holding his *croissants* in their brown tissue paper wrappings, he stammered :

'She hasn't come back.'

Frédo was as big as, and broader in the shoulders than his father, and when he became angry, his nostrils would palpitate, alternately dilating and closing together.

'Where has she gone?' he went on, without taking his suspicious gaze off Jonas.

'I ... but ... to Bourges.'

He added, and perhaps it was a mistake, especially addressed to Frédo :

'At any rate she said she was going to Bourges.'

'When did she say that?'

'Yesterday morning.'

'What time?'

'I don't remember. Before the bus left.'

'Did she take the 7.10 bus yesterday morning?'

'She must have done.'

Why was he trembling in front of a mere boy of nineteen, who was taking liberties in demanding an explanation from him? He wasn't the only one in the neighbourhood to be afraid of Frédo. Since his earliest childhood the Palestri boy had had a sullen character, some even said sinister.

True, he didn't seem to like anybody, except his sister. With his father, when the latter had had too much to drink, he behaved intolerably and the neighbours had overheard some highly unsavoury rows. It was said that once Frédo had hit Palestri, and that his mother had gone for him, locked him up in his room like a ten-year-old.

He had climbed out through the window over the roofs, had stayed away for a week, during which time he had looked in vain for work at Montluçon.

He had not passed his certificate at school and had refused to learn any proper trade. He had worked with a few shopkeepers as errand boy, delivery-man, later as a salesman. Nowhere had he remained for more than a few months or a few weeks.

He was not lazy. As one of his ex-employers said :

'That lad rebels against any form of discipline. He wants to be a general before being a plain soldier.'

As much as Jonas liked the Old Market, Frédo appeared to hate it, just as he despised and hated, in the mass, its inhabitants, as, no doubt, he would have hated anywhere he had happened to be.

Angèle alone liked to treat him as if he were still a child, but it was by no means certain that she wasn't a little afraid as well. When he was fifteen she had found a long clasp-knife in his pocket, which he spent hours fondly sharpening. She had taken it away from him. He had said, unconcerned :

'I'll buy another.'

'I forbid you to do any such thing !'

'By what right?'

'Because I'm your mother !'

'As if you'd become it on purpose ! I bet my father was drunk !'

He didn't drink himself, didn't go dancing, used to frequent a small bar in the Italian quarter, in the shady part of the rue Haute where Poles and Arabs mixed and where there were always to be seen groups of men holding disquieting conferences in the back of the room. The place was called the Luxor Bar. Following Marcel's hold-up the police had taken an interest in it, for Marcel, before Frédo, had been a regular customer.

All they had found had been a retired boxer on probation, whose papers were not in order. Ever since they had nevertheless kept their eye on the Luxor Bar.

Jonas was not afraid in the real sense of the word. Even if Frédo had hit him in a moment of fury, it would not have mattered to him. He was not brave, but he knew that physical pain does not last indefinitely.

It was Gina whom he felt he was defending at this moment, and he had the impression that he was making a mess of it, he could have sworn that his face had reddened to the roots of his hair.

'Did she say she would not be coming back to sleep?'

'I ...'

He thought very rapidly. Once already when the question of Bourges had arisen, he had spoken without thinking. This time he must take care.

'I don't remember.'

The young man sneered derisively.

'So you can't remember whether you were to expect her or not?'

'She didn't know herself.'

'Well then, did she take her travelling-case?'

Think fast, all the time, and not get caught out, not contradict himself. He couldn't help glancing at the staircase.

'I don't think so.'

'She didn't take it,' Frédo stated.

His voice grew hard, became accusing.

'Her case is in the cupboard, and her coat.'

He was waiting for an explanation. What could Jonas reply? Was this the moment to admit the truth? Was it to Gina's brother that he was to make his confession?

He stiffened, managed to say curtly:

'Possibly.'

'She didn't take the bus to Bourges.'

He feigned astonishment.

'I had a friend in the bus and he didn't see her.'

'Perhaps she took the train.'

'To go to see La Loute?'

'I imagine so.'

'Gina didn't go to see La Loute either. I rang her up this morning before coming here.'

Jonas did not know that La Loute had a telephone, or that

Frédo was on speaking terms with her. If he knew her number perhaps he had already been to call on her there himself?

'Where is my sister?'

'I don't know.'

'When did she leave?'

'Yesterday morning.'

He almost added:

'I swear l'

He almost believed it, by sheer force of repetition. What difference did it make if Gina had left on Wednesday evening or Thursday morning?

'Nobody saw her.'

'People are so used to seeing her passing that no one takes any notice now.'

Frédo, who was a whole head taller than he was, seemed to be hesitating whether to seize him by the shoulders and shake him, and Jonas, resigned, didn't move. His eyes didn't flinch until the moment that his visitor turned away to walk over to the door, without touching him.

'We'll soon see ...' Frédo growled heavily.

Never had a morning been so bright and so calm. The Square had scarcely come to life and the sound of the grocer lowering his orange blind could be heard, with the handle squeaking out in the silence.

Standing in the doorway, Frédo was a huge and menacing shadow.

As he turned his back, he opened his mouth, no doubt for some insult, thought better of it, walked across the pavement, and started up his motor-bike.

Jonas was still standing motionless in the middle of the shop, forgetting his *croissants*, forgetting that it was breakfast time. He was trying to understand. Already the day before he had had a premonition of danger hanging over him, and now he had just been threatened under his own roof.

What for? Why?

He had done nothing except to take a wife into his house, whom Angèle had given to him, and for two years he had done his best to give her peace.

'*She's gone to Bourges. . . .*'

He had said it without thinking, to stave off questions, and now it was bringing new ones in its wake. While he was at the baker's, Frédo had not only come into his house, but had gone upstairs, opened the cupboard, searched the wardrobe, since he knew that his sister had not taken her suitcase or coat.

Was it possible that *they* might be thinking what had suddenly come into his mind?

From red, he turned suddenly pale, so absurd and terrible was the notion. Did they really believe it? Had it really occurred to anybody, whether Frédo or not, that he had disposed of Gina?

Didn't they all know, everybody in the Old Market, and in the town as well, that it was not his wife's first escapade, that she had had them before marrying him, when she still lived with her parents, and that this was the reason they had given her to him?

He had no illusions about that. Nobody else would have married her. And Gina did not have the calm, the sangfroid of La Loute, who more or less got away with it in Bourges.

She was a female who could not control herself, that they all knew, including her father.

Why in Heaven's name would he have . . . ?

Even in his mind he hesitated to formulate the word, or to think of it. But wasn't it better to face the reality?

Why would he have killed her?

It was that, he was sure, that Frédo suspected. And perhaps, the day before, the same idea had already come, in a vaguer form, in Palestri's mind.

Otherwise why were they pestering him so?

If he was jealous, if he suffered every time Gina went off after a man, every time he detected an alien smell about her, he had never let anybody see it, not even her. He had never reproached her. On the contrary! When she returned, he was more gentle than ever, to help her forget, to prevent her from feeling uncomfortable in his presence.

He needed her as well. He wanted to keep her. He did not consider that he had the right to shut her up, as Angèle had once shut up her son.

71

Were they really thinking that?

He was on the point of running round to the Palestris' at once to tell Angèle the truth, but he realized that he was too late. He would no longer be believed. He had too often repeated that she had gone to Bourges, had given too many details.

Perhaps she would come back, in spite of everything? The fact that she had not taken her coat perplexed him. For if she had hidden in some part of the town why should she have taken the stamps, which she would not have been able to sell?

Mechanically he had gone into the kitchen, and once again, with mechanical gestures, he was making coffee, sitting down to drink it and eat his *croissants*. The Chaignes's lime tree was full of birds and he opened the door into the yard to throw them crumbs as usual.

If only it had been possible for him to question the clerk at the station, he would know, but it was too late for that, too.

Was somebody waiting for Gina with a car? That would have explained her going off without her coat. He could still present himself to the police and tell them everything, ask them to make inquiries for him. Who could tell? Tomorrow they would very likely reprimand him for not having done so, and see in that a proof against him!

Still unthinking, he went up to the bedroom where the door of the cupboard and the two doors of the wardrobe stood wide open. There was even a pair of his trousers on the floor. He put them back in their place, made the bed, cleaned out the bathroom and changed his dirty towel. It was laundry day and he thought about getting the dirty washing ready, as Gina was not there to do it. In the basket, which he emptied, there were some petticoats and brassières; he had begun to list the various items, when he was interrupted by steps downstairs.

It was Madame Lallemand, the mother of the little invalid girl who had been to Bourges the day before. She had come in to change some books for her daughter.

'What did the doctor say?' he remembered to ask.

'It seems there's a specialist in Vienna who might be able to cure her. It isn't certain and there'd be the business of the journey, and staying there several months in a foreign country without being able to speak the language. It all costs a lot of money. My daughter says she would rather stay as she is, but all the same I'm going to write to her uncle, who has a good business in Paris and may be able to help us.'

While he was choosing the books, the woman seemed to notice the silence in the house where, at that time, Gina would normally have been heard moving about.

'Isn't your wife in?'

He confined himself to a shake of the head.

'Yesterday somebody asked my daughter if she'd been with her on the bus.'

'You don't know who?'

'I didn't ask. I have so little time for other people, you see. . . .'

He did not react. From now on he was prepared for everything. His principal feeling was not even fear, but disappointment, and yet he had never expected anything from other people, had been content to live in his own corner, as humbly as possible.

'I think she would enjoy these two.'

'There's nothing about sick people in them?'

'No. I've read them.'

It was true that he sometimes read novels meant for young girls and actually enjoyed them. On these occasions he would think of Doussia, whom he would picture as each of the heroines in turn.

After that the gas bill was brought and he opened the till, paid, intended to go upstairs to finish off the laundry, when a young man brought in some school books to sell to him. Jonas was sure that he would come in a week or two to buy them back, that he was selling them only because he was short of pocket money. But as other people's affairs were no concern of his, he made an offer.

'Is that all?'

He was still a businessman.

'If they were not in such bad condition . . .'

There were three shelves of them, all school books, and it was these that brought in the most money, because the editions seldom changed, and the same books would pass through his hands a great many times in a few years. There were some he recognized, by a stain on the cover, for example, before he so much as touched them.

In the end he was able to go upstairs, finish off his list, tie up the dirty washing in a pillow case which he hid under the counter to await the arrival of the laundry man. It did not seem odd to him to send Gina's washing to the laundry. In his mind she was still, always would be, part of the household.

At ten o'clock he went over to Le Bouc's bar, where there was only a lorry driver whom he didn't know. He heard the usual:

' 'Morning, Monsieur Jonas.'

And he gave the ritual response:

' 'Morning, Fernand. An espresso coffee, please.'

'There you are.'

He picked up his two bits of sugar and began to unwrap them. The driver held his glass of white wine in his hand and said nothing, all the time keeping an eye on his lorry through the window. Contrary to his usual habit, Le Bouc worked the percolator in silence, and Jonas thought he seemed uncomfortable.

He had been expecting one question, and as it did not come, he volunteered:

'Gina hasn't come back.'

Fernand murmured, placing the steaming cup on the counter:

'So they tell me.'

So they had been talking about it here too. Not Frédo, surely, who did not frequent the bars of the Vieux-Marché. Was it Louis? But how would Louis have known, since his son, when he left, had gone off in the direction of the town?

They had certainly questioned the young cripple as she stepped out of the bus!

He couldn't understand it any longer. There was something entirely beyond him in this undercurrent of distrust. The time that Gina had been away for three days there had been no talk and, at most, a few people had given her a lewd glance.

Only the butcher had commented:

'How's your wife?'

He had replied:

'Very well, thank you.'

74

And Ancel had exclaimed, with a conspiratorial look at the assembled company:

'Heavens above!'

Why were they making a tragedy out of what had amused them only six months earlier? If he had been alone with Le Bouc, he would have been tempted to ask him. He probably would not have done so when all was said and done, from pure shame, but he would have felt like it.

And why did he need to explain himself, as though he felt guilty? Even now, he could not prevent himself from saying, with ill-affected indifference:

'She must have been held up.'

Le Bouc contented himself with a sigh, and avoided his gaze:

'No doubt.'

What had he done to them? Yesterday morning, when Gina had already departed, he still felt he was on good terms with them.

They were letting him drop all of a sudden, without a word of explanation, without letting him show his defence.

He had done nothing, nothing!

Was he going to be forced to shout it out aloud to them?

He was so upset that he inquired, as if he had not always known, the price of his coffee:

'How much is that?'

'The usual: thirty francs.'

They must be talking about him all over the Square. There were rumours of which he knew nothing. Somewhere there must have been a misunderstanding which a few words would suffice to clear up.

'I'm beginning to be anxious,' he went on, with a forced smile.

The observation fell flat. Le Bouc stood before him like a wall.

Jonas was making a mistake. He was talking too much. He gave the impression of defending himself before he had been accused. And nobody would ever dare to accuse him of getting rid of Gina.

Frédo, perhaps. But everyone knew him to be hot-headed.

Once again he was not guilty of anything. He had nothing

to hide. If he had mentioned Bourges, it was out of tact on Gina's behalf. He had not opened the strong-box then, and he envisaged an affair lasting a night or a couple of days. Would he have done better to reply to the people asking him for news of his wife:

'She's in bed with some man or other'?

They must believe him if he affirmed that it was not from vanity or self-respect that he had spoken about Bourges. If he had been vain, he would not have married Gina, whom nobody wanted, and it had given rise to enough laughter in the neighbourhood to see her married in white. Angèle herself had tried to oppose it.

'All my friends were married in white,' she had answered.

'Your friends aren't you.'

'I don't know one who was a virgin when she married, if that's what you mean, and you weren't one either when you married Papa.'

What she said of her friends and her mother was probably quite true. Anyhow, Angèle had made no reply. Only the others had not advertised themselves as much as she had.

If he had been ridiculous, as well, in his get-up, he had none the less looked around him proudly as he left the church with her arm in his.

He was not vain. He was not ashamed of what she was.

And yet he had just tried to lie to himself, by convincing himself that it was for her sake, and not for his own, that he had invented the trip to Bourges.

From what would he have wanted to shield her, since she had never made any secret of her escapades? As for the others, they must have enjoyed seeing her deceive him and been grateful to him for the fun they derived from it.

All the same he had answered:

'*She's gone to Bourges.*'

After that he had stuck to it doggedly.

As he made for his shop, where a stranger was browsing among the books in the cases outside, he was trying to find the answer, or rather to accept, since it gave him no satisfaction to do so.

If he had felt the need to protect Gina, wasn't it ultimately because he felt guilty towards her?

He didn't want to think about it any more. It was quite enough to have gone as far as he had. If he went on in this vein God knows where he would end in his discovery of things better left undiscovered.

Besides, nobody knew about all that. It was not what they were going to accuse him of. He had not killed her. He had not got rid of her. He was not guilty in their sense of the word.

Why, from that moment on, did they all, even Le Bouc, whom he liked best of the lot, to whose bar he went more as a friend than for love of coffee, why did they all look on him with suspicion?

'How much is this?' the customer asked him, holding out a book on underwater fishing.

'The price is marked on the back. A hundred and twenty francs.'

'A hundred francs,' the other suggested.

He repeated:

'A hundred and twenty.'

He must have spoken in an unusual tone of voice, for the man hastily dug into his pocket for the money, looking at him in astonishment.

FIVE

THEY left him alone until the Monday, too much alone in fact, for he was beginning to believe they were creating a vacuum around him. Perhaps he was becoming too susceptible and prone to read non-existent motives into people's actions?

After badgering him for two whole days for news of Gina with as much insistence as if they were dunning him they no longer mentioned it to him, and he was beginning to suspect them, Le Bouc, Ancel, and the others, of deliberately avoiding all reference to his wife.

Why did they abruptly cease taking any interest in her? And

77

if they knew where she was, what reason had they for keeping it from him?

He was on the watch for the slightest nuance. For example, when he had lunched at Pepito's on the Friday, the Widower had then distinctly batted his eyelids at him just as he used to in the old days, whereas yesterday they had scarcely flickered. Was the chief clerk under the impression that Jonas had returned for good and would be once again having his meals opposite him every day?

Pepito was not surprised to see him back, but he hadn't asked for news of Gina.

'There is creamed cod today,' he had announced, knowing that Jonas liked it.

It could not have been said that his manner was exactly cold, but he was certainly more reserved than usual.

'Will you be dining here this evening?' he had asked as Jonas rose to leave.

'I don't think so.'

Logically, Pepito ought to have remarked:

'Is Gina coming back this afternoon?'

For Pepito did not know the reason why Jonas, although he was alone, preferred to have dinner at home. In actual fact it was in order not to resume, all at once, his bachelor's existence, in order not to sever all the links with the other life he had known, and also because getting his meal and washing up afterwards kept him occupied.

The afternoon had been gloomy. The sultry air had penetrated through the open doorway. Jonas had settled down to sorting and marking one of the batches of books he brought down from the stock in the loft, where there were all kinds, the majority of them school prizes, which still bore in faded ink the names of their winners, long since deceased.

There had been few customers. Louis had passed by on his three-wheeler, slowing up, but had not stopped until reaching Fernand's bar.

At four o'clock, by which time he had departed, Jonas had gone for his coffee and Le Bouc had shown the same reserve as he had in the morning. Next he had repaired to Ancel's to buy

78

a cutlet for his dinner. Ancel was not there. His assistant served him and Madame Ancel appeared from the back of the shop to take the money without asking any questions.

He had dinner, tidied up, continued working fairly late on his inventory of the attic stock, which stood in a large pile in a corner, and patching the torn volumes with adhesive paper.

He worked in the shop where there was a light, but he had removed the door handle. The rest of the house was in darkness. Somebody walked past and back again around nine o'clock; he only half saw the figure in the darkness and he would have sworn it was Angèle.

They were spying on him. Without asking him anything, they were coming to see if Gina was back.

He went to bed at ten o'clock, fell asleep, and soon the sounds of an eve-of-market night began. Saturday's market was the most important one and, at certain hours of the day, the cars had to mount the pavement to find a parking space. It was hotter than the day before. The sun, a light yellow hue, no longer had the same airiness, and towards eleven o'clock it was as if a storm were going to break, and the market women could be seen peering anxiously at the sky. It broke somewhere in the country, for there was a rumbling in the distance, after which the clouds became luminous once more and finally disappeared, leaving nothing but an untrammelled blue.

He ate at Pepito's again and the Widower was there with his dog. It was Jonas who this time, as if seeking some sort of sympathy, of support, however vague, was the first to flutter his eyelids, and Monsieur Métras returned the salute with a face devoid of expression.

Pepito's was closed on Sundays and Jonas made the round of the shops to buy his provisions, carrying Gina's straw shopping basket. He did not buy his vegetables at Angèle's but at a shop in the rue Haute. At the butcher's, Ancel served him in person this time, without the remotest suggestion of a friendly jest. He also had to buy some bread, some coffee, and some more salt, which had run out, and, for Sunday evening, he took home some spaghetti. It was a tradition from Gina's day, because it was quick to make.

The floor of the Old Market was washed down with hoses, a few cars came and parked in it and then in the evening, like the day before, he spent his time patching up books and marking the prices in pencil on the back. He had looked through the newspaper. He was not expecting to find news of his wife, nor indeed hoping for it, for that would have meant bad news, but he was nevertheless disappointed.

It was the fourth night that he had slept alone, and as he had gone to bed early, he heard some of the neighbours returning from the cinema; the following morning, before he got up, he heard others, women for the most part, making for St Cecilia's Church.

Ever since he had married Gina, he had accompanied her to Mass on Sundays, always the ten o'clock High Mass, and for this occasion she dressed up in her best clothes, in summer wore a blue suit with a hat and white gloves.

When the question of the wedding had arisen, he had realized that for the Palestri family it would have to take place in church.

Up till then he had never been inside it except for a few funerals, had never observed the rites of any religion, except, up to his mother's departure, the Jewish ones.

He had not said he was a Jew, nor hidden the fact. Immediately after the decision had been taken, he had gone to find the parish priest of St Cecilia's, Abbé Grimault, and had asked to be baptized.

For a period of three weeks he had taken catechism lessons at the priest's house almost every evening, in a little parlour with a round table covered with a crimson velvet cloth with tassels. The air was pervaded with a smell, at once stale and strong, which Jonas had never come across before, and which he was never to find again, anywhere else.

While he was reciting his lessons like a schoolboy, the Abbé Grimault, who was born on a farm in the Charolais, would puff at his cigar and gaze into space, which did not prevent him, however, from correcting his pupil the moment he went wrong.

Jonas had asked that he should not be treated too strictly and the priest had understood. Even so, a godfather and godmother had to be found. Justine, the Abbé's servant, and old Joseph, the sacristan, an engraver by trade, filled these rôles, and Jonas gave them each a handsome present. He gave another to the church. He had written to tell Shepilov that he was getting married, but had not dared mention the christening, nor the religious ceremony.

It had given him pleasure to become a Christian, not only because of the marriage, but because it brought him nearer to the inhabitants of the Old Market, nearly all of whom went to church. At first he stood a little stiffly and made his genuflexions and signs of the cross out of time, but then he had picked up the habit and Gina and he kept to the same places every Sunday, at the end of a row.

He went to Mass that Sunday as on every other Sunday, and it was the first time he had gone alone. They seemed to be watching him as he went to his place, and to nudge one another as he passed.

He did not pray, because he had never really prayed, but he wanted to, and as he watched the dancing light of the candles and breathed the smell of the incense, he thought of Gina and also of his sister Doussia, though he never knew what she looked like.

After the service, groups formed outside the church and for a quarter of an hour the Square was full of life. The Sunday clothes lent a gay note, then, little by little, the pavements emptied and for the rest of the day there was virtually nobody to be seen there.

At noon Ancel, who worked on Sunday mornings, drew his blinds. All the other blinds in the Square were already lowered, except those of the bakery and cake shop which closed at half past twelve.

For Jonas and his wife, it was the day for the backyard. This meant that in good weather they would base themselves in the yard, as long as they were not going out. It was in fact almost impossible to stay in the shop in the summer with the door shut, because of the lack of air, and if the door was left open the passers-by would think they were not observing their Sabbath rest.

Not only did they spend the afternoon in the courtyard but

they lunched there as well, under the lime-tree branch which stretched over the Chaignes's garden wall and gave them some shade.

The whole length of the wall was covered by a vine, old and twisted, its leaves marked with rust, but it none the less produced each year a few bunches of acid grapes.

They had tried keeping a cat. They had had several. All of them, for some reason or other, had gone to seek a home elsewhere.

Gina didn't like dogs. Actually she didn't like any animals, and when they went for a walk in the country, she would eye the cows uneasily from a safe distance.

She didn't like the country either, nor taking walks. She had never wanted to learn to swim. She was only in her element when her extremely high heels came in contact with the hard smooth surface of a pavement, and she had in addition a horror of quiet streets like the one in which Clémence lived; she needed animation, noise, the many-coloured display of shop windows.

When they went to have a drink, she did not choose the spacious cafés of the Place de l'Hôtel de Ville, or the Place du Théâtre, but the bars with juke boxes.

He had bought her a wireless set and on Sundays she would take it out into the yard, using an extension to plug it into the kitchen.

She hardly ever sewed, was content to keep her clothes and linen more or less in disrepair, and her blouses were often missing a button, while a good half of her petticoats had holes in them.

She used to read, listening to the music and smoking cigarettes, and sometimes in the middle of the afternoon she would go up to her bedroom, remove her dress, and stretch out on top of the cover.

He read on this Sunday, too, in one of the two iron chairs which he had bought second-hand for use in the yard. He went back into the shop twice to change his book and in the end became interested in a work on the life of spiders. There was one in the corner, which he had known for a long time, and now and then he raised his eyes to observe it with renewed interest, like a man who has just made a discovery.

The post had brought him no news of Gina the day before or on Friday. He had been hoping, without believing it, that she would perhaps send him a word, and now he was beginning to realize that the idea was ridiculous.

From time to time, without interrupting his reading, his thoughts superimposed themselves on the printed text, without his losing the place. True they were not clear cut, consecutive thoughts. Various images came to his mind, such as that of Angèle, then, straightaway afterwards, for no reason, he pictured Gina lying naked on an iron bed, in a hotel bedroom.

Why an iron bed? And why, all round her, white-washed walls, like those in the country?

It was unlikely that she had taken refuge in the country, which she detested. She was certainly not alone. Since Wednesday evening when she had left she must have bought herself some underclothes, unless she had been content to wash her petticoat and brassière at night and put them on again in the morning unironed.

Clémence, her husband and Poupou must have been with the Ancels, where the whole family used to gather and the youngest of the daughters, Martine, played the piano. They had a very large yard with, at the back, the shed Gina had talked about. She had not told him whether she had allowed the butcher to have her. Probably she had, but it was also probable that Ancel had not dared to go the whole way.

Twice during the afternoon he thought he heard the piano, the sound of which reached his back yard when the wind was in the right direction.

The Chaigne family had a car and were not at home on Sundays. Angèle used to sleep the entire afternoon while Louis, dressed in a navy-blue suit, went to play skittles and did not return until he had made a tour of the town's cafés.

How did a young man like Frédo spend his time? Jonas had no idea. He was the only one in the family not to go to Mass and he was not to be seen all day.

At five o'clock a few old women passed by on their way to

Benediction and the bells rang out for a moment. Le Bouc's bar was closed. Jonas had made himself some coffee and, feeling slightly hungry, he nibbled a piece of cheese.

Nothing else happened. He had dined, after which, not having the heart to work, he had finished his book on spiders. It was only nine o'clock and he had gone for a stroll, closing the door behind him, had headed in the direction of the narrow canal where a lock-gate stood out black against the moonlit sky. Two narrow barges, of the Berry type, were moored to the quay and he could see rings forming around them on the surface of the water.

He passed Clémence's, in the rue des Deux-Ponts, and this time there was a light on the first floor. Did Clémence know something about Gina? Even if she did, she wouldn't tell him anything. He did not stop, as he was tempted to do, but passed quickly by, for the window was open and Reverdi, in shirt sleeves, was moving about the room talking.

The nearer he got to his home, the more the closed shutters in the streets, the deserted pavements, the silence, filled him with a sort of uneasiness, and he caught himself increasing his pace as if to flee from some indefinable menace.

Was it because others, like Gina, felt the same fear that they hurried into the garishly lighted bars, to seek the company of shouts and music?

He could see some of those bars in the distance, in the second part of the rue Haute, on the same side as the Luxor, and he could just make out the couples along the walls.

He slept badly, still with the feeling of a threat, which had pursued him even into his bedroom. He had removed his spectacles and switched off the light when a memory had jangled in his brain, not exactly a personal memory, for the passage of time had confused the fragments of what he had seen and heard with what he had subsequently been told.

He was not six years old when the drama had occurred, and since then there had been no further sensational events in the town until the Marcel hold-up.

He was born in 1916, so it had taken place in 1922, and he was just starting to go to school. It must have been November. The

Maison Bleue was already in existence, so called because the outside was painted in sky-blue from top to bottom.

It had not changed since then. It stood surmounted by a very steep roof, at the corner of the rue des Prémontrés and the Square, just beside Ancel's butcher's shop, two houses from the fishmonger's where Jonas lived at the time.

The sign had not changed either. In letters of a darker blue than the façade was written: '*La Maison Bleue*'. Then, in smaller letters: '*Children's clothing. Baby garments a speciality.*'

The woman now known as the widow Lentin still had her husband at the time, a fair-haired man who wore long moustaches and who, since his wife ran the business, worked at odd jobs outside.

At certain periods, he could be seen sitting all day long on a chair in front of the house, and Jonas remembered a phrase he had heard frequently repeated:

'*Lentin's having one of his bouts.*'

Gustave Lentin had fought in the Tonkin campaign, a name which Jonas had heard for the first time when people were talking of him, and which to Jonas seemed a terrible word. He had caught the fevers there, as the people of the Vieux-Marché put it. For weeks he was like any other man, with a rather dark, at times stormy look in his eyes, and he would embark on some job or other. Then it would get around that he was in bed, 'covered with an icy sweat and trembling in his limbs, his teeth clenched like a dead man's'.

Jonas had not invented this description. He did not know where he had heard it, but it had remained engraved on his memory. Doctor Lourel, since dead, who had worn a beard, came to see him twice a day, striding rapidly, his worn leather bag in his hand, and Jonas, from the pavement opposite, used to glue his eyes to the windows, wondering if Lentin was dying.

A few days later he would reappear, emaciated, his eyes sad and empty, and his wife would help him out on to his chair beside the doorway, would move him during the day, as the sun followed its course.

The shop did not belong to Lentin but to his parents-in-law, the Arnauds, who lived in the house with the couple. Madame Arnaud remained in Jonas's mind as a woman almost entirely round, with white hair gathered in a bun at the back of her head and so sparse that the pink of her skull showed through it.

He could not remember her husband.

But he had seen the crowd, one morning, as he was about to leave for school. There was a wind blowing that day. It was a market day. An ambulance and two other black cars were standing in front of the Maison Bleue and the crowd was shoving so much that one might have thought it was a riot, if it had not been for the oppressive silence which reigned.

Although his mother had dragged him away and assured him afterwards that he could not have seen anything, he was convinced, to this day, that he had seen on a stretcher carried by two male nurses in white smocks, a man with his throat cut. A woman was screaming, he was sure, in the house, in the way that mad women scream.

'You imagine you actually saw what you heard told afterwards.'

It was possible, but it was difficult to admit that that image had not really appeared before his eyes as a child.

Lentin, it was afterwards learnt, suffered from the feeling of being a useless passenger in the house of his in-laws. Several times he was said to have let it be known that things would not go on as they were, and they had imagined suicide. They used to watch him. His wife sometimes followed in the street at a discreet distance.

That night he had not woken her up, even though he was racked with fever. She had been the first down, as usual, imagining him still sleeping and then, silently, a razor in his hand, he had gone into the bedroom of his father- and mother-in-law and had cut their throats one after the other as he had seen done by the Tonkinese soldiers, and as, out there, he had perhaps done himself.

Only old Madame Arnaud had had the time to cry out. Her daughter had rushed up the stairs, but when she reached the open door her husband had finished his work and, standing in

86

the middle of the room and fixing her with a 'mad look', he had in turn severed his own carotid artery.

Madame Lentin was quite white now, diminutive, her hair as thin as her mother's, and she went on selling children's clothing and baby garments.

Why had Jonas thought of this drama just as he was dropping off to sleep? Because he had passed in front of the Maison Bleue a short while ago and had had a glimpse of a shadow behind the curtain?

It disturbed him. He forced himself to think of something else. As he was still not able to sleep after half an hour he got up to take a tablet of gardenal. In fact he took two, and the effect was almost immediate. Only towards four o'clock he awoke in the silence of the dawn and lay with his eyes open until it was time to get up.

He was stiff and uncomfortable. He almost decided against going to the baker for his *croissants*, as he was not hungry, but it was a form of discipline he had imposed on himself and he crossed the deserted Square, saw Angèle laying her baskets out on the pavement. Did she see him? Did she pretend not to see him?

'Three?' the baker's wife asked him from force of habit.

It annoyed him. He had the impression he was being spied on, and above all that the others knew things he did not. Ancel, without taking the cigarette from his lips, was unloading some sides of beef, which did not even cause him to stoop, and yet he must have been five or six years older than Jonas.

He ate, took out his boxes of books, decided to finish off the stock from the attic before going up to his room, and at half past nine he was still working, looking in a bibliography to see whether a dilapidated Maupassant which he had just found in the pile was a first edition.

Somebody came in and he did not immediately raise his eyes. He knew, by the silhouette, that it was a man, and the latter, without pressing him, was examining the books on a shelf.

When he finally looked up, Jonas recognized Police Inspector Basquin, to whom he had on many occasions sold books.

'Excuse me,' he stammered. 'I was busy with . . .'

'How are you, Monsieur Jonas?'

'All right. I'm all right.'

He could have sworn that Basquin had not come that morning to buy a book from him, more especially as he had one in his hand.

'And Gina?'

He reddened. It was unavoidable. The more he tried not to the more he reddened, and he felt his ears burning.

'I trust she's all right, too.'

Basquin was three or four years younger than he and had been born the far side of the canal, in a group of five or six houses surrounding the brickworks. He was fairly often to be seen at the market, and if ever one of the shopkeepers was robbed, it was nearly always he who took charge of it.

'Isn't she here?'

He hesitated, first said no, then, like a man plunging into the water, said all in one breath:

'She left on Wednesday evening telling me that she was going to look after the baby for Ancel's daughter, Clémence. Since then she hasn't come back and I've heard no news.'

It was a relief finally to let out the truth, to dispose once and for all of this fairy tale about the visit to Bourges, which was haunting him. Basquin looked a decent sort of fellow. Jonas had heard tell that he had five children, a very blonde wife with a sickly appearance, who in reality was more hardy than some women who appear outwardly strong.

In this way, often, in the Old Market, one learns the history of people one has never seen, by odds and ends of conversations picked up here and there. Jonas did not know Madame Basquin, who lived in a small new house on the edge of the town, but it was possible that he had seen her when she was doing her shopping, without realizing who she was.

The Inspector did not have a crafty look, as though he wanted to catch Jonas out. He was relaxed, familiar, as he stood by the counter, book in hand, like a customer talking about the rain or the fine weather.

'Did she take any luggage with her?'

'No. Her case is upstairs.'

'And her dresses, her clothes?'

'She was only wearing her red dress.'

'No coat?'

Didn't that prove that Basquin knew more than he wanted to show? Why, otherwise, would he have thought of the coat? Frédo had thought of it, certainly, but only after searching in the bedroom.

Did that mean that Frédo had warned the police?

'Her two coats are in the cupboard as well.'

'Had she any money on her?'

'If she had, it wasn't much.'

His heart was thumping against his constricted chest and he had difficulty in speaking naturally.

'You have no idea where she might have gone?'

'None, Monsieur Basquin. At half past twelve on Wednesday night, I was so worried that I went round to Clémence's.'

'What did she tell you?'

'I didn't go in. There wasn't any light. I thought that they were all in bed and I didn't want to disturb them. I hoped that Gina might have come back another way.'

'You didn't meet anyone?'

That was the question which frightened him most of all, for he realized that what he was being asked for was an alibi. He searched desperately in his memory, then confessed, abashed :

'No. I don't think so.'

A recollection occurred to him.

'I heard a couple talking in the rue de Bourges, but I didn't see them.'

'You didn't pass anyone, either going or coming back?'

'I don't remember. I was thinking about my wife. I wasn't paying any attention.'

'Try to remember.'

'I am trying.'

'Someone, at a window, might have seen you passing.'

He was triumphant.

'There was a lighted window at the corner of the rue des Prémontrés and the rue des Deux-Ponts.'

'Whose house?'

'I don't know, but I could show it to you.'

'Was the window open?'

'No, I don't think so. The blind was lowered. I actually thought of an invalid ...'

'Why an invalid?'

'No particular reason. It was all so quiet. ...'

Basquin was watching him gravely, without severity, without antipathy. On his side, Jonas found it natural that he should be doing his duty and preferred it to be him than anyone else. The Inspector was sure to understand sooner or later.

'It has happened before that Gina ...' he began shamefacedly.

'I know. But she's never been away four days before, has she? And there was always someone who knew where she was.'

What did he mean by that? That when she went on a spree Gina kept some people informed, her brother, for example, or one of her friends, like Clémence? Basquin had not just spoken idly. He knew what he was talking about, seemed to know more about it than even Jonas himself.

'Did you have a quarrel on Wednesday?'

'We never quarrelled, I promise you.'

Madame Lallemand, the mother of the young cripple, came in to exchange her two books and the conversation was left in suspense. Had she heard any rumours? She appeared to know the Inspector, at any rate to know who he was, for she looked embarrassed and said:

'Give me anything of the same kind.'

Had she realized that it was an actual interrogation that the bookseller was undergoing? She left hurriedly like someone who realizes they are not wanted and in the meantime Basquin, having replaced his book on the shelf, had lit a cigarette.

'Not even,' he resumed, 'when she had spent the night out?'

Jonas said forcefully:

'Not even then. I never even reproached her.'

He saw the policeman frown and realized that it was hard to believe. Yet he was speaking the truth.

'You are asking me to believe that it made no difference to you?'

'It did hurt me.'

'And you avoided showing it?'

It was genuine curiosity which had perhaps nothing professional about it, that he read in Basquin's eyes, and he would have liked to make him understand exactly how he felt. His face was covered with sweat and his spectacles were beginning to mist over.

'I didn't need to show it to her. She knew it already. In actual fact she was ashamed, but she wouldn't have let it be seen for anything in this world.'

'Gina was ashamed?'

Raising his head he almost cried out, he was so sure that he was right:

'Yes! And it would have been cruel to add to her shame. It wouldn't have been any good. Don't you understand? She couldn't help it. It was in her nature. . . .'

Stupefied, the Inspector was watching him speak, and for a moment Jonas hoped he had convinced him.

'I had no right to reproach her.'

'You are her husband.'

He sighed wearily:

'Of course . . .'

He realized that his hopes had been premature.

'How many times did it happen in the past two years? For it was two years ago that you got married, wasn't it?'

'Two years ago last month. I haven't counted the number of times.'

It wasn't entirely true. He could have remembered it in a few moments, but it was not important and the question reminded him of the ones the priest asks in the confessional.

'The last time?'

'Six months ago.'

'Did you know who it was with?'

He raised his voice again.

'No! No! Why should I want to know?'

How could it have helped him, to know the man Gina had slept with? To have even more vivid pictures in his mind and suffer all the more?

'You love her?'

He replied almost in a whisper :
'Yes.'

It made him wince to talk about it, because it concerned no one but himself.

'In short, you love her but you're not jealous.'

It wasn't a question. It was a conclusion, and he did not take it up. He was discouraged. It was no longer the more or less marked coldness of the market people that he was up against, but the reasoning of a man who, on account of his profession, ought to have been capable at least of understanding.

'You're sure Gina left the house on Wednesday evening?'

'Yes.'

'At what time?'

'Directly after dinner. She washed up, but forgot to clean the stove, and told me she was going round to the Reverdis.'

'Did she go up to her room?'

'I think so. Yes.'

'You aren't sure?'

'Yes, I am. I remember now.'

'Did she stay there long?'

'Not very long.'

'Did you see her to the door?'

'Yes.'

'So you saw which way she went?'

'Towards the rue des Prémontrés.'

He pictured in his mind's eye the red of her dress in the grey light of the street.

'You're sure your wife didn't spend the night of Wednesday to Thursday here?'

He reddened again as he said :

'Certain.'

And he was about to open his mouth to explain, for he was intelligent enough to know what was coming next. Basquin was too quick for him.

'Yet you told her father that she had taken the bus to Bourges, at 7.10 on Thursday morning.'

'I know. It was wrong.'

'You were lying?'

'It wasn't exactly a lie.'

'You repeated it to different people and you gave details.'

'I was just going to explain ...'

'Answer my question first. Had you any reason for hiding from Palestri the fact that his daughter had gone off on Wednesday evening?'

'No.'

He hadn't had any particular reason for hiding it from Louis, and besides, that was not how it had all started. If only he could have a chance to tell the story the way it had happened, there would be some hope of being understood.

'You admit that Palestri knew all about his daughter's conduct?'

'I think so. ... Yes ...'

'Angèle as well. .... She certainly didn't make any secret of it. ...'

He could have wept at his own impotence.

'It's no use pretending that Gina was ashamed, she never tried to hide it herself, quite the opposite.'

'That's not the same thing. It isn't that sort of shame.'

'What sort is it?'

He was tempted to give up, from weariness. They were two intelligent men face to face, but they didn't speak the same language and they were on completely different planes.

'It was all the same to her what people said. It was ...'

He wanted to explain that it was in regard to herself that she was ashamed, but he was not being given the chance.

'And to you, was it all the same to you?'

'Of course it was!'

The words had been faster than his thoughts. It was true and yet untrue. He realized that that was going to contradict what he had still to explain.

'So you had no reason to hide the fact that she had gone?'

'I didn't hide it.'

His throat was dry, his eyes smarted.

'What difference,' went on Basquin without giving him a chance to go back on what he had said, 'would it make whether she left on Wednesday evening or Thursday morning?'

'Exactly.'

'Exactly what?'

'It doesn't make any difference. That proves that I wasn't really lying.'

'When you said that your wife had taken the bus at 7.10 to go and see La Loute at Bourges? And in repeating it to at least six people, including your mother-in-law?'

'Listen, Monsieur Basquin. . . .'

'I am only too anxious to listen.'

It was true. He was trying to understand, but even so there was in Jonas's manner something which was beginning to irritate him. Jonas noticed it, and that made him lose his bearings even more. As at Le Bouc's during the last few days, there was a wall between himself and the other man, and he was beginning to wonder if he was like other men.

'I was hoping that Gina would come back on Thursday in the morning.'

'Why?'

'Because, most times, she only used to go away for the night.'

It hurt him to say it, but he was ready to suffer more than that for the sake of being left in peace.

'When I saw that she didn't come, I told myself that she would be back during the day and I carried on as if nothing had happened.'

'Why?'

'Because it wasn't worth the bother of . . .'

Would someone else have behaved differently in his place? He had to take advantage of the fact that he was being allowed to get a few words in.

'I went into Le Bouc's around ten o'clock, as I do every day.'

'And you announced that your wife had left for Bourges by the morning bus to go and see her friend.'

Jonas lost his temper, stamped his foot, shouted:

'No!'

'You didn't say so in the presence of five or six witnesses?'

'Not like that. It's not the same thing. Le Bouc asked me how Gina was and I replied that she was all right. Ancel, who was near me, can confirm it. I think it was also Fernand who

94

remarked that he hadn't seen her at the market that morning.'

'What difference does that make?'

'Wait!' he begged. 'It was then that I said she had gone to Bourges.'

'Why?'

'To explain her absence and give her time to come back without there being any fuss.'

'You said just now that it was all the same to her.'

He shrugged his shoulders. He had said so, certainly.

'And that it was all the same to you as well ...'

'Let's say I was caught off my guard. I was in a bar, surrounded by acquaintances, and they were asking me where my wife was.'

'They asked you *where* she was?'

'They mentioned that they had not seen her. I replied that she had gone to Bourges.'

'Why Bourges?'

'Because she used occasionally to go there.'

'And why mention the 7.10 bus?'

'Because I remembered that there wasn't a bus to Bourges in the evening.'

'You thought of everything.'

'I thought of that by chance.'

'And La Loute?'

'I don't even think I was the first to mention her. If I remember rightly, Le Bouc said:

'"Has she gone to see La Loute?"'

'Because everyone knows that La Loute is at Bourges and that Gina and she are friends.'

'Strange!' murmured Basquin, looking at him more closely than ever.

'It's all quite simple,' answered Jonas, forcing a smile.

'Perhaps it isn't as simple as all that!'

And the Inspector pronounced these words in a grave tone, with an expression of annoyance on his face.

SIX

WAS Basquin hoping that Jonas would change his mind and make a confession? Or was he simply anxious to underline the unofficial character of his visit? Whatever the case, he behaved before leaving as he had done on his entry, like a customer who has dropped in, glancing through a few books with his back turned to the bookseller.

Finally he looked at his watch, sighed, picked up his hat from the chair.

'It's time I was getting along. No doubt we shall have another opportunity to talk all this over again.'

He did not say it as a threat, but as if the two of them had a problem to solve.

Jonas followed him to the door, which had been open all the time, and with a reflex action common to all shopkeepers, glanced up and down the street. He was still shaken. The sun shone full upon him when he turned to the right and he could not make out the faces around Angèle. What he was sure of was that there was a group on the pavement, round the greengrocer's wife, most of them women, and that everybody was looking in his direction.

Turning to the left, he caught sight of another group, in Le Bouc's doorway with, as a focal point, Ancel's working overalls with their narrow blue and white stripes and his bloodstained apron.

So they had known what was going on ahead of him and had been keeping an eye open for the Inspector's visit. Through the wide open door of the shop they must have caught fragments of conversation, when Jonas had raised his voice. Perhaps some of them had even approached softly without being noticed?

He was even more shocked than he was frightened by the thought. They were not behaving decently to him and he did not deserve it. He was ashamed of giving the impression of

96

running away or retreating abruptly into his shop, but there and then, without warning, he was in no fit state to face their hostile curiosity.

For that their silence was hostile there could be no doubt. He would have preferred whistles and insults.

Well, this was the silence that he was going to have to endure for the next few days, during which he lived as if in a universe detached from the rest of the world.

He made himself go on with his work, without realizing precisely what he was doing, and, a few minutes before four o'clock, instinct made him look at his watch. It was time for his cup of coffee at Le Bouc's. Was he going to change his routine? He was tempted to do so. That was the simplest solution. But in spite of everything that Basquin might think, it was from loyalty to Gina, it was for Gina's sake that he was so anxious for life to continue as before.

When he came out of the door, there was no longer anybody spying on him, and the Chaignes's red-haired dog, which had been sleeping in the sun, struggled lazily to its feet and came over to sniff his heels and offer its head to be patted.

In Le Bouc's bar he found only a stranger, and the old beggar-woman who was eating a hunk of bread and a piece of sausage in a corner.

''Afternoon, Fernand. An espresso coffee, please,' he said, carefully noting the inflexions of his own voice.

He was striving to remain natural. Without a word, Fernand placed a cup under the chromium tap and let the steam escape, avoiding his eyes, ill at ease, as if he were not convinced that they weren't all behaving rather cruelly.

He couldn't act differently from the others. Jonas understood that. All the Old Market, at the moment, was forming a bloc against him, including, in all likelihood, people who didn't know anything about the affair.

He didn't deserve it, not only because he was innocent of everything they might accuse him of, but because he had always tried, discreetly, quietly, to live like them, with them, and to be like them.

He believed, only a few days before, that he had succeeded

by dint of patience and humility. For he had been humble as well. He did not lose sight of the fact that he was a foreigner, a member of another race, born in far-off Archangel, whom the fortunes of wars and revolutions had transplanted to a small town in the Berry.

Shepilov, for instance, did not possess this humility. Having fled to France, he did not think twice before taking it on himself to criticize the country and its customs, even its politics, and Constantin Milk himself, when he had his fishmonger's shop, did not hesitate to talk to Natalie in Russian in front of the customers.

No one had resented it, in his case. Was it because he had asked nothing and did not worry about what his neighbours thought? The ones who had known him talked of him still with affection, as of a strong and colourful personality.

Jonas, perhaps because his first conscious memories had been of the Vieux-Marché, had always tried to become integrated. He did not ask the people to recognize him as one of themselves. He felt that that was impossible. He behaved with the discretion of a guest, and it was as a guest that he saw himself.

They had let him be, let him open his shop. In the morning they called out their ritual:

' 'Morning, Monsieur Jonas!'

There had been about thirty of them at his wedding reception, and outside the church the whole of the market had ranged themselves in two rows on the steps.

Why were they suddenly changing their attitude?

He would have sworn that things would not have turned out the same if what had happened to him had happened to one of themselves. He had become a foreigner again over-night, a man from another clan, from another world, come to eat their bread and take one of their daughters.

It did not anger him, nor embitter him, but it caused him pain, and like Basquin, he, too, repeated insistently:

'Why?'

It was hard to be there, at Fernand's bar, which was like a second home to him, and see the latter silent, distant, to be obliged to remain silent himself.

He didn't ask what he owed, as he had done last time, but put the money down on the linoleum of the counter.

'Good night, Fernand.'

'Good night.'

Not the usual:

'*Good night, Monsieur Jonas.*'

Only a vague and cold:

'*Good night.*'

It was Monday, and this was to go on for four days, until the Friday. Gina sent no word of herself. There was nothing about her in any of the papers. At one moment he thought that Marcel might have escaped and that she had rejoined him, but an escape would probably have attracted a certain amount of publicity.

During those four days he managed, by sheer will-power, to remain the same, rose every morning at the usual time, went across to the other side of the Square for his three *croissants*, made his coffee, then, a little later in the morning, went up to do his room.

At ten o'clock he would go into Le Bouc's, and when Louis was there one time, on the Wednesday, he had the strength of mind not to retreat. He was expecting to be harangued by Palestri, who had already had a few drinks. On the contrary, he was greeted by an absolute silence; on seeing him everyone stopped talking, except for a stranger who was talking to Le Bouc and who uttered another remark or two, looking round him in surprise, only to end up in an embarrassed silence.

Each day at noon he went round to Pepito's, and neither he nor his niece once engaged him in conversation. The Widower went on blinking his eyelids, but then hadn't he, too, been living in a world of his own for a long time?

Customers still came to his shop, fewer than usual, and he did not see Madame Lallemand, whose daughter ought to have finished her last two books.

Often two whole hours would pass without anyone coming in through the doorway, and to keep himself occupied, he undertook the cleaning of his shelves, one by one, dusting book after book, so that he came across various works which had been there for years and which he had forgotten about.

99

He spent hours thus occupied on his bamboo steps, seeing the Square outside now deserted, now enlivened with the colourful bustle of the market.

He hadn't spoken to Basquin about the missing stamps. Was that going to recoil upon him too? The Inspector had only asked him whether Gina had any money, and he had replied that she could not have had much, which was true.

He, too, was beginning to be afraid that some accident had befallen Gina. Once at least, he was sure, she had spent the night in a squalid furnished room in the rue Haute, with a North African. Mightn't she have fallen this time on a sadist or a madman, or one of those desperadoes who kill for a few hundred francs?

It comforted him to think that she had taken the stamps for it enabled him almost for sure to dismiss this theory.

He felt so alone, so helpless, that he was tempted to go and seek the advice of the Abbé Grimault, in the tranquility of his parlour, where the smell and the semi-obscurity were so soothing. What could the priest have said to him? Why should he understand any better than Basquin, who at least had a wife himself?

In the evening he made his supper, did the washing up. He did not again touch the album of Russian stamps, which reminded him that he was of another race. He was feeling almost guilty, by now, for having amassed this collection as if it were an act of treason towards the people amongst whom he lived.

However, it was not from patriotism or nostalgia for a country which he did not know, that he had gathered all these stamps together. He could not have said exactly what impulse he had obeyed. Perhaps it was because of Doussia? He had talked about her to Gina, one Sunday afternoon, in the back yard, and Gina had asked:

'Is she older than you?'

'She was two when I was born. She would be forty-two now.'

'Why do you say *would be*?'

'Because she may be dead.'

'Did they kill children so young?'

'I don't know. It's possible that she's still alive.'

She had looked at him wonderingly.

'How strange!' she had murmured finally.

'What?'

'Everything. You. Your family. Your sisters. All these people who are perhaps living quietly over there without your knowing it and may very well be wondering what's happened to you. Haven't you ever wanted to go and see them?'

'No.'

'Why not?'

'I don't know.'

She hadn't understood and she must have thought that he had disowned his family. It wasn't true.

'Do you think they shot your father?'

'They may have sent him to Siberia. Perhaps again they've let him go back to Archangel.'

How ironical if all the family had been reunited out there in their town, in their own house – who could say? All except him!

On one occasion he found himself next to Constable Benaiche at Le Bouc's bar and Benaiche pretended not to see him. Now though he went three times a week to the market on duty, he was not part of the market and he must know what they thought of Jonas at the police station.

Basquin had given him to understand that they would be meeting again, and Jonas was hourly expecting his arrival. He had forced himself to prepare answers to the questions he anticipated. He had even summarized, on a scrap of paper, his movements on the Thursday, the day he had talked so much about the visit to Bourges, with a list of people he had spoken to.

Four days of living as though in a glass frame, like certain animals on which experiments are being made in laboratories and which are observed hour by hour. There was a violent storm on the Thursday morning, when the market was at its height, which caused a stampede, for the rain fell in huge drops mixed with hailstones, and two women he didn't know took refuge in his shop. The downpour lasted nearly an hour and activities outside were almost suspended; he was himself unable to go to Le Bouc's at ten o'clock and it was about half past eleven before he went to have his coffee in the bar, which smelt of damp wool.

He was still compelling himself to say, as usual, as if nothing had happened :

'Morning, Fernand.'

And he ordered his coffee, while unwrapping his two pieces of sugar.

That afternoon, towards five o'clock, a policeman on a bicycle stopped outside the shop and came in, leaving his machine propped up at the edge of the pavement.

'You are Jonas Milk?'

He said yes, and the man handed him a yellow envelope, then a notebook like the ones postmen used for registered packages.

'Sign here.'

He signed, waited until he was alone again before opening the envelope, which contained an official letter printed on coarse paper, summoning him to the police station for the following day, Friday, at ten o'clock in the morning.

They were not going to continue coming to question him with an air of casually passing by. They were summoning him. On the dotted line followed the word : 'Reason' there was written in indelible pencil :

'*Personal Matters.*'

He felt a desire, that evening, to put in writing all that had happened since the Wednesday evening, and in particular, during the whole of Thursday, with a sincere explanation of every one of his actions, every one of his words, but it was in vain that he sat at his desk and tried to decide where to start.

They had not yet accused him of anything whatsoever. They had merely asked him insidious questions and created a vacuum around him.

Perhaps it would be better after all for him at last to have an opportunity to explain everything from beginning to end. He did not know who, over there, would see him. The summons was signed by the superintendent, whom he knew by sight. He was called Devaux and, if only from the hair in his nostrils and ears, he looked like Monsieur Métras. He was a widower, too, lived with his daughter who had married a young doctor from Saint-Amand, with a house in the rue Gambetta.

He slept badly, woke up almost every hour, had confused nightmares, and dreamed, among other things, of the canal and the lock-gate, which had been raised to allow a barge to pass and which would not go down again. Why was he to blame? It was a mystery, but everybody was accusing him and he had been given a ridiculously short time to make the bridge work; he was bathed in sweat, gripping the operating handle with his hands, while Ancel, who was carrying a quarter of beef on his shoulder, was sneering at him.

They were treating him like a convict. That is what emerged clearly from his dream. There was also some talk of Siberia.

'You who come from Siberia . . .'

He endeavoured to explain that Archangel is not in Siberia, but they knew better than he did. Siberia, God knows why, had something to do with the fact that he was the person who had to turn the handle, and Madame Lentin came into it too, he could not recall how, perhaps because he remembered her pale face behind her lace window curtains.

He was almost afraid to go back to sleep, so much did these nightmares exhaust him, and at five o'clock in the morning, he preferred to get up and go out in the street for some air.

In this way he reached the Square outside the station, where there was a bar open, and he had a cup of coffee and ate some *croissants* which had just arrived and were still warm. Would the baker's wife be surprised when he did not come for his three *croissants* as on other days? He passed by the bus station, too, where two large green coaches, one of them for Bourges, were waiting for the time to go, without anyone in them.

At eight o'clock he opened his shop, carried out the two boxes, took them in again at half past nine and then, with his hat on his head, his summons in his pocket, he went out and locked his shop.

It was not quite time to go to Le Bouc's, but since he would be at the police station at ten o'clock, he went in and drank his coffee.

They must have noticed his hat. They must have seen, too, that he locked his door. However, they did not ask him any questions, but ignored him as they had ignored for the past four days. Nevertheless he said :

'See you later.'

He took the rue Haute. About five hundred yards up on the left there was a square, in the middle of which stood the grey building of the Town Hall.

Here also there was a market, much less important than the one opposite his shop, a few barrows of vegetables and fruit, two or three stalls, a woman selling baskets and bootlaces.

To reach the police station one did not go in by the main entrance but by a small door in the side street, and he went into the first room which smelled like a barracks and was divided in two by a sort of black wooden counter.

Five or six people were waiting on a bench and, out of humility or timidity, he was going to sit in the queue, when a police sergeant called to him :

'What do you want?'

He stammered :

'I've had a summons.'

'Let's see.'

He glanced at it, disappeared through a door, and said on returning a little later :

'Wait a minute.'

Jonas remained standing to start off with, and the hands of the clock, on the rough white wall, pointed to ten past ten, a quarter past ten, twenty past ten. Then he sat down, fiddling with his hat, wondering whether, as at the doctor's, all the people ahead of him had to go in first.

It was not the case, for when they called a name, a woman rose and was led in the opposite direction to the one the sergeant had taken a short time before. Then they said another name and told an elderly man who was going towards the desk :

'Sign here. . . . Now here . . . . You've got four hundred and twenty-two francs?'

He held the money in his hand and, in exchange, was given a pink piece of paper which he folded carefully and put in his wallet before leaving.

'Next!'

It was an old woman, who leaned towards the sergeant and spoke to him in a low voice, and Jonas was unconsciously straining his ears to hear, when a bell rang.

'One moment!' the man in uniform interrupted her. 'Monsieur Milk! This way please.'

He went down a corridor on to which there opened a number of offices, until he came to the one where the superintendent, sitting in front of a piece of mahogany furniture, had his back to the window.

'Sit down,' he said, without looking up.

He wore spectacles for reading and writing, which Jonas did not know, only having seen him in the street, and he took them off each time he looked at him.

'Your name is Jonas Milk, born at Archangel on 21 September 1916, naturalized a Frenchman on 17 May 1938?'

'Yes, Superintendent.'

The man had in front of him some closely written sheets of paper which he appeared to be perusing in order to refresh his memory.

'Two years ago you married Eugénie Louise Joséphine Palestri.'

He nodded his head and the superintendent leaned back in his chair, played with his spectacles for a moment, before asking him:

'Where is your wife, Monsieur Milk?'

To hear himself addressed by that name, to which he had become unaccustomed, was enough to discompose him.

'I don't know, Superintendent.'

'I see here' – and he tapped the papers in front of him with his horn-rimmed spectacles, which he had folded up – 'that you have provided at least two different accounts of her departure.'

'Let me explain.'

'One moment. On the one hand, to several of your neighbours you declared spontaneously and in the presence of witnesses, on Thursday morning, then on Thursday afternoon and on Friday, that your wife had left the town by the 7.10 bus.'

'That is correct.'

'She did take the bus?'

'No. It is correct that I said so.'

It was starting all over again. The huge sheets of official paper contained the report from Inspector Basquin, who must have, back in his office, reconstructed their conversation from memory.

'On the other hand, when you were questioned afterwards by one of my colleagues, you changed your wife's departure to Wednesday evening.'

As he was opening his mouth, a sharp rap of the glasses on the dossier interrupted him.

'One moment, Monsieur Milk, I am bound to warn you first that we have been requested to start a search for her as a missing person.'

Was it Louis who had come and asked for this? Or Angèle? Or Frédo? He didn't dare inquire, although he was burning to know.

'These affairs are always delicate, especially when it concerns a woman, and, even more so, a married woman. I summoned you to ask you a certain number of questions and I shall be obliged to go into somewhat intimate details. It is understood that I am not accusing you of anything and you have the right not to reply.'

'I only ask to ...'

'Please let me do the talking. I shall first of all outline the position as briefly as possible.'

He put on his spectacles, looked for another piece of paper on which he had apparently jotted down a few notes.

'You are forty years old and your wife, better known under the name of Gina, is twenty-four. If I understand rightly, she did not pass for a model of virtue before she met you and, as a neighbour, you were aware of her conduct. Is that correct?'

'That is correct.'

Life, described thus, in official language, how odious it became!

'Nevertheless you married her, in the full knowledge of the facts and, in order that the wedding should take place in church, a condition without which the Palestris would not have given their consent, you became converted to Catholicism and were baptized.'

This was another shock, for it revealed that an intensive inquiry had been going on about him during the empty days he had just passed. Had they been to question the Abbé Grimault, and others as well, whose names were perhaps yet to emerge?

'By the way, Monsieur Milk, I should like to ask you a question which has nothing to do with this matter. You are a Jew, I believe?'

For the first time he replied as if he were ashamed of it:

'Yes.'

'You were here during the occupation?'

'Yes.'

'So you remember that at one time the German authorities made it compulsory for your co-religionists to wear a yellow star on their clothes?'

'Yes.'

'How is it that you never wore this star and yet did not get into trouble?'

In order to remain calm he had to dig his nails into the palms of his hands.

What could he reply? Was he to renounce his own people? He had never felt himself to be a Jew. He had never believed himself to be different from the people who surrounded him at the Old Market and they, just because of his fair hair and blue eyes, had never thought that he was of another race.

It was not in order to deceive them that he had not worn the yellow star, at the risk of being sent to a concentration camp or condemned to death. He had taken the risk, naturally, because he wanted to remain like the others.

The superintendent, who did not know him, had not found all this out on his own. Nor was it Basquin, who at the time was a prisoner-of-war in Germany.

It had come from somebody else, from somebody at the market, one of the people who used to give him a friendly greeting every morning.

'Did your wife know that you were a Jew?'

'I never talked about it to her.'

'Do you think that would have affected her decision?'

'I don't think so.'

As he said it, he thought bitterly of the Arab with whom she had once spent the night.

'And her parents?'

'It never occurred to me to wonder.'

'Let's leave that on one side. Do you speak German?'

'No.'

'Russian, of course?'

'I used to speak it once, with my parents, but I have forgotten it and I could hardly even understand it now.'

What had this to do with the disappearance of Gina? Was he finally going to discover what they had against him?

'Your father came to France as an émigré, at the time of the Revolution.'

'He was a prisoner in Germany and when the armistice was signed, in 1918 ...'

'Let's call him an émigré, since at that time he did not return to Russia. I suppose he formed part of some White Russian group?'

He seemed to remember that at first Shepilov had made him a member of some political society, but Constantin Milk had never been an active member and had dedicated himself entirely to his fishmonger's business.

Without waiting for his answer, Superintendent Devaux went on:

'Yet in 1930 he did not hesitate to go back to his country. Why?'

'To find out what had become of my five sisters.'

'Did you hear any news of him?'

'Never.'

'Not a letter, or by word of mouth, nor through friends?'

'In no way at all.'

'How is it, in that case, that your mother went off in her turn?'

'Because she could not live without her husband.'

'Have you ever indulged in political activities?'

'Never.'

'You don't belong to any group, or party?'

'No.'

Devaux put on his spectacles to consult his notes once again. He looked put out. One would have said that it was only with a certain reluctance that he was asking certain questions.

'You carry on a considerable correspondence with foreign countries, Monsieur Milk.'

Had they questioned the postman as well? Who else?

'I am a philatelist.'

'Does that call for such an extensive foreign correspondence?'

'Given my method of work, yes.'

He felt the desire to explain the mechanics of his operations, the research work among the raw material which he had sent to him from the four corners of the earth, for stamps with peculiarities which had escaped his colleagues.

'We'll leave that on one side,' the superintendent said once again, apparently in a hurry to get to the end of the interview.

Nevertheless he added :

'How are your relations with your neighbours?'

'Good. Very good. I mean up to the last few days.'

'What has happened in the last few days?'

'They have been avoiding me.'

'You received, I believe, a visit from your brother-in-law, Alfred Palestri, known as Frédo?'

'Yes.'

'What do you think of him?'

He said nothing.

'Are you on bad terms?'

'I don't think he likes me.'

'For what reason?'

'Perhaps he wasn't pleased that I married his sister.'

'And your father-in-law?'

'I don't know.'

After a glance at his notes, the superintendent resumed :

'It would appear that both of them were opposed to your marriage. Gina, at the time, was in your service, if I am not mistaken?'

'She was working in my house as my servant.'

'Did she sleep in the house?'

'No.'

'Did you have intimate relations with her?'

'Not before we were married.'

'The idea of starting a family never came to you before?'

'No.'

It was true. It had never occurred to him.

'I am going, for my own guidance, to ask you another indiscreet question and you are perfectly entitled to refuse to answer. How did you manage?'

He did not understand at once. The superintendent had to elucidate:

'A man has his needs . . .'

Before the war there was a house, not far from the Town Hall, in the rue du Pot-de-Fer to be precise, which Jonas visited regularly. The new laws had upset his arrangements for a time, then he had discovered a street corner, near the station, where four or five women walked their beat of an evening in front of a private hotel.

He admitted to it, since he was in any case being forced to strip his soul bare.

'According to what you said, you were not jealous of your wife?'

'I didn't say that. I said I did not let her see it.'

'I understand. So you were jealous?'

'Yes.'

'What would you have done if you had caught her in the arms of another man?'

'Nothing.'

'You wouldn't have been furious?'

'I should have suffered.'

'But you wouldn't have used violence, either against her or against her partner?'

'Certainly not.'

'Did she know that?'

'She must have known it.'

'Did she take advantage of the fact?'

He felt like replying:

'It's all written down in front of you!'

But if he had already been overawed once when Inspector

Basquin had interrogated him in his shop, which he had entered with the casual air of a customer, he was very much more so in this formal office where, on top of everything else, they had just touched on sensitive points, and left him as if he had been flayed alive.

There were words, sentences, which went on resounding in his head and he had to make an effort to understand what was being said to him.

'You never threatened her?'

He started.

'What with?'

'I don't know. You never uttered any threat against her?'

'Never in my life. It would never have occurred to me to do so!'

'Not even during a quarrel at home, for example, or perhaps after a few drinks?'

'We never had any quarrels and you must have been told that I only drink coffee.'

The superintendent slowly lit his pipe, which he had been filling, and leant back in his armchair, his spectacles in his hand.

'In that case, how can you explain that your wife is frightened of you?'

He thought he had misheard him.

'What did you say?'

'I said "that she is frightened of you".'

'Gina?'

'Your wife, yes.'

He started to his feet, overawed though he was by his surroundings. It was with some difficulty that he was able to pronounce clearly the words that came, in a confused torrent, to his lips.

'But, Superintendent, she was never frightened of me .... Frightened of what? ... When she came back, on the contrary, I ...'

'Sit down.'

He was twisting his hands together. It was meaningless, as if he was living one of his nightmares of the night before.

'Afraid of me!' he repeated. 'Of me!'

Whoever could be afraid of him? Not even the stray dogs of the market, or the cats. He was the most inoffensive being on the face of the earth.

The superintendent, meanwhile, who had put his spectacles on again, ran his eyes over a report while his fingers underlined a passage.

'On several occasions, your wife declared that you would end up by killing her.'

'When? Who to? It's not possible.'

'I am not at liberty, at present, to disclose the name of the person to whom she made these confidences, but I can assure you that she made them, and not just to one person.'

Jonas was capitulating. It was too much. They had just gone too far. That the neighbours had turned against him he could endure, by gritting his teeth.

But that Gina ...

'Listen, Superintendent ...'

He stretched out his hands in supplication, in a final outburst of energy.

'If she was afraid of me, why ...?'

What was the use? In any case, the words failed him. He had forgotten what he was going to say. It no longer mattered.

Afraid of him!

'Keep calm. Once again I am not accusing you of anything. An inquiry has been opened as a result of your wife's disappearance and it is my duty not to neglect anything, to listen to all the evidence.'

Without realizing, he nodded his approval.

'The fact is that for some mysterious reason, ever since the morning when your wife's disappearance was noted, you have been lying.'

He did not protest, as he had done with Inspector Basquin.

'Afraid of me!' he kept repeating to himself with bitter obstinacy.

'This has inevitably given rise to certain rumours.'

His head went on nodding affirmatively.

'All I am asking is to clear the matter up with your help.'

The face and outline of the superintendent suddenly danced

in front of his eyes and he felt himself being overcome by a weakness which he had never known before.

'You ... you haven't a glass of water?' he had time to stammer.

It was the first time in his life that he had fainted. It was very hot in the room. The superintendent rushed to the door and Jonas had time to hear water flowing from a tap.

He could not have been unconscious for more than a few seconds, for when he opened his eyes, the glass was clinking against his teeth and the cold water was trickling down his chin.

He looked without resentment, his eyes half-closed, at the man who had just caused him so much pain, who now stood bending over him.

'Do you feel better?'

He blinked his eyelids, as he did to greet the Widower, who was rather like the superintendent to look at. Perhaps after all the superintendent was a decent fellow and was sorry for him?

'Have another drink.'

He shook his head. He was embarrassed. A nervous reaction made him suddenly feel like crying. He mastered himself, but it was a good minute before he was able to speak. Then it was to stammer:

'I am sorry.'

'Relax and keep quiet.'

The superintendent opened the window, suddenly letting in the noises from the street, went and sat down in his place again, not knowing what to do or say.

SEVEN

'I DON'T think, Monsieur Milk,' the superintendent was saying, 'that you have quite grasped the point. Once again for some reason or other, your wife has disappeared, and we have been asked to investigate. We have had no choice but to collect statements and check certain rumours which were circulating.'

Jonas was calm again now, too calm, and the smile on his face looked as if an india-rubber could have wiped it away. He was looking at the other politely, his mind elsewhere; in actual fact he was listening to the crowing of a cock, which had just broken, strident and proud, into the noises from the street. At first it had surprised him so much that he had a feeling of unreality, of floating, until he recalled that just opposite the police station there was a man who dealt in birds and farmyard animals.

By rising from his chair he could have seen the cages piled on top of one another on the pavement, hens, cocks, and pedigree ducks underneath, then on top, parakeets, canaries and other birds, some bright red, others blue, whose names he did not know. To the right of the door, a parrot stood on its perch and passers-by were constantly amazed that it was not attached.

In the Square a woman with a shrill voice, a costermonger, was calling on the world at large to buy her fine salads and the intervals in her monotonous cry were roughly regular, so that he ended up by waiting for it.

'I went about it a bit brutally, perhaps, and I am sorry. . . .'

Jonas shook his head as if to say that all was well.

Gina was frightened of him. The rest did not matter. He could stand up to anything now, and the superintendent had no need to approach the question in a roundabout way.

'I will not conceal from you that there is another somewhat disturbing piece of evidence. On Wednesday, shortly before midnight, a woman was leaning out of her window, in the rue du Canal, a quarter of a mile from where you live. She was waiting for her husband who, for reasons that need not concern us, had not returned home at the usual time. Anyway, she saw a rather small man, about your size, who was carrying a large sack on his shoulder, heading towards the lock and keeping close to the wall.'

'Did she recognize me?'

He was not angry, or indignant.

'I did not say that, but clearly it is a coincidence.'

'Do you think, Superintendent, that I would have had the strength to carry my wife from the Place du Vieux-Marché to the canal?'

If Gina was very little bigger than he was, she was heavier and he was not a strong man.

Monsieur Devaux bit his lips. Since Jonas had fainted, he was less at his ease and was minding how he went, without realizing that it was no longer necessary. Isn't there a moment when the intensity of pain brings on insensitivity? Jonas had passed that crisis and, while he listened to what was being said, he was concentrating on the noises from the street.

It wasn't the same sound as in his quarter. The cars were more frequent, the pedestrians in more of a hurry. The light itself was different, and yet it was not ten minutes' walk from here to the Vieux-Marché.

The cupboards, behind the superintendent, were made of mahogany like the desk, with green baize cloth stretched behind gold-coloured lattice work, and above, in a wooden frame, could be seen a photograph of the President of the Republic.

'I thought of that objection, Monsieur Milk. But you are not unaware, if you read the papers, that this problem has often, alas, been overcome.'

He did not understand straight away.

'You cannot have failed to read or hear stories of dismembered bodies being found in rivers or waste land. Once again, I am not accusing you.'

He was not being accused of cutting Gina into pieces and carrying them into the canal!

'What we have to do now, unless you wife reappears or we find her, is to exculpate you from the affair, and therefore to study all the possibilities calmly.'

He was replacing his spectacles in order to cast an eye over his notes.

'Why, after her disappearance, were you in such a hurry to take your washing and hers to the laundry?'

They knew his slightest acts, as if he had been living in a glass cage.

'Because it was laundry day.'

'Was it you who normally counted the washing and made up the parcel?'

'No.'

No and yes. Which proved how difficult it is to express an absolute truth. It was among Gina's duties, as in other households, and Gina usually attended to it. Only she never knew which day of the week it was and sometimes Jonas reminded her, while she was doing their room:

'Don't forget the laundry.'

It was also a habit of theirs to put the pillow-case with it under the counter, so as not to hold up the van driver, who was always in a hurry.

Gina lived in disorder. Indeed, had she not forgotten, before leaving, to wash the pan in which she had cooked the herrings? Jonas, who had lived alone a long time and had not always had a maid, had kept up the habit of thinking of everything and often, when Gina was away, of doing the chores she ought to have taken on.

'Your wife has just disappeared, Monsieur Milk. You told me a short while ago that you were in love with her. Yet you took the trouble to devote yourself to a job which men do not normally do.'

He could only repeat:

'It was laundry day.'

He felt that the other was examining him curiously. Basquin, too, had looked at him like that at certain moments, as a man who is trying to understand, but without success.

'You were not trying to hide compromising traces?'

'Traces of what?'

'On the Friday or the Saturday, you also turned out your kitchen.'

How often this had happened before Gina's day, when the maid was ill, and even after his marriage!

'These are details of no significance individually, I agree, but which added together are nothing if not disturbing.'

He nodded in agreement, a submissive schoolboy.

'You have no idea what liaisons your wife may have formed of late?'

'None.'

'Has she been away more often than usual?'

'No.'

As always in the morning, she would roam about the market, preferably in dressing-gown and slippers. In the afternoon she would probably dress, powder her face, put on scent and go and do her shopping in the town, or see one of her girl friends.

'Hasn't she received any letters either?'

'She never has had any letters at the house.'

'Do you think she received them somewhere else, at the poste restante, for example?'

'I don't know.'

'What you must admit is curious, seeing that you are an intelligent man, is that she should have gone off without taking any clothes, not even a coat and, according to your own statement, almost without any money. She didn't take a bus, nor the train, we have confirmed that.'

In the end he felt it better to mention the stamps. He was tired, he was in a hurry to get outside this office, and not have to listen to any more of these questions which had so little relation to reality.

'My wife,' he said, smarting at being finally driven to it, and with a sense of betrayal, 'had premeditated her departure.'

'How do you know, and why didn't you say so to Inspector Basquin?'

'In the wardrobe with the looking-glass in our bedroom there is a box which used to contain my rarest stamps.'

'Did she know about it?'

'Yes.'

'Are these stamps of any great value?'

'Several million francs.'

He wondered if he had been wise to speak, for the superintendent's reaction was not what he had expected. He was being looked at, not with incredulity, but with a hint of suspicion.

'You mean that you possessed several million francs' worth of stamps?'

'Yes. I began collecting them at school, when I was about thirteen, and I have never given it up.'

'Who, apart from your wife, has seen these stamps you possess?'

'Nobody.'

'So that you cannot prove that they were in the cupboard?'

He had become calm, patient, detached almost, as if it were no longer anything to do with Gina and himself, and that was perhaps because he was on professional ground.

'I can prove, as far as most of them are concerned, that I acquired them at a particular moment, either by purchase or by exchange, some of them fifteen years ago, some two or three years ago. Philatelists form a fairly small circle. It is nearly always known where the rarer specimens are to be found.'

'Excuse me interrupting you, Monsieur Milk. I know nothing about philately. I am trying, at present, to put myself in the position of a jury. You are saying that while still living in a manner which I would, with all due respect, describe as very modest, and I hope I don't offend you, you say that you had several millions' worth of stamps and that your wife has taken them away with her. You go on to say that as far as most of them are concerned, you are able to establish that they came into your possession a number of years ago. Is that correct?'

He nodded his head, listening to the cock which was crowing once more, and the superintendent, exasperated, got up to close the window.

'Do you mind?'

'As you wish.'

'The first question that will arise is whether, last Wednesday, these stamps were still in your possession, for there was nothing to stop you from reselling them a long time ago. Is it possible for you to prove this was not so?'

'No.'

'And can you prove that you have not still got them?'

'They are no longer in the box.'

'We are still in the realms of theory, aren't we? What was there to prevent you from having put them somewhere else?'

'Why should I?'

In order to incriminate Gina, that is what the superintendent was thinking. To make it seem that she had gone off taking his fortune with her.

'Do you see now how difficult and delicate my task is? The

inhabitants of your neighbourhood, for some reason unknown to me, seem to have a grudge against you.'

'Up to these last few days, they have been very nice to me.'

The superintendent was studying him closely and Jonas found the explanation in his eyes. He did not understand either. Human beings of all sorts had been in and out of his office and he was accustomed to the most unusual kinds of confidences. But Jonas baffled him, and he could see him pass from sympathy to irritation, amounting at times to aversion, only to start again and try to find a fresh point of contact.

Had it not been the same with Basquin? Didn't that go to prove that he was not like other men? Would it have been different in the country where he was born, at Archangel, among the people of his own race?

All his life he had sensed it, intuitively. Even at school he made himself inconspicuous, as if in order to be forgotten, and he had been uncomfortable when, against his will, he came top in his class.

Hadn't they encouraged him to consider himself at home in the Vieux-Marché? Hadn't they suggested, at one moment, that he should join a shopkeepers' defence committee, and even become the treasurer? He had refused, feeling that it was not his place.

It was not without good reason that he had shown such humility. He could only assume that he had not shown enough, since they were turning against him.

'When did these stamps disappear, according to your story?'

'Normally I keep the key to the box in my pocket, with the key to the front door and the one for the till.'

He displayed the silver chain.

'On Wednesday morning I dressed as soon as I got up, but the day before I went down in my pyjamas.'

'So that your wife would have taken the stamps on the Tuesday morning?'

'I presume so.'

'Are they easy to sell?'

'No.'

'Well?'

'She doesn't know it. As I told you, dealers know one another. When a rare specimen is brought to them, they usually make inquiries about its origin.'

'Have you alerted your colleagues?'

'No.'

'For what reason?'

He shrugged his shoulders. He was beginning to sweat, and missed the noises from the street.

'So your wife went off without a coat, without luggage, but with a fortune she will not be able to realize. Is that right?'

He nodded.

'She left the Old Market on Wednesday evening, over a week ago now, and no one saw her go, no one saw her in the town, she didn't take the bus, nor the train: in short, she melted into thin air without leaving the slightest trace. Where, in your opinion, would she have the best chance of selling the stamps?'

'In Paris, obviously, or in a big city like Lyons, Bordeaux, Marseilles. Abroad, too.'

'Can you furnish me with a list of the stamp dealers in France?'

'The principal ones, yes.'

'I will send them a circular letter warning them. Now, Monsieur Milk ...'

The superintendent rose to his feet, hesitated, as if he had not yet discharged the most disagreeable part of his task.

'It remains to me to ask your permission to instruct two of my men to accompany you and pay a visit to your house. I could obtain a search warrant but, at this stage of the affair, I prefer to keep matters on a less official footing.'

Jonas had also risen to his feet. He had no reason for refusing since he had nothing to hide and since, in any case, he was not the stronger of the two.

'Now?'

'I should prefer it that way, yes.'

To prevent him from covering up traces?

It was at once laughable and tragic. All this had started with an innocent little remark:

'She has gone to Bourges.'

It was Le Bouc who, innocently too, had asked:

'On the bus?'

From there, little by little, there had grown ripples, then waves, which had invaded the market and finally reached as far as the police station, in the centre of the town.

He was no longer Monsieur Jonas, the bookseller in the Square whom everybody greeted cheerfully. For the superintendent, and in the reports, he was Jonas Milk, born at Archangel, Russia, on 21 September 1916, naturalized French on 17 May 1938, exempted from military service, of Jewish origin, converted to Catholicism in 1954.

There remained one more facet of the affair to be revealed, which he was far from expecting. They were standing up. The conversation, or rather the interrogation, seemed to be at an end. Monsieur Devaux was playing with his spectacles, which now and then caught a ray from the sun.

'Anyway, Monsieur Milk, you have a simple way of establishing that these stamps were in your possession.'

He looked at him uncomprehendingly.

'They amount, you said, to a capital value of several million francs. They were bought from your income, and consequently, it must be possible to find, in your income-tax returns, a record of the sum you invested. Naturally this does not concern me personally, and it falls in the province of the Direct Taxation authorities.'

They would corner him there, too, he knew in advance. He wouldn't be able to get them to accept a perfectly simple truth. He had never bought a stamp for fifty thousand francs, or a hundred thousand, or three hundred thousand, even though he had possessed stamps of that value. He had discovered some by examining them with his magnifying glass, stamps whose rarity other people had failed to spot, and some of the others he had acquired by a series of exchanges.

As the superintendent had said, he lived very modestly.

What was the use of worrying about it, in the state he was already in? Only one thing counted. *Gina was afraid of him*. And, in the doorway of the office, he in his turn timidly asked a question.

'She really said I would kill her one day?'

'That is what emerges from the evidence.'

'To several people?'

'I can assure you so.'

'She didn't say why?'

Monsieur Devaux hesitated, reclosed the door, which he had just opened.

'Do you insist on my replying?'

'Yes.'

'You will note that I made no allusion to it during the course of the conversation. Twice, at least, when talking about you, she declared:

'*He's vicious.*'

He turned scarlet. This was the last word he had been expecting.

'Think about it, Monsieur Milk, and we will resume the discussion another day. For the present, Inspector Basquin will accompany you with one of his men.'

The superintendent's statement did not shock him, and he finally felt he was beginning to understand. Often Gina had watched him stealthily when he was busy, and when he raised his head, she had seemed confused. The look on her face was similar then to certain of Basquin's and the superintendent's looks.

All the same she lived with him. She saw him in all his behaviour, day and night.

Despite this, she had not grown used to it, and he remained an enigma to her.

She must have wondered, when she was still working with him as a maid, why he did not treat her as other men used to treat her, including Ancel. She was never overdressed and there was a wanton freedom in her movements which might have been taken as a provocation.

Had she thought him impotent, at that time, or did she attribute special tastes to him? Had she been the only one during the years, to think so?

He could picture her, serious-faced, preoccupied, when he had spoken of marrying her. He could picture her undressing the first evening and calling to him as, fully dressed, he was pacing the room without daring to look at her.

'Aren't you going to undress?'

It was almost as if she was expecting to discover something abnormal about him. The truth was that he was ashamed of his over-pink, plump body.

She had turned down the bed, lain down with her knees apart, and watching him undress, as he was approaching awkwardly, she had exclaimed with a laugh, which in reality was perhaps just uneasiness:

'Are you going to keep your glasses on?'

He had taken them off. All the time he had lain upon her, he had felt that she was watching him, and she had not taken part, nor made any pretence at taking part in his pleasure.

'*You see!*' she had said.

What exactly did that mean? That, in spite of everything, he had got what he wanted? That, despite appearances, he was almost a normal man?

'Shall we go to sleep?'

'If you like.'

'Good night.'

She had not kissed him and he had not dared to do so either. The superintendent forced him to reflect that in two years they had never kissed. He had tried twice or three times and she had turned her head away, not abruptly, with no apparent revulsion.

Although they slept in the same bed, he approached her as seldom as possible, because she did not participate, and when, towards morning, he would hear her panting near to him, finally subsiding in the depths of the bed with a sigh that almost rent her in two, he used to keep his eyes closed and pretend to be asleep.

As the superintendent had just told him, they had not yet questioned him about that, but it would come.

What was it that frightened Gina?

Was it his calm, his gentleness, his abashed tenderness when she came back from one of her escapades? One would sometimes have said that she was defying him to beat her.

123

Would she then have been less afraid of him? Would she have stopped thinking of him as vicious?

'Basquin!' called the superintendent, who had moved towards the corridor.

In an office, Jonas saw the inspector at work in his shirt-sleeves.

'Take somebody with you and accompany Monsieur Milk.'

'Right, Superintendent.'

He must have known what he had to do, for he did not ask for instructions.

'Dambois!' he called out in his turn, addressing someone out of sight in another office.

Neither of them were in uniform but everyone, in the Old Market as in the town centre, knew them.

'Think it over, Monsieur Milk,' Monsieur Devaux was saying again by way of good-bye.

What he was thinking over was not what the superintendent imagined. He was no longer trying to defend himself, to reply to the more or less grotesque charges which they had levelled against him.

It was an inner debate which occupied his mind, a debate infinitely more tragic than their tale about a woman being cut up into pieces.

In a curious way they were right, but not in the way they imagined, and Jonas suddenly felt himself really guilty.

He had not effected Gina's disappearance or thrown her body into the canal.

He was not vicious either, in the sense they understood him to be, and he knew of no peculiarity in himself, no sexual abnormality.

He hadn't yet registered the point, for the revelation had been too recent, it had just come at the moment he least expected it, in the neutral atmosphere of an official building.

'Do you mind waiting for me a moment, Monsieur Jonas?'

Basquin went on giving the name he was used to, but it did not even please him any longer.

That stage was past. He had reached the office divided by a dark wooden counter where some new visitors were waiting on the bench, and he pretended, to keep up appearances, to be reading an official notice advertising the sale of some horses and oxen in the main square.

Wasn't it to her brother, to start with, that Gina had confided that she was frightened of him? Very probably. That explained Frédo's fierce opposition to the marriage.

Who else had she spoken to? Clémence? La Loute?

He tried to remember the words the superintendent had repeated to him:

'*That man will kill me one of these days....*'

Why? Because he did not react as she had expected when she ran after other men? Because he was too soft, too patient?

Did she think to herself that he was acting and that one day he would give free reign to his real instincts? He had told her, when he had talked to her about marriage:

'I can at least offer you *peace and quiet.*'

Those words or something like them. He had not talked to her of love, or happiness, but of peace and quiet, because he was too humble to imagine that he could give her anything else.

She was beautiful, full of vitality, and he was sixteen years older, a dusty, lonely little bookseller whose only passion in life was collecting stamps.

That was not entirely true. That was how it seemed, what people must think. The truth is that he lived intensely, in his inner self, a rich and varied life, the life of the entire Old Market, the entire neighbourhood, of which he knew the minutest movements.

Behind the shelter of his thick spectacles, which seemed to isolate him and give him an inoffensive air, was it not rather as if he had stolen the lives of the others, without their noticing it?

Was that what Gina had discovered on entering his house? Was that why she had spoken of vice and been afraid?

Did she hold it against him that he had bought her?

For he had bought her, he knew it and she knew it. Angèle knew it better than anyone, for she had sold her, and Louis as well, who had not dared to say anything for fear of his wife, and Frédo, who had revolted against it.

They had not sold her for money, but for peace and quiet. He was so well aware of it that he had been the first to use the words as a bait, a temptation.

With him, Gina would have a front of respectability and her escapades would be covered up. Her material needs would be assured and Angèle would tremble no more at the thought of seeing her end up on the streets.

Had the neighbours who had been at the wedding thought of it? Their smiles, their congratulations, their contentment, especially at the end of the feast, were they sincere?

Weren't they, too, a little ashamed of the bargain which, in a sense, they had just countersigned?

The Abbé Grimault had not openly tried to dissuade him from his designs. Doubtless he, too, preferred to see Gina married. Nevertheless even Jonas's conversion had evoked little enthusiasm in him.

'I daren't ask you whether you have faith, since I would not wish to induce you to tell a lie.'

So he knew that Jonas didn't believe in it. Did he also guess that it had not been simply to marry Gina that he had become a Catholic and that he had sometimes thought about it long before he met her?

'I hope you will be happy with her, and bring her happiness.'

The good wish was genuine, but it could be seen that he placed little confidence in it. He did his duty as a priest in joining them together as he had done in receiving the little man from Archangel into the bosom of the Roman Catholic church.

How was it that during the two years it had never once occurred to Jonas that Gina could be afraid of him?

Now the scales had fallen from his eyes and details he had taken no notice of were coming back to him.

He was realizing, at last, that he was a foreigner, a Jew, a solitary, a man from the other end of the world who had come like a parasite to embed himself in the flesh of the Old Market.

'If you will come this way. . . .'

The two men were ready with their hats on, and with Jonas between them, half a head smaller than either, they set off for the rue Haute in the hot, sun-soaked air.

'Did it go off all right?' asked Basquin, who had obviously been to have a word with his chief.

'I suppose so. I'm not sure.'

'The superintendent is a man of remarkable intelligence, who would have had an important post in Paris a long time ago if he didn't insist on living with his daughter. He was called to the bar at the age of twenty-three and started off his career with the prefecture. It was sheer accident that he joined the police.'

From time to time Basquin returned the greeting of a passer-by and people turned to stare at Jonas, who was walking between the two policemen.

'During the last four days, since the day I came to see you, we have been circulating your wife's description everywhere.'

The inspector was surprised at Jonas' lack of reaction and kept shooting him little glances out of the corner of his eye.

'True, there are plenty of pretty dark girls in red dresses. Quite apart from the fact that she may have bought herself a new dress.'

As he passed the restaurant, Jonas saw the top of Pepito's head above the curtains, and Pepito was looking at him. Would he be lunching there? Would they give him the chance? It was already half past eleven. They were probably going to search the house from top to bottom and the corners were full of odd bits and pieces, for Jonas never threw anything away.

Who could say, at this stage, that they were not going to arrest him?

It remained for him to pass Le Bouc's, and he decided to turn his head away, not from shame, but to spare them embarrassment.

For despite everything they must have been embarrassed. They must have egged one another on. Any one of them, on their own, with the exception of Frédo, would not have dared to turn against him so brutally.

'If you'll say it, then I'll say so too. . . .'

Why not, since he had taken them in? He took the keys from his pocket and opened the door, under which he found a yellow cinema programme.

127

'Come in gentlemen.'

The shop, which had had the sun all the morning and in which the air was stagnating, was like a furnace. Two great black flies were flying clumsily about.

'Presumably you would rather I left the door open?'

The smell of books was stronger than usual and, in order to create a draught, he went and opened the door into the yard, where a blackbird was hopping about. He knew it. The blackbird came every morning and was not afraid of Jonas.

'Call me if you need me.'

It was Basquin who took the lead.

'I'd like to visit the bedroom first. I suppose it's this way?'

'Go on up. I'll follow.'

He wanted a cup of coffee, but didn't dare ask for permission to go and make himself one, still less to go and have one at Le Bouc's.

The bedroom was tidy, the counterpane carefully spread on the bed, and the dressing-table immaculate. As he went in Jonas's eye fell immediately upon Gina's comb which was dirty, with one or two hairs caught in it. He was so used to seeing it in the same place that he had not noticed it during the past few days, nor washed it.

'Is this the only bedroom in the house?'

'Yes.'

'So that this is the bed you both slept in?'

'Yes.'

Through the open window Jonas thought he could hear stealthy footsteps on the pavement, muffled whispers.

'Where does this door lead to?'

'The lavatory and bathroom.'

'And that one?'

He pushed it open. It had once been a bedroom looking out on to the yard, but it was so tiny that there was only just room for a bed. Jonas used it as a loft and box-room for his shop. It contained broken chairs, an old chest with the lock torn off, dating from their flight from Russia, a dress-maker's model, which he had bought for Gina and which she had never used, cracked crockery, piles of books, the ones which he had no hope of ever selling, and even a chamber pot. No one ever dusted this room. The skylight was not opened more than once a year and the air was musty, everything was covered with a layer of grey powder.

The two policemen exchanged glances. Presumably it meant that nobody could have gone in there recently without leaving traces. They had kept their hats on and Basquin was finishing a cigarette, the stub of which he went and threw down the lavatory.

'Are these the clothes?' he asked, pointing to the wardrobe with the looking-glass.

Jonas opened its two doors and the inspector ran his hand over the dresses, the coats, then over Jonas's two suits and overcoat.

'She didn't have another coat?'

'No.'

In the bottom of the wardrobe stood three pairs of Gina's shoes, a pair of slippers and a pair of his own shoes. That was their entire wardrobe.

'Is that the famous strong-box?'

He was thus admitting that the superintendent had spoken to him while Jonas was waiting in the front office.

'Do you mind opening it?'

He took out his keys again, put the strong-box onto the bed and raised the lid.

'I thought it was empty!' exclaimed Basquin.

'I never said that.'

There were in fact still about fifty transparent packets each containing a stamp or a stamped card.

'Well, what did she take?'

'About a quarter of the stamps which were in here. The whole lot, with the packets, wouldn't have fitted into her bag.'

'The rarest ones?'

'Yes.'

'How could she have recognized them?'

'I had shown them to her. And also because they were on top of the others, as I had just been looking at them.'

The two men exchanged glances behind his back, and they must have been thinking he was a lunatic.

'You don't have any weapons in the house?'

'No.'

'You have never possessed a revolver?'

'Never.'

The detective with Basquin was examining the floor, the woven carpet of blue and red flowers, the blue curtains, as if in search of traces of blood. He made an even more careful study around the dressing-table and went off to pursue his investigations in the bathroom.

Basquin stepped on to the straw-bottomed chair to look on top of the wardrobe, then he pulled open the drawers of the chest one by one.

The top one was Gina's drawer, and everything was in chaos, her three nightdresses, petticoats, brassières, combinations which she scarcely ever wore, stockings, an old bag, a powder case, two boxes of aspirin, and a small rubber object.

In the bag the inspector found a handkerchief stained with lipstick, some coins, a propelling-pencil, and a receipt for two hundred and twenty-seven francs for a purchase she had made at Prisunic.

Jonas's drawer was in better order, with the shirts on one side, the pyjamas on the other, the socks, underpants, handkerchiefs, and vests in the middle. There was also a brand new wallet which Gina had given him for his birthday and he never used because he considered it too smart. It still smelled of new leather and was empty.

Lastly, the bottom drawer contained, thrown in anyhow, everything that had not found a home elsewhere, medicines, the two winter blankets, a silver-mounted hat brush given to them as a wedding present, some hairpins, and two advertisement ashtrays which they didn't use.

Basquin did not forget the drawer of the bedside table, where he found a pair of broken glasses, some gardenal, a razor, and finally a photograph of Gina naked.

It was not Jonas who had taken it, nor he who had put it there. It dated back to well before their marriage, for Gina could not have been more than twenty at the time and, if her bosom was already well-developed, her waist was narrower, her hips less powerful.

'Look,' she had said to him one day when, by a miracle, she was tidying up her things. 'Do you recognize me?'

The features were not very clearly defined. True, the photograph was blurred. Gina was standing at the foot of a bed, in a hotel bedroom probably, and it was obvious that she did not know what to do with her hands.

'Don't you think I was better looking than I am now?'

He had said no.

'It amuses me to keep it, because I can compare myself. The day will come when people will no longer believe it's me.'

She looked at herself in the glass, displaying her bosom, feeling her hips.

'I didn't take that photograph,' he told Basquin hurriedly. 'She was much younger then.'

The inspector glanced at it again, curiously.

'So I see,' he said.

Then, after a glance at his colleague:

'Let's take a look at the ground floor.'

It was rather like a public sale, when the most personal furniture and objects of a family are piled up in the street for inquisitive passers-by to come and finger them.

What did it matter now that they should turn his home inside out, after what had already been done to him?

Not only was he no longer at home in his own house, but he was no longer at home in his own skin.

EIGHT

As they passed through the little room on their way from the bedroom to the kitchen, Jonas glanced automatically in the direction of the shop and saw some faces pressed to the window; he even caught a glimpse of one urchin who must have ventured into the house, hurriedly beating a retreat and causing a burst of laughter.

The detectives examined everything, the cupboard where the groceries, the scales and the coffee-grinder were kept, the brooms hanging from its doors, the contents of the other cupboards, the table drawer, and they studied with particular attention the meat axe and the carving knives as if in search of telltale signs.

They went into the yard as well, where Basquin pointed to the windows of the Palestris' house.

'Isn't that Gina's home?'

'Yes.'

One of the windows actually belonged to the bedroom, now Frédo's, which she occupied as a young girl.

The little room took longer. The drawers were full of papers of all sorts, envelopes crammed with stamps, marked with signs which the inspector had to have explained, and for a long time he turned over the pages of the Russian album, with a series of sidelong glances at Jonas.

'You haven't done the same for the other countries, have you?'

He could only reply that he hadn't. He knew what they would deduce from that.

'I see you have the entire Soviet series. It's the first time I've had a chance of seeing them. How did you get hold of them?'

'You can pick them up everywhere in the trade.'

'Ah!'

The inquisitive eavesdroppers did not disappear until the two men set to work on the shop, where they ran their hands behind the rows of books.

'Have you dusted here recently?'

Was it also going to count against him that in order to keep himself occupied, he had undertaken a spring-cleaning of the shelves? It was all the same to him. He was no longer trying to defend himself.

At a particular moment during the morning, he could not have said precisely which moment, and in any case it did not matter, something had snapped. It was as if someone had cut a wire, or better still, perhaps, as if he had suddenly become independent of the law of gravity.

He could see the two of them, the inspector and Dambois, who were carrying out their duty conscientiously, but their comings and goings, their actions, the words they spoke, no longer had any connexion with himself. A little knot of people outside continued to watch the house, and he did not even glance up to see whom it was composed of; for him they were nothing more than a patch of life in the sunlight.

He was beyond everything. He had passed to the other side. He was waiting, patiently, for his companions to finish, and when they finally made up their minds to depart, he removed the door handle and locked the door behind them. It was no longer his own house. Furniture and objects were still in the same place. He could still have placed his hand on each thing with his eyes closed, but all real contact had ceased to exist.

He was hungry. The idea of going to eat at Pepito's did not occur to him. In the kitchen he found the remains of some cheese from the day before and a hunk of bread, and he began to eat, standing in front of the door into the back yard.

At that particular moment he had decided nothing, at least not consciously, and it was when his gaze alighted on a clothes line stretched between the house and the Chaignes' wall that his thoughts took a definite shape.

He had come by a long road, from Archangel to here, by way of Moscow, Yalta, and Constantinople to finish up in an old house in the Market Place. His father had gone back again. Then his mother.

'*I insist on this one at least remaining!*' Constantin Milk had said, pointing to Jonas at the moment of setting out on his adventure.

Now it was his turn. His decision was taken, but he still finished his cheese and bread with his eye first on the clothes line, which was made of twisted steel wire, then on the branch of the lime-tree which projected from the grocer's garden next door. One of the two iron chairs stood, by chance, directly beneath the branch.

It was true, as he had told the inspector, that he had never possessed a weapon and had a horror of all violence, so much so that the noise of children's pistols in the Square made him jump each time he heard it.

He was reflecting, wondering whether he had anything still to do upstairs, or in the shop or the little room.

He had nothing left to do anywhere. They hadn't understood him, or else he hadn't understood the others, and this latest misunderstanding was now beyond all hope of being cleared up.

He had a momentary impulse to explain everything in a letter, but it was a last vanity of which he was ashamed, and he rejected the idea.

He had some difficulty in undoing the knots by which the metal cord was attached and he had to fetch the pliers from the kitchen drawer. He was not sad, nor bitter. He felt, on the contrary, a serenity which he had never known before.

He was thinking of Gina, and now it was no longer Gina as other people saw her and as she saw herself, it was a disembodied Gina, confused in his mind with the image he had created of his sister Doussia, a woman such as probably does not exist : Woman.

Would she find out that he had died because of her? He was trying to lie to himself again, and it made him blush. It was not on her account that he was departing, it was on his own account, perhaps in fact it was because he had been forced, in his own eyes, to stoop too far.

Could he go on living after what he had discovered about himself and about the others?

He climbed on to the iron chair to attach the cord to the branch of the tree and grazed his finger-tip on a loose strand of wire; it bled, and he sucked it, as he used to do when he was a little boy.

Although you could see the kitchen door from the Palestris' window, from the bedroom that used to be Gina's, the Chaignes' party wall blocked the view from where he was standing. All he had to do now was to make a slip knot and he used the pliers so as to be sure that it would hold.

A hot nausea suddenly rose to his head at the sight of the

loop which hung suspended, and he wiped his brow and upper lip, had difficulty in swallowing his saliva.

He felt ridiculous standing on the iron chair, hesitating, trembling, seized with panic at the thought of the physical pain which he was going to feel, and worse still, of the slow choking, of the struggle which his body, hanging in mid-air, would instinctively make against suffocation.

What was preventing him from living, after all? The sun would continue to shine, the rain to fall, the Square to be filled with the sounds and smells of market day. He was still capable of making himself coffee, alone in the kitchen, listening to the songs of the birds.

The blackbird, just then, his blackbird, came and perched on the box where the chives were growing, beside a tuft of thyme, and as he watched it hopping about, Jonas's eyes filled with tears.

There was no need for him to die. Nobody was forcing him. With patience and an extra effort of humility, he could still come to terms with himself.

He stepped down from the iron chair and suddenly ran into the house in order to flee from the temptation, to be sure of not turning back. He struck a match over the gas ring, poured some water into the kettle to make himself some coffee.

He would find good reasons for acting as he was. Who could tell? Perhaps Gina would come back one day and would need him. Even the people from the market would understand, in the end. Hadn't Fernand Le Bouc already shown signs of embarrassment?

In the semi-darkness of the cupboard, he ground the coffee-mill, which was fixed to the wall. It was a china mill, with a Dutch landscape in a blue on a white background, and a picture of a windmill. He had never been to Holland. He, who as a baby had covered such immense distances, had never travelled since, as though he had been afraid of losing his place in the Old Market.

He would be patient. The superintendent, Basquin had told him, was an intelligent man.

Already the smell of coffee was doing him good, while the

steam misted over his glasses. He mused to himself, whether he would have kept his glasses on to hang himself, then he thought of Doussia again, telling himself that perhaps it was thanks to her that he had not taken the final step.

He did not yet dare to return to the yard to undo the knot. The alarm-clock, on the mantelpiece, pointed to ten to two and it comforted him to hear its familiar tick.

He would come to terms with himself, avoid thinking about certain subjects. He felt an urge to see his Russian stamps again, as though to cling on to something, and, taking his cup with him, he went and sat at his desk in the little room.

Was he a coward? Would he regret not having done today what he had decided to do? If life became too burdensome later on, would he still have the courage to do it?

There was nobody in sight outside. The Square was empty. The clock of St Cecilia's struck two and according to the rites, he ought to have replaced the handle in the door.

It no longer had the same importance as it had before, and he had plenty of time to return to his old habits bit by bit. He opened the drawer and took out the album, on the first page of which he had gummed a photograph of his father and mother outside their fishmongery. He had taken it with a cheap camera which he had been given for Christmas at the age of eleven. He was just going to turn over the page when a shadow outlined itself against the shop-window. A woman he did not know was knocking at the door, trying to see inside, surprised to find the shop shut.

He thought it was a customer and almost did not open the door. It was a working-class woman about forty years old, and she must have borne several children and worked hard all her life for one could see in her the deformities, the lassitude of women of that type, grown old before their time.

Shielding her eyes with her hand, she was peering into the obscurity of the shop, and in the end he rose to his feet, almost out of charity.

'I was afraid there was nobody at home,' she said, looking at him curiously.

He said quietly:

'I was working.'

'You are Gina's husband?'

'Yes.'

'Is it true they mean to arrest you?'

'I don't know.'

'They told me so this morning, and I wondered if I would be too late.'

'Won't you sit down?' he said, pointing to a chair.

'I haven't time. I must get back to the hotel. They don't know I've come out yet, as I took the back door. The management's new in the business and seem to think they've got to be strict.'

He listened without understanding.

'I work as a chambermaid at the Commercial Hotel. Do you know it?'

It was there that he had attended the wedding reception of Ancel's daughter. The walls were painted in imitation marble and the hall was bedecked with green plants.

'Before my husband went to the factory I used to live in this area, at the corner of the rue Gambetta and the rue des Saules. I knew Gina well when she must have been about fifteen years old. That's why I recognized her at once when she came to the hotel.'

'When has she been to the hotel?'

'Several times. Each time the traveller from Paris comes here, that's to say nearly every two weeks. It's been going on for months now. He's called Thierry, Jacques Thierry. I looked up his name in the register, and he's in chemical products. Seems he's an engineer, though he's still young. I'd bet he's not yet thirty. He's married and has two lovely children, I know because to start with he always put a photo of his family on the bedside table. His wife's a blonde. His eldest, a boy, is five or six, like my youngest.

'I don't know where he met Gina but one afternoon I saw him in the corridor with her and she went into his bedroom.

'Since then, every time he's come, she stops in to see him at the hotel for an hour or two, all according, and I'm the last one to be in the dark about what goes on, since it's me that has to remake the bed. Begging your pardon for telling you, but they say you've been in trouble and I thought it might be better for you to know.

'Gina was like that at fifteen, if that's any consolation, and I should add something that you perhaps don't know but I'm told by people who ought to know, and that is that her mother was the same before her.'

'Did she go to the hotel on Wednesday last week?'

'Yes. Around half past two. When they told me the story, this morning, I wasn't sure of the day and went and looked at the register. He arrived early on Tuesday and left again on Wednesday evening.'

'By train?'

'No. He always comes by car. I gather he has other factories to visit on his way.'

'Were they together a long time, on Wednesday?'

'Same as usual,' she replied, with a shrug.

'What dress was she wearing?'

'A red dress. You couldn't help noticing.'

He wanted to be sure.

'Now I would rather not get mixed in the affair because as I told you before, the management's got its own ideas. But if they really mean to put you in prison and there isn't any other way, I will repeat what I've told you.'

'You haven't got the address of this man in Paris?'

'I copied it down on a piece of paper and brought it with me.'

She seemed surprised to see him so unmoved and so gloomy, when she must have expected him to feel relieved.

'It's number 27 rue Championnet. I don't suppose he'll have taken her home. When I think of his wife, who looks so delicate, and his children. . . .'

'I am most grateful to you.'

'My name is Berthe Lenoir, in case you need me. I would rather no one came to the hotel. We live in the housing estate opposite the factory, the second block on the right, the one with blue shutters.'

He thanked her again and, when he was left alone, felt more disconcerted than ever, rather like a prisoner who, recovering his freedom after many long years, does not know what to with it.

He could furnish them with proof now that he had not disposed of Gina and that he had not thrown her body into the canal. What surprised him most was what he had been told about the man she had gone off with, for he did not correspond to the type she usually chose.

Their affair had been going on for about six months and during the whole of that time she had not run away once.

Was she in love with him? And he, was he going to break up his household? Given her situation, why had Gina taken the stamps?

Mechanically he had put on his hat and was heading for the door, in order to go to the police station. This seemed to him to be the only logical thing to do. It could do no harm to Gina who, the moment the complaint was withdrawn, had nothing to answer the police for. He would not claim back his stamps. They had nothing against her lover either.

It was a curious sensation to find himself on the pavement once more, in the sun, which was even hotter than in the morning, and to pass Le Bouc's, telling himself that he would be going back there again.

For there was nothing to stop him going back. The people of the market would soon find out what had happened and, instead of holding it against him, would be sorry for him. They would be a bit ashamed at first, for having deserted him so quickly, but it only needed a few days for everything to be once again as it had been in the past, and for them to call out cheerfully:

'Good morning, Monsieur Jonas!'

Would Angèle be cross with him for not having kept a better watch on her daughter? Had she been able to do so herself, before Gina's marriage?

Only Frédo would not change his attitude, but there was a very small chance of Frédo becoming reconciled with the human race. He would sooner or later go off, God knows where, far away from the Vieux-Marché which he hated, and would be just as unhappy somewhere else.

He very nearly went into Fernand's there and then, as if it were all forgotten already, then he told himself that it was too soon, and set off up the rue Haute.

He was convinced that Gina would come back, as she had always done before, only more marked this time, and that then she would need him.

Hadn't everything become easy? He would go into the police station, walk over to the black wooden counter dividing the first room in two.

'I want to speak to Superintendent Devaux, please.'

'What name?'

Unless it was the same sergeant as that morning, who would be sure to recognize him.

'Jonas Milk.'

For here they called him Milk. It hardly mattered, this time, if they kept him waiting. The superintendent would be surprised. His first thought would be that he had resolved to make a clean breast of everything.

'I know where my wife is,' Jonas would announce.

He would provide him with the name and address of the chambermaid and advise him not to go and see her at the hotel; he would also hand over the piece of paper with the address of the traveller in chemical goods.

'You can check up, but I must insist on their not being troubled. Madame Thierry may very well know nothing, but there's no point in telling her the truth.'

Would they understand him this time? Were they going to look on him again as a man from another planet? Or would they at last condescend to consider him as a human being, like other human beings?

The rue Haute, at that hour, was almost deserted. In the Place de l'Hôtel de Ville the costermongers' carts had disappeared and a few pigeons were still foraging among the cobblestones.

He saw the bird-cages in the distance, opposite the police station, but he could not hear the cock crowing.

That morning in the superintendent's office he had fainted for the first time in his life and it had not been an unpleasant sensation; it had even seemed to him at one moment that his body no longer weighed anything, as if he were in the process of becoming disembodied. At the moment of losing consciousness he had thought of Doussia.

He was slowing his pace without realizing. He had only another twenty yards to cover and he could see distinctly the round eyes of the parrot on its perch. A policeman came out of the station and mounted a bicycle, possibly on his way to deliver a summons on coarse paper like the one he had received the day before.

Was it really the day before? It seemed such a long way off! Hadn't he lived since then, almost as much as during the rest of his existence?

He had stopped ten paces from the door with the blue lantern above it and, with his eyes wide open, stood staring at nothing. A boy of about fifteen who was running by collided with him, almost knocked him down, and he just caught hold of his glasses in time. What would have happened if they had broken on the pavement?

The bird-seller, wearing a dark grey smock like an iron-monger's, was watching him, wondering perhaps if he had been taken ill, and Jonas turned about, once again crossed the Square with the small cobblestones and went down the rue Haute.

Pepito, who was sweeping out his restaurant with his door open, saw him pass. So did Le Bouc. There was only a little girl with very fair hair, who was playing dolls all by herself beneath the slate roofs of the Old Market, to watch him as he removed the handle from his door.

NINE

It was a dull grey day. A small lorry was parking, two of its wheels on the pavement, opposite the bookseller's shop. The baker's wife hadn't noticed that he had not appeared that morning to buy his three *croissants*. The boy who had taken a book on bees the week before and was bringing in his fifty francs, tried to open the door and looked inside without seeing anything.

At a quarter past ten, in Le Bouc's, Ancel remarked:

'Odd! Jonas hasn't been in this morning.'

He added, but without malice:

'Little bastard!'

Le Bouc had said nothing.

It was only at eleven o'clock that, in Angèle's shop, a woman who had tried to go in the shop to buy a book had asked:

'Is your son-in-law ill?'

Angèle had retorted, leaning over a basket of spinach, with her great behind in the air:

'If he is, I hope he croaks!'

Which had not prevented her from asking:

'Why do you say that?'

'His shop's shut.'

'Can they have arrested him already?'

A little while later, when she was free of customers, she went to have a look for herself, pressed her face to the window, but everything appeared to be in order within the house except for Jonas's hat, which stood on a straw-bottomed chair.

'Have you seen Jonas, Mélanie?' she asked, on her way past the Chaignes.

'Not this morning.'

When Louis came back, and parked his three-wheeler, she told him:

'It seems Jonas has been arrested.'

'So much the better.'

'The handle isn't in the door and I couldn't see anything going on inside.'

Louis went for a drink at Le Bouc's.

'They've arrested Jonas.'

Constable Benaiche was there, having a glass of white wine.

'Who?'

'The police, I presume.'

Benaiche frowned, shrugged his shoulders, said:

'Strange.'

Then he emptied his glass.

'I didn't hear anything up at the station.'

The only one to seem uneasy was Le Bouc. He said nothing, but, after a few minutes' thought, he retired to the back room where there was a telephone on the wall by the lavatory door.

'Get me the police station, please.'

'The number's ringing now.'

'Police here.'

He recognized the sergeant's voice.

'That you, Jouve?'

'Who's that?'

'Le Bouc. I say, is it true that you've arrested Jonas?'

'The bookseller?'

'Yes.'

'I haven't heard anything about him this morning. But it doesn't concern me. Wait a second.'

His voice came back, a little while later:

'No one here knows anything about it. The superintendent's out to lunch, but Basquin, who's here, would have heard.'

'His door's closed.'

'So what?'

'I don't know. No one's seen him this morning.'

'I'd better put you on to the inspector. Hang on.'

Another pause, and it was Basquin's voice:

'Jouve tells me Jonas hasn't been seen today?'

'Yes. His shop's shut. There's nothing going on inside.'

'Do you think he would have gone?'

That was not what Fernand had in mind, but he preferred not to volunteer any opinion.

'I don't know. It seems odd to me. He's a queer chap.'

'I'll be right round.'

When he arrived ten minutes later, several people emerged from the bar and walked over to Jonas's shop.

The inspector knocked at the door, normally at first, then louder and louder, finally called out, looking up towards the open window on the first floor:

Angèle, who had come up, had lost her habitual caustic wit.

'Monsieur Jonas!'

At Fernand's, Louis, who was gulping down two glasses of *grappa* one after the other, growled:

'I'll bet he's gone to earth in some corner, like a rat.'

He didn't believe it. He was blustering, uneasiness reflected in his red-rimmed eyes.

'Is there a locksmith nearby?' asked Basquin, who had tried shaking the door in vain.

'Old Deltour. He lives in . . .'

Madame Chaigne interrupted the woman who was speaking.

'It's not worth the trouble of forcing the door. You only have to get over the wall of the yard by climbing on a chair. Follow me, Inspector.'

She led him through her shop, then through the kitchen where a stew was simmering, as far as the yard, which was littered with barrels and crates.

'It's Jonas!' she called out as she passed her husband, who was hard of hearing.

Then:

'Look! A barrel will do even better than a chair.'

She remained standing, in her white apron, her hands on her hips, watching the inspector hoisting himself on to the wall.

'Can you get down the other side?'

He did not reply at once, for he had just found the little man from Archangel hanging from the branch which grew out over the yard. The kitchen door was open with, on the wax tablecloth, a cup containing the remains of some coffee, and a blackbird crossed the doorstep, coming from inside the house, and flew off to the top of the lime-tree where it had its nest.

Monsieur Monde
Vanishes

To Professors Lian and Giroire,
To Doctor Ériau, in memory of February 1944

ONE

It was five o'clock in the afternoon, or a trifle after – the minute hand was leaning slightly towards the right – on 16 January, when Madame Monde swept into the waiting-room at the police station, bringing with her a gust of freezing air.

She must have jumped out of a taxi, or perhaps a private car, darted like a shadow across the pavement of the Rue La Rochefoucauld, and stumbled, no doubt, on the ill-lit staircase; and she had pushed open the door so authoritatively that everyone had started with surprise as the grimy grey panel fitted with an automatic closing device swung slowly back behind her, its slowness seeming absurd by contrast – so much so, indeed, that one working-class woman, shawled and hatless, who had been standing waiting for over an hour, instinctively pushed forward one of the children clinging to her skirts with a muttered: 'Go and shut the door.'

Until Madame Monde's entry, the atmosphere had been snug enough. On one side of the railing, clerks in police uniform or plain clothes were writing or warming their hands at the stove; on the other side, some people were sitting on a bench alongside the wall, others were standing; when anyone went out, carrying a brand-new sheet of paper, the rest moved up one place, the first clerk lifted his head; everyone was resigned to the bad smell, the feeble light shed by two green-shaded lamps, the monotony of waiting and of filling in forms in purple ink; and no doubt if some unforeseeable catastrophe had cut off the police station, for any length of time, from the outside world, those who happened to be assembled there would have ended by living together like a tribe.

Without jostling anyone, the woman had made her way to the front row; she was dressed in black, and under its heavy powder her face looked very white and her nose had a mauvish tinge.

Without seeing anyone, she groped in her handbag with black-gloved fingers like sticks of ebony, as precise in their movement as the beak of a bird of prey; and everyone was waiting, everyone was watching her as she thrust her visiting-card across the railing.

'Will you please tell the Superintendent I wish to see him.'

There was plenty of time to examine her in detail and yet nobody formed more than a general impression.

'A kind of widow,' the clerk told the Superintendent, who was sitting in his office amid a cloud of cigar-smoke, having a friendly chat with the general secretary of the Théâtre de Paris.

'In a moment.'

The clerk went back, and before resuming his seat and picking up the identity cards that were being held out to him he repeated the message:

'In a moment.'

She remained standing. No doubt her two feet, in their trim shoes with inordinately high heels, were resting on the dirty floor; none the less she gave the impression of being perched on one leg, like a heron. She saw nobody. She stared icily down at nothing in particular, perhaps at the cinders that had rolled out of the stove, and her lips were quivering like those of old women at prayer in church.

A door opened. The Superintendent appeared.

'Madame? . . .'

He closed the door behind her, waved her to a chair upholstered in green cloth, then walked slowly round his Empire-style desk, with her visiting-card in his hand, and sat down.

'Madame Monde?' he queried.

'Yes, Madame Monde. I live at 27b, Rue Ballu.'

And she glared at the smouldering cigar-butt which the Superintendent had crushed out in the ash-tray.

'And what can I do for you?'

'I have come to let you know that my husband has disappeared.'

'Very good. . . . Excuse me . . .'

He reached out for a writing-pad and picked up a silver propelling-pencil.

'Your husband, you said? . . .'

'My husband disappeared three days ago.'

'Three days. . . . Then he's been missing since 13 January.'

'Yes; it was on the 13th that I saw him last.'

She was wearing a black astrakhan coat which gave out a faint scent of violets, and her gloved fingers were twisting a flimsy handkerchief steeped in the same perfume.

'A sort of widow,' the secretary had announced.

But she was not a widow, or at least she had certainly not been one on 13 January, since at that date she still had a husband. Why did the Superintendent feel that she ought to have been one?

'Forgive me if I don't know Monsieur Monde, but I was only appointed to this district a few months ago.'

He was waiting, ready to take notes.

'My husband is Norbert Monde. You have no doubt heard of the firm of Monde and Company, brokers and exporters, whose offices and warehouses are in the Rue Montorgueil?'

He nodded, more from politeness than from conviction.

'My husband was born and has always lived in the house in the Rue Ballu where we still live.'

He nodded again.

'He was forty-eight years old. . . . I've just remembered: it was actually on his forty-eighth birthday that he disappeared . . .'

'January 13. . . . And you've not the slightest idea? . . .'

No doubt the visitor's stiff bearing and tight-lipped air implied that she had not the slightest idea.

'I suppose you want us to investigate?'

Her contemptuous pout might mean that this was obvious or, on the other hand, that she did not care.

'So then. . . . January 13. . . . You must forgive me for asking: had your husband any reason to attempt suicide?'

'None whatever.'

'His financial position?'

'The firm of Monde, which was founded by his grandfather Antonin Monde in 1843, is one of the soundest in Paris.'

'Your husband did not speculate? or gamble?'

On the mantelpiece, behind the Superintendent, there stood a black marble clock which had permanently stopped at five minutes past twelve. Why did this always suggest twelve midnight rather than twelve noon? The fact is that one always thought of five minutes past midnight when one looked at it. Beside it there stood a noisy alarm-clock which told the right time. It was right in front of Madame Monde's eyes, yet she kept twisting her long thin neck to look at the time on a tiny watch which she wore fastened to her bodice, like a locket.

'If we rule out money worries. . . . I suppose, madame, your husband hadn't any personal problems? . . . I'm sorry to be so persistent.'

'My husband hadn't a mistress, if that's what you mean.'

He dared not ask her if she herself had a lover. It was too improbable.

'His health?'

'He's never been ill in his life.'

'Good. . . . Very good. . . . Right. . . . Will you tell me what were your husband's movements that day, 13 January?'

'He got up at seven as usual. He has always gone to bed and risen early.'

'Excuse me; do you share the same bedroom?'

A curt, unfriendly 'Yes.'

'He got up at seven and went to his bathroom where in spite of . . . never mind . . . where he smoked his first cigarette. Then he went downstairs.'

'You were still in bed?'

The same stony 'Yes'.

'Did he speak to you?'

'He said good-bye as he always does.'

'Did you remember then that it was his birthday?'

'No.'

'He went downstairs, you said . . .'

'And had breakfast in his study. It's a room which he never uses for work, but which he's fond of. The big bay window has stained glass in it. The furniture is more or less Gothic.'

She must have disliked stained glass windows and Gothic furniture, or perhaps she'd had other plans for the use of that room which her husband had insisted on keeping as a study.

'Have you many servants?'

'A concierge and his wife; she does the rough work and he

acts as butler. We have a cook and a housemaid as well. I don't include Joseph the chauffeur, who is married and lives out. I usually get up at nine, after I have given Rosalie the orders for the day. . . . Rosalie is my maid. . . . She was with me before my marriage. . . . I mean before my second marriage . . .'

'So Monsieur Monde was your second husband?'

'I was first married to Lucien Grandpré who was killed fourteen years ago in a motor accident. . . . Every year he used to compete, as an amateur, in the twenty-four hour race at Le Mans . . .'

In the waiting-room, the people sitting on the greasy bench moved up one place from time to time, and others slipped out humbly, barely opening the door.

'In short, everything was just as usual that morning?'

'Just as usual. I heard the car start off about half-past eight to drive my husband to the Rue Montorgueil. He liked to read his mail himself and that's why he went to the office so early. His son left a quarter of an hour after him.'

'Your husband had a son by a first marriage?'

'We each had one. He has a married daughter, too. She and her husband lived with us for a while, but now they're living in the Quai de Passy.'

'Good . . . very good. . . . Did your husband actually go to his office?'

'Yes.'

'Did he come home to lunch?'

'He nearly always lunched in a restaurant close to the Halles, not far from his office.'

'When did you begin to feel anxious?'

'That evening, about eight o'clock.'

'In short, you've not seen him again since the morning of 13 January?'

'I rang him up soon after three to ask him to send Joseph along with the car, as I had to go out.'

'Did he sound his usual self when he spoke to you over the telephone?'

'Absolutely.'

'He did not tell you he would be late back, or mention the possibility of a journey?'

'No.'

'He just failed to come home to dinner at eight o'clock? Is that right?'

'That's right.'

'And since then he's given no sign of life. I suppose they've seen nothing of him in the office either?'

'No.'

'And what time did he leave the Rue Montorgueil?'

'About six. He never told me, but I knew that instead of coming straight home he used to stop at the Cintra, a café in the Rue Montmartre, for a drink.'

'Did he go there that evening?'

With dignity: 'I have no idea.'

'May I ask you, madame, why you have waited three whole days before coming to inform us of Monsieur Monde's disappearance?'

'I kept hoping he would come back.'

'Was he liable to go off like this?'

'It never happened before.'

'Did he never have to go off into the provinces suddenly on business?'

'Never.'

'And yet you went on waiting for him for three days?'

Without replying, she stared at him with her little black eyes.

'I suppose you informed his daughter who, so you tell me, is married and lives in the Quai de Passy?'

'She came to the house herself and behaved in such a way that I had to throw her out.'

'You don't get on with your step-daughter?'

'We never see one another. At least, not for the last two years.'

'But your husband still saw her?'

'That's to say she used to hunt him out in his office when she needed money.'

'If I understand you correctly, your step-daughter recently needed money and went to the Rue Montorgueil to ask her father for some. I suppose he usually gave it her?'

'Yes.'

'And there she learnt that Monsieur Monde had not re-appeared.'

'Probably.'

'And then she rushed off to the Rue Ballu.'

'Where she tried to get into the study and search the draw-ers.'

'Have you any idea what she wanted to find?'

Silence.

'In short, supposing Monsieur Monde should be dead, which seems to me unlikely . . .'

'Why?'

'. . . unlikely, the question would arise whether he had left a will. What were the terms of your marriage?'

'Separate maintenance. I have an income of my own and some property in the Avenue de Villiers . . .'

'What is your stepson's opinion about his father's disap-pearance?'

'He hasn't got one.'

'Is he still in the Rue Ballu?'

'Yes.'

'Did your husband make any arrangements before he left? About his business affairs, for instance. I suppose these require some working capital . . .'

'The cashier, Monsieur Lorisse, had his signature . . .'

'Did the cashier find the usual sums in the bank?'

'No. That's the point. On 13 January, just before six, my husband went to the bank.'

'It must have been closed?'

'To the general public, yes. Not to him. The clerks work late, and he went in by the side door. He withdrew three hundred thousand francs, which he had had in his current account.'

'So that next day the cashier was in difficulties?'

'No, not next day. He had no important deal to put through that day. It was not until yesterday that he needed to pay out certain sums, and then he learnt that the money had been with-drawn.'

'If I understand correctly, your husband, when he disap-peared, left no money either for his business or for yourself and his children?'

'That's not quite correct. The greater part of his fortune, represented by various securities, is in his safe at the bank. Now he has withdrawn nothing from the safe lately, he has not even visited it, so the bank manager tells me. As for the key, it was in its usual place at home, in a small drawer in his bureau.'

'Have you powers of attorney?'

'Yes.'

'In that case . . .' he said, with unintentional offhandedness.

'I went to the bank. I had promised the cashier to let him have the money. I was refused access to the safe on the pretext that I could not certify that my spouse was still living, according to the accepted formula.'

The Superintendent heaved a sigh, and nearly took a cigar out of his case. He had understood. There was nothing for it.

'So you want us to undertake investigations?'

She merely stared at him once again, then rose, twisting her neck to look at the time.

A minute later she walked through the waiting-room, where the woman in the shawl, leaning sideways under the weight of the baby she was carrying on her arm, was humbly explaining that for the last five days, ever since her husband had been arrested during an affray, she had been penniless.

When Madame Monde had crossed the pavement, on which the police-station lamp shed a red glow, and when Joseph the chauffeur had swiftly opened the door of the car and closed it behind her, she gave him the address of her solicitor, whom she had left an hour previously and who was expecting her return.

Everything she had told the Superintendent was true, but sometimes nothing is less true than the truth.

*

Monsieur Monde had woken at seven o'clock in the morning; noiselessly, and without letting any cold air under the covers, he had slipped out of the bed where his wife lay motionless. This was his invariable habit. Each morning, he pretended to believe she was asleep. He avoided lighting the bedside lamp, and crept round the huge bed in the darkness, which was streaked by faint gleams of light filtering through the shutters; barefooted, holding his slippers in his hand. And yet he knew that if he glanced at the pillow he would see his wife's little black eyes gleaming.

Only when he reached the bathroom did he take a deep breath; he turned the bath taps on full and plugged in his electric razor.

He was a stout, or more precisely a corpulent man. His scanty hair was fair, and in the morning, when it was ruffled, it gave his rosy face a childish look.

Even his blue eyes, all the time he watched himself in the glass while shaving, wore an expression of surprise which was like a child's. It was as if every morning, when he emerged from the ageless world of sleep, Monsieur Monde felt surprised to meet in his mirror a middle-aged man with wrinkled eyelids and a prominent nose topping a sandy toothbrush moustache.

Pouting at himself to stretch the skin under the razor, he invariably forgot the running bathwater, and would rush to the taps just as the sound of the overflow betrayed him, through the door, to Madame Monde.

When he had finished shaving he would look at himself a little longer, complacently yet with a certain regretful pang because he was no longer the chubby, somewhat ingenuous lad he had once been, and could not get used to the idea of being already embarked on the downward slope of life.

That morning, in the bathroom, he had remembered that he was just forty-eight years old. That was all. He was forty-eight. Soon he would be fifty. He felt tired. In the warm water he stretched out his muscles as though to shake off the fatigue accumulated during all those years.

He was nearly dressed when the ringing of an alarm-clock overhead told him that his son Alain was now about to get up.

He finished dressing. He was meticulous about his appearance. He liked his clothes to be uncreased and spotless, his linen soft and smooth, and sometimes in the street or in his office he would look down with satisfaction at his gleaming shoes.

He was forty-eight years old. Would his wife remember? his son? his daughter? Nobody, most likely. Perhaps Monsieur

Lorisse, his old cashier, who had been his father's cashier, would say to him solemnly: 'Best wishes, Monsieur Norbert.'

He had to go through the bedroom. He bent over his wife's forehead and brushed it with his lips.

'You won't be needing the car?'

'Not this morning. If I need it in the afternoon I'll ring you at the office.'

His house was a very odd one; as far as he was concerned, there was no other like it in the world. When his grandfather had bought it, it had already had a number of owners. And each of them had altered it in some way, so that there was no longer any recognizable plan. Some doors had been blocked up, others let in in different places. Two rooms had been thrown into one, a floor had been raised, and a passage introduced with unexpected twists and even more unexpected steps on which visitors were apt to stumble, and on which Madame Monde herself still stumbled.

Even on the sunniest days the light in the house was dim and soft as the dust of time, and as though imbued with a fragrance that may have been insipid but that seemed sweet to one who had always known it.

Gas pipes still lay along the walls, and there were some burners on the back staircase, while in the attic lay dozens of oil lamps of every sort of date.

Some of the rooms had become Madame Monde's province. Alien, characterless pieces of furniture mingled with the old things that belonged to the house, and she had sometimes driven them out into the lumber-room, but the study had remained intact, just as Norbert Monde had always known it, with its red, yellow and blue stained-glass windows which lit up one after the other as the sun ran its course, and awakened bright little coloured flames in every corner.

It was not Rosalie but the cook who brought up Monsieur Monde's breakfast, because of a strict timetable decreed by Madame Monde which determined where every member of the household had to be at various times of day. This was all to the good, for Monsieur Monde disliked Rosalie, who despite the image her name suggested, was a gaunt and sickly girl who vented her spite on everyone except her mistress.

That morning, 13 January, he read his papers while dipping croissants in his coffee. He heard Joseph opening the main gate to take out the car. He waited a little, staring at the ceiling, as though he hoped his son might be ready to set off at the same time as himself, but this practically never happened.

When he went out it was freezing, and a pale winter sun was rising over Paris.

No thought of escape had as yet crossed Monsieur Monde's mind.

'Morning, Joseph.'

'Morning, monsieur.'

As a matter of fact, it started like an attack of 'flu. In the car he felt a shiver. He was very susceptible to headcolds. Some winters they would hang on for weeks, and his pockets would be stuffed with wet handkerchiefs, which mortified him. Moreover that morning he ached all over, perhaps from having slept in an awkward position, or a touch of indigestion due to last night's supper?

'I'm getting 'flu,' he thought.

Then, just as they were crossing the Grands Boulevards, instead of automatically checking the time on the pneumatic clock as he usually did, he raised his eyes and noticed the rosy chimney pots outlined against a pale blue sky where a tiny white cloud was floating.

It reminded him of the sea. The harmony of blue and rose-red suddenly brought a breath of Mediterranean air to his mind, and he envied people who, at that time of year, lived in the South and wore white flannels.

The smell of the Halles came to meet him. The car stopped in front of a porch over which was written in yellow letters: 'Norbert Monde Ltd., brokers and exporters, founded 1843.'

Beyond the porch lay a former courtyard which had been covered over with a glass roof and looked like the hall of a railway station. It was surrounded by raised platforms on which lorries were being loaded with cases and bundles. Warehousemen in blue overalls were pushing trolleys and greeted him as he went by: 'Morning, Monsieur Norbert.'

The offices stood in a row along one side, just as in a railway station, with glazed doors and a number over each of them.

'Morning, Monsieur Lorisse.'

'Morning, Monsieur Norbert.'

Was he going to wish him a happy birthday? No. He hadn't remembered it. And yet yesterday's page in the calendar had already been torn off. Monsieur Lorisse, who was sixty-six, was sorting letters without opening them and setting them out in little heaps in front of his employer.

The glass roof over the courtyard was yellow this morning. It never let the sunlight through because of the layer of dust that covered it, but on fine days it was yellow, almost pale yellow, though sometimes, in April for instance when a cloud suddenly hid the sun, it turned so dark that the lights had to be switched on.

The question of sunlight proved to be an important one that day. And then there was a complicated business about a flagrantly untrustworthy client from Smyrna, with whom they had been at law for the past six months or more and who always found a way to evade his obligations, so that although he was in the wrong they would end, out of sheer weariness, by allowing him to be in the right.

'Is the consignment for the "Maison Bleue" of Bordeaux ready?'

'The van will be leaving presently.'

About twenty minutes past nine, when all the employees were at their posts. Monsieur Monde saw Alain come in and make his way to the Foreign Trade Department. Alain, although his son, did not come in to say good morning to him. It was like that every day. And yet every day it made Monsieur Monde unhappy. Every day he felt like telling Alain: 'You might at least look in at my office when you get here.'

A sort of diffidence, of which he was ashamed, prevented him from doing so. Apart from which, his son would have misinterpreted such a suggestion as an attempt to keep a check on his punctuality, for he was invariably late. Heaven knows why: five minutes earlier, he could have gone with his father in the car.

Was it from a spirit of independence that he travelled to the office alone, by bus or by metro? And yet a year ago, when in view of his patent inability to pass his *bachot* he had been asked what he would like to do, he had replied of his own accord, 'I'd like to join the business.'

Not until ten or eleven o'clock would Monsieur Monde pay an apparently unpremeditated visit to the office of the Foreign Trade Department, and laying a casual hand on Alain's shoulder murmur: 'Good morning, son.'

'Good morning, Father.'

Alain was as delicate as a girl. He had a girl's long curling eyelashes, that fluttered like a butterfly's wings. His ties were always in pale pastel shades, and his father disliked the lace-edged handkerchiefs that adorned his jackets.

No, it wasn't 'flu. Monsieur felt uncomfortable all over. At eleven his daughter rang him. There happened to be two important clients in his office.

'Excuse me, please.'

And his daughter, at the end of the line: 'Is that you? ... I'm in town. ... Can I call in at your office? ... Right away, yes ...'

He could not see her right away. He would have to spend at least an hour longer with his clients.

'No, this afternoon I can't. ... I'll look in tomorrow morning. ... It can wait.'

Money, obviously! Yet again! Her husband was an architect. They had two children. They were always short of money. What on earth did they do with it?

'Tomorrow morning, right.'

Well! she hadn't remembered his birthday either.

He went to lunch all by himself in a restaurant where his place was always reserved and where the waiters called him Monsieur Norbert. The sun was shining on the tablecloth and the carafe.

He caught sight of himself in the glass as the cloakroom attendant was handing him his heavy overcoat, and thought he looked older. The mirror must have been a poor one, for he always saw himself with a crooked nose.

'See you tomorrow, Monsieur Norbert.'

Tomorrow. ... Why did the word remain so firmly fixed in his mind? The year before, at about this same date, he had felt tired, listless, ill at ease in his clothes, just as he was feeling now,

He had mentioned it to his friend Boucard, who was a doctor and whom he frequently met at the Cintra.

'Are you sure there's no phosphate in your water?'

He had taken a glass jar from the kitchen furtively, without saying a word; he remembered it had held mustard. Next morning he had urinated into it and had seen a sort of fine white powder dancing in the yellow liquid.

'You ought to take a holiday, have a change. In the meantime, swallow this night and morning . . .'

Boucard had scribbled out a prescription. Monsieur Monde had never dared piss into the glass again; he had thrown it out into the street, after deliberately breaking it so that nobody could think of using it. He knew that wasn't what was the matter with him.

Today, at three o'clock, feeling disinclined to work, he was standing in the courtyard on one of the platforms, vaguely watching the comings and goings of warehousemen and drivers. He heard the sound of voices in a tarpaulin-covered lorry. Why did he listen? A man was saying:

'The boss's son is always after him, making propositions. . . . Yesterday he brought him flowers . . .'

Monsieur Monde felt himself turn quite white and stiffen from head to foot, and yet he had really learnt nothing new. He had suspected the truth for some time. They were talking about his son and a sixteen-year-old assistant warehouseman who had been taken on three weeks before.

So it was true!

He went back to his office.

'Madame Monde wants you on the phone.' She needed the car.

'Will you tell Joseph . . .'

From that moment onward he stopped thinking. There was no inner conflict, no decision to be reached, indeed nothing was ever decided at all. All that happened was that his face grew more expressionless. Monsieur Lorisse, who was working opposite him, glanced furtively at him several times and thought he was looking better than in the morning.

'Do you know, Monsieur Lorisse, that I'm forty-eight today?'

'Goodness! monsieur, I'm very sorry I forgot. I've had this Smyrna business on my mind . . .'

'It doesn't matter, Monsieur Lorisse, it doesn't matter!'

He spoke more lightly than usual, as Monsieur Lorisse was later to remember, and to confide in the chief warehouseman, who had been with the firm almost as long as himself: 'It's funny. He seemed somehow detached from his worries.'

At six o'clock he visited the bank and went into the manager's office, where he was welcomed as usual.

'Will you find out what I have in my current account?'

There were three hundred and forty thousand odd francs to his credit. He signed a cheque for three hundred thousand and received the money in five-thousand-franc notes. He divided these among his various pockets.

'I could have them sent to you . . .' commented the assistant manager.

He understood later, or rather he thought he understood, for as a matter of fact Monsieur Monde was, even then, on the point of leaving the money behind, taking away only a few thousand-franc notes. Nobody ever guessed this.

He thought of the securities in his safe. They were worth over a million.

'With that,' he thought, *'they'll* be in the clear.'

For he knew that the key was in his bureau, that his wife knew where to find it and that she had powers of attorney.

His first idea had been to go off without any money. It seemed to him an act of cowardice to take any. It spoilt the whole thing. As he left the bank he felt ashamed of it, and nearly retraced his steps.

Then he decided to think no more about it. He began to walk along the streets. Occasionally, he looked at himself in shopwindows. Near the Boulevard Sébastopol he noticed a third-rate hairdresser's, and went in, took his place in the queue behind other customers and, when his turn came to sit down in the hinged chair, he told the barber to shave off his moustache.

TWO

He stared at himself in the glass, pouting like a child, and trying not to look at the other people but to concentrate on his own reflection. He felt that he was very different from the rest, that he had somehow betrayed them by coming amongst them. He almost wanted to apologize.

The barber's assistant, however, behaved towards him with indifference; he had merely given his colleagues a wink as Monsieur Monde leaned back in the chair, but it had been a wink so brief, automatic and unsmiling as to seem more like a sort of Masonic sign.

Was Monsieur Monde so very unlike the rest, with his sleek flesh, his expensive suit, his custom-made shoes? He thought so. He longed for the transformation to have taken place.

And meanwhile he was distressed because the assistant had a pink plaster on the nape of his neck, a bulging plaster which must conceal a horrid purplish boil. It distressed him, too, to see a tobacco-stained forefinger moving to and fro under his eyes, and to breathe the sickening smell of nicotine mingled with shaving soap. And yet there was something pleasurable about this slight pain!

He was still too new to it all. The transformation was not yet complete. He didn't want to look to the right or the left, in the chalk-scrawled mirror, at the row of men behind him, all reading sporting papers and, from time to time, glancing unconcernedly at the occupants of the armchairs.

On the day of his First Communion, at the Lycée Stanislas, after he had walked gingerly back to his seat with downcast eyes, he had stayed motionless for a long time with his face buried in his hands, waiting for the promised transformation.

What was happening now was so much more essential! He could not possibly have explained it, or even thought about it in a logical way.

When, a short while before, he had decided.... But he hadn't decided anything! He had had nothing to decide. What he was living through was not even a completely new experience. He must have dreamed about it often, or have thought about it so much that he felt he had done it all before.

He looked at himself, as the barber's fingers held his cheek taut, and he said to himself: 'That's that! The die is cast!'

He felt no surprise. He had been expecting this for a long time, all his life long. But his nostrils were still unaccustomed to the cheap scents that he was now inhaling deeply, whereas hitherto he had only caught a whiff of them as some workman in his Sunday best passed by. He was offended by the tobacco-stained finger, and the plaster, and the towel of dubious cleanliness round his neck.

He was the odd man out, the one who felt surprised, for instance, to see ten people deep in the same sporting papers; it was he who must seem strange, whom others would maybe point at?

If he had not yet experienced the ecstasy of release, it was because the transformation had barely begun. He was still too new to it, of course.

'Dry shampoo?'

He heard, yet he did not answer immediately; then he said, very fast:

'Excuse me. . . . Yes. . . . If you like . . .'

Once before he had got rid of that toothbrush moustache which had just been shaved off. It was a long time ago, two or three years after his second marriage. He'd gone home, to the Rue Ballu, in high spirits, feeling rejuvenated. His wife had looked at him with those little black eyes – they were hard eyes already – and had said: 'What's come over you? You look indecent.'

He did not look indecent, but he looked a different man. There was suddenly something ingenuous about his expression, due to the pouting upper lip and the alternately pleading or sulky look of his whole mouth.

He paid and went out awkwardly, apologizing yet again as he brushed against the crossed legs of those who were waiting.

Initiations are always painful, and this was an initiation. He dived into the street and began walking through districts he hardly knew. He was haunted by the feeling that everybody was watching him and he felt guilty; guilty, for instance, of having shaved off his moustache, like a criminal who's afraid of being recognized, and guilty, too, because of the three hundred thousand francs with which his pockets were bulging.

Suppose that policeman at the corner of the boulevard were to stop him and ask him . . .

He sought out the darkest, most mysterious streets, those where the lights reminded him somewhat of those of his youth.

Wasn't it extraordinary to be doing at the age of forty-eight, exactly forty-eight, what he had nearly done thirty years earlier, when he was eighteen? And to be feeling almost the same man, to such an extent that he never gave a thought to his wife nor to his children, nor to everything that had happened in between?

He remembered that first temptation very clearly. It had been a winter's evening, too. He was living in the Rue Ballu – he had never lived anywhere else; but he'd had a room on the second floor then, over his father's study, the room which was now Alain's. The house was still lit by gas.

It must have been eleven at night. He had dined alone with his mother. She was an extremely gentle woman, with delicate features, a smooth skin, a melancholy smile. That evening she was paler than usual, with eyes reddened by tears, and around them the huge house seemed deserted. The servants trod noiselessly, and spoke in low voices, as people do in a house of mourning.

His father had not come home. That often happened. But why, at about five o'clock, had he sent the coachman to collect his valise and his fur-lined cloak?

He had always had mistresses. For some time lately there had been one, a little actress whose picture was on all the walls of Paris, who seemed more dangerous than the rest.

He was an invariably good-humoured man, always spick and span; the barber called to shave him every morning, and afterwards he would go off to fence at his club, and in the afternoons he was to be seen at the races, in a grey top hat and morning coat.

Had he gone for ever?

Norbert would have liked to comfort his mother.

'Go to bed,' she told him with a somewhat mournful smile. 'It's all right.'

That evening he had stayed for a long while with his face pressed against the window-pane in his bedroom. He had turned out the gas. He was looking out. A fine drizzle was falling. The Rue Ballu was deserted, and there were only two lights to be seen: a gas lamp fifty yards from the house, and the glowing rectangle of a blind in front of a window, a sort of luminous screen behind which a shadow passed from time to time.

Over by the Rue Clichy life was flowing by; and Norbert Monde, his burning forehead pressed against the pane, felt a shiver run through him. Behind him there reigned a calm so deep, so absolute, that it frightened him. This house that was his home, these rooms that he knew so well, these things that he had always seen about him, seemed to be alive, with a menacing and terribly still life. The air itself was coming to life, becoming a threat.

It was a dark world, peopled with ghosts, that enclosed him, seeking to hold him back at all costs, to prevent him from going elsewhere, from discovering another life.

Then a woman passed by. He could see only her black silhouette, with an umbrella. She was walking fast, holding up her skirt with one hand, over the wet gleaming pavement, she was about to turn the corner of the street, she had turned it, and he felt a longing to run, to get out of the house; it seemed to him that he could still do it, that one great effort would be enough, that once outside he would be saved.

He would rush forward, would plunge head foremost into that stream of life that was flowing all around the petrified house.

He gave a start because the door was opening noiselessly in the darkness. He was terrified, and opened his mouth to scream, but a gentle voice said softly: 'Are you asleep?'

That day, the choice had still been open to him. He had missed his opportunity.

He was to miss another, later, during his first marriage.

It was with a strange sense of pleasure mingled with dread that he thought about it, now that he had at last achieved what had been ordained from the beginning.

He had been thirty-two; in appearance much like today, as stout or even stouter. At school his companions had nicknamed him Podge; and yet there was nothing flabby about him.

It was a Sunday. A winter Sunday yet again, but as far as he could remember it was at the onset of winter, which always seems gloomier because it suggests lingering Autumn rather than approaching Spring.

Why, on this occasion, was the house in the Rue Ballu empty? The servants had gone out; obviously, because it was Sunday. But his wife Thérèse, who looked so fragile and so guileless? Thérèse . . . well! . . .

The two children were ill. Not just the girl, who was five and had whooping cough. As for Alain, who was only one, he was going through a phase of bringing up whatever he drank.

Their mother had gone out, none the less. She had invented some excuse or other. In those days she seemed the picture of innocence, and nobody suspected.

In short, he was all alone. It wasn't quite dark yet. It was freezing. Not only the house but the whole of Paris seemed empty, with the occasional rumble of a car along the paved streets. The little girl was coughing. Sometimes he gave her a spoonful of linctus from a bottle which stood on the mantelpiece, he could still point out the exact spot.

The day before, that morning, just an hour previously, he had adored his wife and children.

Dusk was spreading through the house, ash-grey, and he forgot to put on the lights. He walked to and fro, always returning to the window with its floral-patterned lace curtains. That was yet another sensation which he recalled with obsessive accuracy: the mesh of the lace between his forehead and the cold pane.

Suddenly, as he looked down into the street at the man in a greenish overcoat who was lighting the only gas-lamp within his field of vision, he was seized by a sense of detachment from everything: his daughter had coughed and he had not turned round, the baby might have been vomiting in his cradle; he stared at the figure of the man going off, and felt himself as it were impelled forward, he had an irresistible longing to go off too, to go straight ahead.

To go somewhere!

He had even been downstairs into his study, for no apparent reason, perhaps with some thought of going away? He had stayed there motionless for a long while, as though dazed, in the same place, and he had given a start when the cook – the one who had been there before he was born, and who had since died – had exclaimed, with her hat still on her head and mittens on her frozen hands:

'Have you gone deaf? Don't you hear the child screaming her head off?'

And now he was in the street. He walked along, gazing with something akin to terror at the shadowy figures that brushed against him and at the endless tangle of dark streets, crammed with invisible life.

He had a meal somewhere near the Bastille – he remembered crossing the Place des Vosges diagonally – in a little restaurant where there were paper napkins on the marble tables.

'Tomorrow!'

Then he went for a walk along the Seine. In this, again, he was involuntarily performing an old-established rite.

He still felt diffident and awkward. He was really too new to it. To do the thing properly, to carry it through, he ought to have gone down one of the flights of stone steps leading to the water's edge. Whenever he crossed the Seine in the morning he used to glance under the bridges, in order to revive another very ancient memory, dating from the days when he went to the Lycée Stanislas and would sometimes make his way there leisurely on foot: under the Pont Neuf he had caught sight of two old, or ageless, men, grey and shaggy as neglected statues; they were sitting on a heap of stones and while one of them ate a sausage, the other bandaged his feet with strips of cotton.

He did not know what time it was. He had not thought about it once since leaving the bank. The streets were emptying. Buses were becoming fewer. Then groups of people passing him talking very loudly, presumably on their way back from theatres or cinemas.

His plan was to choose a third-rate hotel like the one he had noticed a short while before in a little street close to the Place des Vosges. He still felt reluctant to do so, because of the way he was dressed and because of the three hundred thousand francs.

He found a humble, but decent, place near the Boulevard Saint-Michel, and went in. There was a smell of cooking. A night porter in slippers fiddled for a long time with the keys before handing him one.

'Fourth floor ... the second door. ... Try and not make a noise.'

For the first time, at forty-eight – as though he had made himself a present of it, on that birthday that everyone had forgotten! – he was a man all alone, but he was not yet a man in the street.

*

He was still apprehensive of giving offence, of seeming out of place. For it was not shyness. He was not embarrassed for his own sake, but he was afraid of embarrassing other people.

For ten minutes, at least, he had been prowling round the narrow house which he had found without too much difficulty. The sun was shining; the butchers' and dairymen's shops were full of provisions which, exuding their mingled smells, overflowed on to the pavement, and it was difficult to make one's way through the bustling crowd of housewives and vendors in the street-market of the Rue de Buci.

From time to time, with an instinctive gesture of which he was ashamed, Monsieur Monde felt his pockets to make sure nobody had stolen his bank notes. In fact, how was he going to manage when he had to change clothes in front of someone?

The problem worried him for some time. Then he found a solution, but he needed paper and string. Paper was easy enough. He merely had to buy a newspaper from the first stall he saw. Wasn't it rather odd to buy a whole ball of string in order to use only a scrap of it?

That was what he did. He walked about for a long time, through a district selling exclusively food, before he discovered a stationer's shop.

And he couldn't do it in public. He went into a bistro, ordered a coffee and went down to the lavatory; this was in the cellar, next to the bottles, and the door did not shut. There was only a grey concrete hole in the ground and the space was so narrow that his shoulders touched the walls.

He made a parcel of the bank notes, tied it up securely, and threw the rest of the paper and string down the hole; when he pulled the chain the water spurted over his shoes and splashed his trousers.

He forgot to drink his cup of coffee. He was conscious of looking like a criminal, and turned back to make sure that the proprietor was not staring after him.

He had to go into the narrow house with its blue-painted façade, on which was inscribed in large black letters: *Clothing for sale and hire.*

'Do you know what Joseph does with the clothes you give him?' his wife had remarked one day, in an aggressive tone. '... He sells them in a shop in the Rue de Buci. As they're nearly new when you give them to him ...'

She was exaggerating. She always exaggerated. She hated seeing money spent.

'I don't see why, considering we pay him, and pay him well, far better than he deserves, we should give him this bonus ...'

He went in. A little man who must have been an Armenian received him without a trace of the surprise he had anticipated. And he said hesitantly:

'I would like a suit ... something very simple, not showy. ... I don't know if you see what I mean? ...'

'A good class of thing, all the same?'

If he'd dared, he would have said: 'A suit like everybody else's.'

There were clothes hanging everywhere throughout the house, in every room, town suits, evening dress clothes particularly, riding habits and even two policemen's uniforms.

'A darkish cloth, please. ... Not too new ...'

He felt worried, shortly after, because he had laid down his parcel in the first room and now had gone up to the second floor. Suppose someone stole it?

He was shown suits, but almost all of them were too narrow, or too long in the sleeves or in the leg. He was standing in his underpants in the middle of the room when a woman came in, the shopkeeper's wife, who had something to say to her husband but paid no attention to him.

Whatever must they take him for? Surely for a man who was trying to hide; for a thief, a bankrupt, a murderer! He felt wretched. It was the change-over that was painful. Afterwards, in less than an hour, he would be free.

'Now here's a jacket that might have been made for you. Unfortunately I don't know if I've got the trousers to go with it. No. But wait a minute . . . this grey pair . . .'

Monsieur Monde submitted, for he dared not argue. It was all rather better quality than he'd have liked. Dressed thus, he looked like a respectable clerk, a careful accountant.

'Would you like shoes and linen too?'

He bought some. A small fibre suitcase of an ugly brown, also second-hand, was finally provided.

'Are you going to keep it on?'

'If you don't mind I should even like to leave you my other clothes . . .'

He saw the Armenian glance at the tailor's label, and reflected that he had made a mistake. He was not afraid of being followed. The thought had not occurred to him. And yet it vexed him to leave this sort of trace behind.

When he emerged, his parcel was still in the first room. The shopkeeper handed it to him. Couldn't he guess from the feel of it that it contained bank notes?

It was ten o'clock. The time when. . . . No, no. He didn't want to think about what he usually did at such or such a time. The jacket was rather tight over the shoulders. The overcoat was made of thinner cloth than his own, and this gave him a feeling of lightness.

Why did he go unhesitatingly to wait for a bus, at the corner of the Boulevard Saint-Michel, that would take him to the Gare de Lyon? He had not thought about it beforehand; he had not said to himself that he would do this or that.

Once again, he was following a preordained plan, for which he was not responsible. Nor had he taken any decision the day before. It all came from much further back, from the beginning of things.

Standing on the platform of the bus, he patted his pockets; he leaned forward to see his reflection in the window. He felt no surprise. But he was still waiting, as he had waited after his First Communion, for something he longed for, which was slow in coming.

It felt odd to be following the crowd through the main hall of the station, carrying only a small suitcase like so many other travellers, then to take his place in the queue at the ticket office and, when his turn came, to say meekly: 'Marseilles'.

He was not asked which class. He was handed a mauve third-class ticket, which he examined with curiosity.

He kept on following the crowd. One merely had to drift along with it. He was pushed and jostled, suitcases were flung against his legs and a child's pram shoved into his back, the loud-speaker shouted orders, train whistles blew, and he climbed like the rest into a third-class compartment where three soldiers already sat eating.

What embarrassed him chiefly was his parcel, which he had not thought of putting away in his case. It is true that the latter was already full, but he opened it and packed the contents closer so as to set his mind at rest.

Was life beginning at last? He did not know. He was afraid to question himself. The smell in the compartment upset him, like the plaster and the stained forefinger of the barber's assistant, and when the train started he went out into the corridor.

A magnificent sight, magnificent and sordid, met his eyes: the soaring blocks of blackened houses between which the train was threading its way, with hundreds and thousands of windows open or closed, linen hanging out, wireless aerials, a prodigious accumulation, in breadth and in height, of teeming lives, from which the train suddenly broke away after a glimpse of the last green-and-white bus in a street which already seemed like a main road.

After that, Monsieur Monde stopped thinking. The rhythm of the train took possession of him. It was like some music with a regular beat, the words for which were provided by scraps of phrases, memories, the passing images that met his eyes, a lonely cottage in the countryside where a stout woman was washing clothes, a station-master waving his red flag in a toy station, people passing ceaselessly behind him on their way to the toilet, a child howling in the next compartment and one of the soldiers asleep in his corner, his mouth wide open in a ray of sunlight.

He did not know where he was going, nor what he would do. He had set off. Nothing lay behind him any more: nothing lay before him as yet. He was in space.

He felt hungry. Everyone was eating. At a station he bought some dry sandwiches and a bottle of beer.

At Lyons it was dark already. He nearly got off the train, without knowing why, tempted to plunge right away into the spangled darkness, but the train moved off again before he had time to make up his mind.

There were so many things within him which he must settle later, when he'd got used to it, when the train stopped, when he reached some destination at last.

He was not afraid. He had no regrets. In most of the compartments the lights had been put out. People had fallen asleep leaning against one another, mingling their smells and their breath.

He dared not, as yet. And despite his weariness he went on standing in the draughty corridor. He kept his eyes averted from the next coach, where red carpets could be glimpsed.

Avignon. . . . He stared in amazement at the big clock, which only said nine o'clock. . . . From time to time he cast a glance into his compartment, where he had left his suitcase in the rack beside various odd bundles.

Saint-Charles . . .

He went on foot, very slowly, towards the harbour. The big brasseries of La Canebière were still open. He stared at them with a sort of amazement, particularly at the men whom he could see through the lighted windows, sitting round their tables, as though he found it strange that life still went on.

These people were at their usual tables, as on any other evening. They had been in no train. They had just finished playing cards or billiards, or talking politics, and they were calling the waiter, or else the waiter, who knew them all by name, was telling them that it was closing time.

Some of them were coming out already, lingering on the edge of the pavement to finish the conversation they had begun, shaking hands, going off in various directions, each of them towards his home, his wife, his bed.

Iron shutters clattered down over windows. In the Old Port District, too, the little bars were being closed.

He saw the water quite close to him, small boats packed close together and lifted by the gently-breathing sea. Reflected lights stretched out, and somebody was rowing, yes, even at this hour somebody was rowing in the cool darkness of the dock, somebody who was not alone, for there was a sound of whispering voices. Lovers, perhaps, or else smugglers?

He turned up the collar of his overcoat, that overcoat that was still unfamiliar to him, the feel of which he could not recognize. He raised his head to look at the starry sky. A woman brushed up against him, saying something, and he moved quickly away, took a small street to the right, and caught sight of the lighted doorway of a hotel.

It was warm inside, even in the entrance hall. There was a mahogany reception desk and a formal-looking gentleman in black, who asked him:

'Are you alone?'

He was offered a pad of registration forms, and after a moment's hesitation he wrote down some name or other, the first that came into his mind.

'We still have one room vacant overlooking the Old Port.'

The clerk picked up the little suitcase and Monsieur Monde felt ashamed. Surely the man must be surprised at the meagreness of his luggage?

'It's on the second floor. The lift doesn't work at this time of night. . . . If you'll come this way . . .'

It was a comfortable room, with a *cabinet de toilette* beyond a glass partition. Over the mantelpiece there was a large mirror and Monsieur Monde looked at himself in it, a long, serious look, shook his head, started to heave a sigh but suppressed it, and took off his somewhat tight-sleeved jacket, his tie, his shirt.

Then he inspected his lonely room and felt a slight regret, which he hardly dared admit to himself, for not having listened to the woman who had spoken to him a short while before, by the water's edge.

Finally he got into bed and pulled the blanket right up to his nose.

THREE

Tears were gushing from behind his closed eyelids, swelling them as they streamed forth. They were no ordinary tears. They gushed in a warm, endless flow from some deep spring, they gathered behind the barrier of his lashes and then poured freely down his cheeks, not in separate drops but in zigzagging rivulets like those that run down windowpanes on rainy days; and the patch of wetness beside his chin spread ever wider on his pillow.

Monsieur Monde could not have been asleep, could not have been dreaming, since he was conscious of a pillow and not of sand. And yet, in his thoughts, he was not lying in the bedroom of some hotel of which he did not even know the name. He was lucid, not with an everyday lucidity, the sort one admits, but on the contrary the sort of which one subsequently feels ashamed, perhaps because it confers on supposedly commonplace things the grandeur ascribed to them by poetry and religion.

What was streaming from his whole being, through his two eyes, was all the fatigue accumulated during forty-eight years, and if they were gentle tears, it was because now the ordeal was over.

He had given up. He had stopped struggling. He had hurried from far away – the train journey no longer existed, there was only a sense of endless flight – he had hurried here, towards the sea which, vast and blue, more intensely alive than any human being, the soul of the earth, the soul of the world, was breathing peacefully close to him. For, in spite of the pillow, which was real enough but unimportant, he had ended his journey lying by the sea, he had collapsed beside it, exhausted and already pacified, he had lain down full length on warm golden sand, and there was nothing else in the universe but sea and sand, and himself speaking.

He was speaking without moving his lips, for he had no need

to. He was telling of his infinite aching weariness, which was
due not to his journey in a train but to his long journey as a
man.

He was ageless now. He could let his lips quiver like a
child's.

'Always, for as long as I can remember, I've had to make
such efforts ...'

No need to go into details here, as when he complained of
anything to his wife.

Hadn't the servants whispered among themselves, when he
was a tiny boy, that he would never be able to walk because he
was too fat? He had been bow-legged for quite a long time.

At school he used to stare intently, painfully, at the letters on
the blackboard, and the teacher used to say: 'You're day-
dreaming again!'

It may well have been true, for he usually ended by falling
asleep, willy-nilly.

'It's pointless trying to make him study ...'

He remembered standing still in a corner of the playground
at Stanislas, while all the others were running about, or sitting
at his desk ignored by contemptuous schoolmasters.

And yet, by dint of patient and fierce effort, he had passed
his *bachot*.

Lord, how tired he was now! And why were the heaviest
burdens laid on his shoulders, when he had done no harm to
anyone?

His father, for instance, had never had to make the slightest
effort. He played with life, with money, with women, he lived
for his pleasure alone, and he was invariably light-hearted when
he rose in the morning, his son had always seen him go by
whistling to himself, his eye sparkling with the pleasure he had
just enjoyed or that which he anticipated.

In this way he had squandered his wife's dowry, and his
wife had borne him no grudge. He had almost ruined the
business inherited from his father and grandfather, and it
was his son who'd had to labour year after year to set it on its
feet again.

In spite of it all, when this man had at last succumbed to
illness, his family had rallied round him, and he'd enjoyed the

devotion of a wife who had never uttered one word of reproach and had spent her life waiting for him.

The whole thing was so overwhelming, out of all proportion with words, on the scale of the sea, the sand and the sun. Monsieur Monde felt like a great caryatid released, at long last, from its burden. He did not complain. He did not recriminate. He bore no resentment against anyone. Only, for the first time, now that it was over, he let his weariness flow out, like streams of rainwater blurring the window-pane, and he felt his body grow warmer and more peaceful.

'Why have you treated me so harshly?' he longed to whisper in the sea's ear.

He had tried so hard to do the right thing! He had married so as to have a home and children, he had wanted to be a fruitful, not a sterile, tree; and one morning his wife had left him; he had found himself with a baby in one cot, a small girl in the other, without understanding, without knowing; he had been in despair, and those whom he questioned had smiled at his innocence; and finally, in forgotten drawers, he had discovered horrible drawings, obscene photographs, unspeakable things which had revealed to him the true nature of the woman he had thought so guileless.

In his heart of hearts he had borne her no resentment, he had pitied her for the demon she had inside her. And for the children's sake he had married again.

He stretched out his whole frame in deep relief, and the little shining waves came up to lick the sand by his side; perhaps one of them would soon reach him for a caress.

He had borne his burden as long as his strength had lasted. How horrible it all was! His wife, his daughter, his son. . . . And then money! . . . His money or their money, he no longer knew, he no longer wanted to know. . . . What was the good, since it was over and done with, and now at last . . .

Somebody was walking about. Loud footsteps that seemed to go right through him, a floor reverberating cruelly, a door opening and shutting, an agonizing silence; he was aware of two people face to face, two people looking one another up and down, who were both on the very verge of tragedy.

'No!'

He passed his hand over his face, and his face was dry; he passed it over the pillow, without encountering the damp patch under his chin. His eyelids were smarting, but it was from fatigue, and perhaps, too, from the smuts in the train; and the train was responsible, too, for the ache in his limbs.

Who had said 'No'? He sat up, his eyes wide open, and saw a slender ray of light under a door, the door next to his in a Marseilles hotel whose name he had forgotten.

The man who had said 'No' was striding back and forth on the other side of the wall. The catch of a suitcase clicked open.

'Jean!'

'I said no!'

'Please, Jean! Listen to me! Let me explain, at least . . .'

'No!'

The words came from the darkness outside. The man's movements were quick and unhesitating. Probably he was taking his scattered belongings out of the wardrobe and cramming them into the suitcase. . . . Probably the woman was clinging to him, for there was a soft thud followed by a moan. He must have pushed her away, and she had collapsed somewhere or other.

'Jean, for pity's sake . . .'

She must have been frantic. For her, too, the petty considerations of everyday life and conventional behaviour no longer existed.

'I'll explain. . . . I swear to you . . .'

'Slut!'

'Yes, I'm a slut. . . . You're right. . . . But . . .'

'D'you want to wake up the whole hotel?'

'I don't care. . . . If there were a hundred people here it wouldn't stop me from going on my knees to you and begging you to forgive me, imploring you . . .'

'Shut up . . .'

'Jean!'

'Shut up! D'you hear?'

'I didn't do it on purpose, I promise you . . .'

'Oh no! It was all my fault . . .'

'I needed a breath of air . . .'

'You needed a man, that's all . . .'

'It's not true, Jean. . . . For three days I'd not stirred from this room, I'd been looking after you like . . .'

'Like a mother, I suppose you're going to say, you trollop?'

'You were asleep, and I went out for a moment . . .'

'To hell with you!'

'You won't go away, will you? . . . You're not going to leave me alone? . . . I'd rather you killed me . . .'

'I felt like doing so a little while back . . .'

'Well then, kill me . . .'

'You're not worth it. . . . Get off. . . . Let me go. . . . D'you hear?'

He must have pushed her away once again, she must have fallen on to the floor, there was a silence, then the voice, whose pathetic tone had already become monotonous, the everlasting plea that was almost like a parody:

'Jeaaan!'

'When you've done bleating my name . . .'

'I can't go on living without you . . .'

'Go to hell!'

'How can you talk like that! . . . How can you have forgotten already . . .'

'Forgotten what? What you did for me or what I did for you? . . . Eh? . . . Tell me that. . . . Or rather, hold your tongue. . . . Where are my shirts? Where the devil have you put my shirts?'

And just as, between the acts of a tragedy, the players resumed their normal voices, she simply muttered: 'I sent three to the wash. The others are on the top shelf in the bathroom cupboard. . . .' Then, reverting to her former tone: 'Jean . . .'

He did not try to vary his response: 'To hell with you!'

'What are you going to do?'

'That's my own business.'

'I swear, since I've known you I've not let a man touch me . . .'

'Except the one you were coming out of the dance-hall with when I turned up . . .'

'I'd asked him to bring me back here. . . . I was frightened . . .'

He burst out laughing. 'That's the best yet!'

178

'Don't laugh, Jean. . . . If you go away, you'll be sorry for it tomorrow . . .'

'Is that a threat?'

He sounded threatening himself. More than threatening, for there was a loud thud – perhaps he had struck her – then another silence, and a moan:

'You've not understood. . . . I'm the one who. . . . Oh no, after all. . . . I'd rather make an end to it right now . . .'

'Just as you like.'

Footsteps; a door closing. It was not the door into the passage but probably the bathroom door. The sound of water pouring into a glass.

'What're you doing?'

She did not answer. He was panting, presumably as he tried to shut a suitcase that was too full. Then he went round the room to make sure he had forgotten nothing.

'Good-bye!' he flung out at last, with a hysterical laugh.

Immediately the door opened again and a terrified voice exclaimed:

'Jean. . . . Jean . . . for pity's sake!'

'To hell with you!'

'One second, Jean. . . . You can't refuse me that now. . . . Listen . . .'

He was walking towards the door.

'Listen. . . . I'm going to die . . .'

He went on walking. She was crawling on the floor. One could guess that she was crawling on the floor, on the grubby red carpet of the hotel bedroom; one could imagine her clinging to the man's trouser-leg, and being kicked away.

'I swear. . . . I swear. . . . I swear . . .'

She was gasping, and only blurred syllables rose to her lips.

'. . . that I've taken poison . . .'

The door opened and slammed shut. Footsteps sounded along the corridor and then moved away down the stair. From below there could be heard the faint sound of a conversation between the departing guest and the black-clad clerk at the reception desk.

Monsieur Monde was standing in the middle of his room, in the dark. He groped along the unfamiliar walls to find the switch, and was surprised to see himself in his shirt, barefooted. He moved close to the communicating door to listen, and heard nothing, not a sob, not a breath.

Then, resignedly, he picked up his trousers from the foot of the bed, trousers which did not seem to be his own. Having no bedroom slippers he put on his shoes, leaving them unlaced.

He went out of his room noiselessly, hesitated in front of the neighbouring door and then knocked timidly. No voice answered. His hand turned the door-knob, but he still dared not push it open.

At last he heard a barely perceptible sound, as though some-one were choking and trying to swallow a little air.

He went in. The room was just like his own, or a little larger. The wardrobe was wide open, as was the bathroom door, and a woman was sitting on the floor, curiously hunched up, some-what like a Chinese mandarin. Her bleached hair hung over her face. Her eyes were red, but dry. She was clasping both hands over her breast and staring blankly in front of her.

She did not seem surprised to see him. Yet she watched him come close without making a single movement or saying a word.

'What have you done?' he asked.

He didn't know what he must look like, with his trousers unfastened, his sparse hair ruffled on his head, as it was when he got up in the mornings, and his gaping shoes.

She gasped: 'Close the door.'

Then: 'He's gone, hasn't he?'

And after a silence: 'I know him; he won't come back. . . . How stupid it all is!'

She screamed out these last words with the frenzy she had shown earlier, raising her arms to heaven as though reproaching it for the idiocy of men.

'How stupid it all is!'

And she got up, leaning on her hands so that at one point he saw her on all fours on the carpet. She was wearing a very short, tight-fitting dress of black silk from which emerged long legs clad in flesh-coloured stockings. Her lipstick and mascara had run a little, so that she looked like a washed-out doll.

'What are you doing here?'

She could scarcely stand upright. She was weary. She was about to lie down on the bed, the coverlet of which had been turned down, but before doing so she looked suspiciously at the man who had come into her room.

'I heard . . .' he stammered. 'I was afraid. . . . Have you . . .'

She made a grimace, as a spasm of nausea seized her. And she whispered to herself: 'I must try and be sick.'

'You've taken something, haven't you?'

'Barbiturates. . . .' She was walking to and fro, concerned with what was happening inside her, an anxious frown on her brow. 'I always kept some in my bag, because he slept badly. . . . Oh God!'

She clasped her hands, as though to wring them in renewed frenzy.

'I never can be sick! . . . Perhaps it's better so. . . . I thought when he knew I'd . . .'

She was frightened. Panic was visibly overwhelming her. And her terrified eyes eventually settled on the stranger, while she besought him:

'What am I to do? Tell me what I must do!'

'I'll send for a doctor . . .'

'No, not that! . . . You don't know. . . . That would be the worst thing. . . . It would be enough to get him arrested, and he'd blame me again . . .'

She could not keep still, she was walking ceaselessly to and fro in the confined space of the bedroom.

'What do you feel!'

'I don't know. . . . I'm frightened. . . . If only I could be sick . . .'

He didn't know, either. The idea of leaving her and rushing off to a chemists' to get an emetic did not occur to him, or rather it seemed too complicated.

'How many tablets have you taken?'

She flared up, infuriated by his uselessness and perhaps by the absurdity of his appearance.

'How should I know? What was left in the tube. . . . Six or seven. . . . I'm cold . . .'

She flung her coat over her shoulders and glanced at the door, as though tempted to go and seek help elsewhere.

'To think he left me ...'

'Listen. I'm willing to try. .... I did it once before, when my daughter had swallowed a ...'

They were both equally incoherent, and to crown everything the people on the third floor, assuming that the original scene was still going on, banged on the floor to demand silence.

'Come here. .... Open your mouth. .... Let me do it ...'

'You're hurting me.'

'That's nothing. .... Wait a minute ...'

He was looking for something with which to tickle the back of her throat, and his inexperience was such that he almost used his own handkerchief. She had one in her hand, a tiny one screwed up into a tight ball, which he unfolded and rolled into a tapered twist.

'Oh, you're choking me. .... Oh!'

He was obliged to hold her head in a firm grip, and was surprised at the slightness of her skull.

'Don't stiffen yourself. .... My daughter was just the same. ... There! Just another minute. .... D'you feel it coming?'

Spasms shook her chest, and suddenly she vomited, without noticing that part of her vomit went over the stranger. Tears filled her eyes and prevented her from seeing. She was vomiting reddish stuff, and he held her by the shoulders, encouraging her like a child:

'There! ... There! ... You see you'll feel better. ... Go on. ... Don't hold it back. On the contrary, let yourself go ...'

She was looking at him through blurred eyes, like an animal that has had a bone removed from its throat.

'Does your stomach feel empty yet? ... Let me try once more. .... It'd be wiser ...'

She shook her head. She went limp. He had to help her to the edge of the bed, where she lay down, her legs dangling, and now she was uttering little regular moans.

'If you promise not to move, to be very good, I'll go down to the office. They must have a gas ring or some other method of heating water. .... You've got to drink something hot to wash out your stomach ...'

She nodded her willingness, but before leaving the room he went into the bathroom to make sure there was no poison left.

She followed him with her gaze, anxiously wondering what he was doing. She was even more surprised when he rummaged in her handbag, which contained crumpled notes, powder and rouge.

He wasn't a thief, though. He put the bag down on the bedside table.

'Don't stir. . . . I'll be back immediately.'

And on the staircase, where he endeavoured to make as little noise as possible, he smiled rather bitterly. Nobody had ever done as much as this for him! All his life, as far back as he could remember, it was he who'd had to help other people. In vain he had often dreamed of being ill so that somebody might bend over him with a gentle smile and relieve him, for a brief while, of the burden of his existence.

*

'Forgive me for bothering you' – he had always been exaggeratedly polite, through fear of giving offence – 'my neighbour isn't feeling very well. Would you be kind enough to boil a little water for her? If you had any sort of infusion . . .'

'Come this way.'

It was night. The whole hotel was asleep. Somewhere in the darkened city could be heard the heavy rumble of a passing cart, and from time to time the carter cracked his whip to waken the drowsy horse.

'Did you know them?' asked the clerk, who had promptly realized that the people in room 28 were involved.

'No.'

'Wait a sec. . . . I'm looking for matches . . .'

There was a percolator in a dingy, crowded closet that served as pantry, but the clerk lit a tiny gas ring, with that calm, rather mournful air common to those who live by night, always alone, while others are asleep.

'I was surprised to see him go. . . . He's been ill for the last few days. . . . She used to spend all day up in the bedroom with him. . . . She took his meals up herself . . .'

Monsieur Monde found himself asking, to his own surprise: 'Is he young?'

'Twenty-two, maybe? . . . I'd have to look at his form. . . .

This evening they went out one after the other, and she went first. .... When they came in again an hour later, I could see there was going to be some nasty ...' He ended with a coarse word.

'He's dropped her, hasn't he?'

The water was simmering already. The man looked through his tins, and eventually found some lime-flowers for a tisane.

'If you like I'll take it up to her.'

'I'll do it myself ...'

'Some sugar?'

'Perhaps ... yes. .... Thank you.'

'Nothing very high-class there, you know ...'

He meant the girl, obviously. Why did he say that? Did he suspect Monsieur Monde of some ulterior motive?

'If you need anything else, don't hesitate to ask. I'm here until six o'clock in the morning.'

And he went back to lean on his elbows on the mahogany counter, pulled out an open book from under it and started reading it again.

When Monsieur Monde returned to the bedroom with a teapot in his hand, the woman had fallen asleep, or was pretending to sleep. He felt embarrassed, because her dress was hitched up very high, showing part of her thigh above her stocking. He felt no desire, he had no secret thoughts.

'Mademoiselle ...'

She barely raised her listless lids.

'You've got to drink this. .... I'd even advise you, if you feel brave enough, to bring some of it back, for safety's sake, so as to clear out your stomach ...'

It worried him to see the misty, faraway look in her eyes. She did not stir. He raised her body and held the cup to her lips.

'Drink ...'

'It's hot ...'

The syllables were blurred and indistinct, as if her tongue had been too thick.

'Drink it all the same ...'

He forced her to, made her vomit once more, but this time she shook with painful hiccups for a long time and seemed to bear him a grudge for this additional suffering.

'We shall feel safer now . . .'

Probably because she was choking, she passed one hand over her shoulder, slipped it under her dress, unfastened her brassière and, in a gesture which was unfamiliar to him and which shocked him, managed to pull it off and throw it on to the floor.

'Lie down. . . . If you want to undress I'll go out for a moment.'

She did not give him the chance, but with an air of complete indifference pulled her dress over her head, peeling it off her body like some superfluous skin. He had turned his face to the wall, but caught sight of her none the less in the wardrobe mirror. Under her dress she wore nothing but narrow pink briefs and an even narrower suspender-belt. When she bent forward to remove her stockings, her little pointed breasts seemed to hang in space.

Next she removed the briefs, and the elastic band left a reddish mark on her skin. When she stood there naked (only a faint shadow darkened her belly between the thighs) she tiptoed, after a moment's hesitation, into the bathroom, where she behaved as if there had not been a man in the next room.

She came back wrapped in a faded blue dressing-gown, and her eyes were still misty, her lips pursed with nausea.

'I feel ill . . .' she sighed as she lay down.

Then, as he tucked the bedclothes round her: 'I'm fagged out.'

She fell asleep directly, curled up in a ball, her head right at the bottom of the pillow so that only her bleached hair could be seen. A few minutes later she was snoring, and Monsieur Monde crept noiselessly back to his room to put on his jacket and overcoat, for he had felt cold.

Not long after he had settled down in the armchair beside the bed he noticed light shining through the cracks in the venetian blinds. Noises began, some in the hotel, others outside. Particularly, outside, the sound of engines trying to start up, motor-boat engines as he realized, for he heard the splash of oars in the water, and the boats in the Old Port knocking together; a factory whistle blew; sirens, in the distance, in the harbour where steamships and cargo-boats lay, were moaning interminably.

He switched off the electric lamp which he had left burning, and the bright streaks of the venetian blinds patterned the floor.

The sun was shining. He'd have liked to see. Standing at the window, he tried to peer between the laths of the shutters, but could make out only thin slivers of things, part of the trolley-pole of a passing tram for instance, some pink and purple shells on a little cart.

The girl had stopped snoring. She had flung off the covers and now her cheeks were crimson, her lips puffed, her whole face distorted with suffering. The gleam of her skin counteracted the effect of her make-up, so that she no longer seemed the same woman; this was a far more human face, something very youthful, very poor, and rather common. She must have been born in some shanty in the city outskirts; as a small child she probably sat, with bare bottom and running nose, on some stone doorstep, and later ran about the streets on her way back from the council school.

One after the other, the guests were leaving the hotel; cars were passing in the street, and all the bars must be open by now, while in the still empty brasseries the waiters were sprinkling sawdust on the grey floors and polishing the windows.

He had had time to shave and dress. He went into his own room, after making sure that his companion was still asleep. He drew up the blinds and flung the windows wide open, in spite of the tingling cold of the morning air, and he felt life come pouring in; he could see the blue water, white rocks in the distance, a boat with a red-ringed funnel putting out to sea, leaving a wake of incredible whiteness.

He had forgotten the immense sea, and the sand, and the sun, and the secrets he had whispered to them, and if a faint after-taste of tears still lingered, he was ashamed of it.

Why had they given him a room without a bathroom, when he longed for clean water to stream over his body and purify it? Probably because of his clothes, those drab, badly-cut clothes in which he now felt so ill at ease.

He had brought no razor, no soap, no toothbrush. He rang. A

pageboy knocked at his door. He felt reluctant to entrust this errand to him, to give up the imminent realization of his dream.

'Will you go and buy me. . . .' And while he waited for the return of the uniformed messenger, whom he could see hopping along the pavement, he looked at the sea which was no longer last night's sea, which had become a harbour furrowed by motor-boats and where fishermen were sinking their nets.

For a long time, dazzled by the morning light, he stared at the transporter-bridge, whose gigantic metal carcase blocked out the horizon and on which, from a distance, he could just make out minute human figures.

FOUR

Monsieur Monde had waited, because it seemed to him impossible to act otherwise. From time to time he went to lay his ear against the communicating door and then went back to his place beside the window; because of the biting cold, he had put on his overcoat and thrust his hands deep into the pockets.

At about ten o'clock it struck him that the noise from the town and the harbour would prevent him from hearing a call from the next room, and he regretfully closed the window. His heart was heavy then; he wore a queer smile as he looked at himself in the glass, wearing his overcoat, beside an unmade bed in a hotel bedroom where he didn't know what to do.

He ended by sitting down on a chair as though in a waiting-room, beside the communicating door and (again as though in a waiting-room) he indulged in hypotheses and threats, he counted to a hundred, then to a thousand, tossed coins to decide whether to stay there or not, until at last he gave a start, like a man suddenly awakened, for he must have dozed off. Somebody was walking, not with soft bare-foot steps, but on high heels that made a sharp tapping sound.

He hurried round and knocked.

'Come in!'

She was fully dressed already, with a little red hat on her head, her handbag in her hands, and she was just about to go out. A few minutes later and he'd have missed her. She had spruced herself up as if nothing had happened, her make-up was spick and span with a strange mouth painted on, smaller than the real one, so that the pale pink of her own lips showed below it like an undergarment.

He stood awkwardly in the doorway, while after glancing sharply at him – as though to make sure he really was last night's visitor, whose face she could hardly remember – she hunted for her gloves.

'Are you feeling better?'

'I'm hungry,' she said.

She found her gloves at last – they were red, like her hat – left the room, and showed no surprise at his following her down the stairs.

The hotel looked quite different. By daylight the vestibule which served as an entrance hall seemed more luxurious. The reception clerk behind the mahogany counter was wearing a morning coat, the walls were covered with laminated wood panelling, there were green plants in the corners and a green-uniformed commissionaire outside the door.

'Taxi, *messieurs-dames*?'

The girl refused, while Monsieur Monde, without knowing why, avoided meeting the eyes of the reception clerk, although the latter did not know him. The fact was that Monsieur Monde was ill at ease in his skimpy clothes. He felt awkward. Perhaps he regretted the loss of his moustache?

Once on the pavement he walked on the left of his companion, who stepped out briskly, paying no attention to him yet showing no surprise at his presence. She turned left immediately, and they found themselves on the corner of the Canebière and the Old Port; she pushed open a glazed door and threaded her way between the tables of a restaurant with the ease of a regular customer.

Monsieur Monde followed. There were three floors of huge, wide-windowed rooms where people were eating, where hundreds of people were eating, packed close together, while between the tables, along the passages, up and down the stairs ran waiters and waitresses bearing dishes of bouillabaisse or cray-fish, plates of shell-fish stacked in pyramids.

The sun poured in through the bay windows, which went right down to the floor like those in big stores, so that the whole roomful could be seen from outside. Everyone was eating. People stared at one another with blank or curious eyes. Sometimes someone would raise a hand, calling out impatiently: 'Waiter!'

A strong odour of garlic, saffron and shell-fish assaulted one's senses. The dominant note was the red of the crayfish gleaming on the waiters' outstretched arms and on nearly every table, and whose slender empty shells lay piled on the plates of departing guests.

The young woman had found two places by a wall. Monsieur Monde sat down opposite her. He immediately wondered what she was looking at so insistently behind his back and, on turning round, discovered a mirror in which she could see herself.

'I'm looking pale,' she said. 'Waiter!'

'Coming!' Running up, he thrust into their hands a huge mimeographed menu, scrawled over with red and violet ink. And she studied this menu with the utmost gravity.

'Waiter!'

'Madame?'

'Are the andouillettes good?'

Monsieur Monde raised his head. He had just made a discovery. If he had asked the same question, for instance, he was convinced that the waiter, any waiter on earth, would naturally have answered yes, thus doing his duty as waiter. Can one imagine a waiter telling his customers: 'They're horrible! Don't eat any!'?

The waiter was, in fact, saying 'Yes' to the young woman, but not a meaningless 'Yes'. You could feel that he was telling her the truth, that he regarded her differently from the hundreds of customers thronging the three floors of the vast eating-factory.

With her he was both respectful and familiar. He recognized somebody of his own sort. He congratulated her on her success. He did not want to do her a disservice. It was therefore necessary to understand the situation, and he turned to Monsieur Monde, sizing him up.

'If you'll allow me to advise you . . .'

He never lost contact with the girl. Between these two, imperceptible signs were enough. He seemed to be asking her: 'Playing high?'

And as she remained impassive, he bent forward to point out certain dishes on the menu card.

'Shellfish, of course, to start with. . . . It wouldn't be worth coming to Marseilles and not eating shellfish. . . . D'you like sea-urchins?'

He spoke with an exaggerated accent.

'And then some of our own bouillabaisse, with crayfish.'

'I'll have crayfish by itself!' she interrupted. 'Without mayonnaise. I'll make my own dressing.'

'And an andouillette to follow . . .'

'Have you gherkin?'

'And what wine?'

Somewhere near the Chaussée d'Antin there was a restaurant that bore some resemblance to this one, and in which, from outside, you could see through the windows large numbers of people munching their food. Now, heaven knows why, Monsieur Monde had sometimes envied them, although he did not really know what for – perhaps for sitting there in a crowd, all more or less alike, side by side, feeling at ease in an atmosphere of facile glitter, of stimulating vulgarity.

The customers, for the most part, must be visitors from the country, or people of moderate means who had decided to treat themselves to a good meal. At the next table to theirs, in the full sunlight, there sat in state a huge middle-aged woman, whose fur coat made her look even huger, wearing diamonds, real or sham, in her ears and on her fingers, giving her orders in a loud voice, drinking hard and laughing heartily, her companions being two youths who could hardly have been more than twenty.

'Were you following us?'

He gave a start. His companion, whose name he did not know, was looking sternly at him, with a stubborn frown, and there was such cold lucidity in her gaze that he reddened.

'You'd better tell me the truth. Are you police?'

'Me? I give you my word of honour . . .'

She believed him readily; she probably knew a policeman

when she saw one. But she went on, none the less: 'How did you happen to be there last night?'

And he explained volubly, as though to justify himself: 'I'd just arrived from Paris. . . . I wasn't asleep. . . . I'd only just dozed off. . . . I heard . . .'

'What did you hear?'

He was too honest to lie. 'Everything you said.'

The waiter was covering their table with overlapping dishes of hors d'oeuvres and shellfish and bringing them white wine in a champagne bucket. So his unpretentious appearance had not discouraged the waiter; perhaps this was the sort of place where unpretentious people came to enjoy themselves.

'I've asked the chef to take special care over your andouillette,' the waiter whispered, leaning over towards the young woman.

She remarked, as she spooned out the pale pink granular flesh of a sea-urchin: 'You're married . . .'

She was staring at his wedding-ring, which it had not occurred to him to remove.

'That's all over,' he said.

'Have you left your wife?'

'Yesterday . . .'

She pursed her lips contemptuously. 'For how long?'

'For ever.'

'That's what they always say . . .'

'I assure you . . .'

And he blushed, realizing that he must be giving a misleading impression of boasting of his liberty, as though he intended to take advantage of it.

'It's not what you think. . . . It's more complicated . . .'

'Yes. . . . I know . . .'

What did she know? She looked at him, then she looked at herself in the glass just as ruthlessly, then she turned to glance at the bejewelled woman and the two young men.

'You'd have done better perhaps to leave me alone,' she sighed. 'It'd all be over by now.'

None the less she went on meticulously shelling her crayfish with her lacquered fingernails.

'Are you from these parts?' he asked her.

She shrugged her shoulders. No woman would have asked such a stupid question.

'I'm from the North, from Lille. And you're from Paris yourself, aren't you? What's your line?'

She was examining his suit, his shirt, his tie. And as he hesitated in some embarrassment before replying, she went on in an altered, almost threatening voice:

'You didn't run off with the cash-box, I should hope?'

Before he had taken in the meaning of this challenge, she went on as though she was quite prepared to drop him flat: 'Because I've had more than enough of *that* . . .'

'I'm not an officer worker.'

'What are you?'

'I've private means.'

She looked him up and down again. What did she find reassuring about her companion's appearance?

'Good . . .'

'Moderate private means.'

She must have interpreted this as miserly, for she cast a peculiar glance at the table loaded with food and the bottle of expensive wine.

Monsieur Monde felt his head in a whirl. He had had nothing to drink, had barely dipped his lips in his misted glass, and yet he felt drunk with all the dazzling light and the bustling crowds, with the red of the crayfish and the dizzy speed of the waiters rushing to and fro, and the din of all those conversations, of those possibly confidential remarks that people had to yell out to be heard above the noise of other voices and the clatter of plates and cutlery.

'I wonder where he's got to now . . .'

And as, with naïve thoughtlessness, he asked who, she shrugged her shoulders; she had him sized up now.

'It'll be his loss more than mine . . .'

She seemed to feel the need to talk about it. Not necessarily to him, but to anyone. The lobster had been served, and she was mixing herself a vinaigrette in her plate, carefully proportioning the ingredients.

'Mayonnaise doesn't agree with me. I don't know why I shouldn't tell you the whole story. Seeing what he's done! I crawled at his feet, which I've never done to any other man, and he kicked me here. . . . Look, you can still see the mark . . .'

It was true. At close quarters, a slight swelling on the left side of her upper lip was visible under her make-up.

'Real trash he was. . . . His mother sold vegetables in the street; she was still pushing her barrow, only a few years ago. . . . It wasn't as if I'd run after him! But I was quite happy as I was. . . . D'you know Lille?'

'I've been through it . . .'

'You didn't go to the Boule Rouge? It's a little dive in a basement near the theatre. . . . The boss used to run a night-club in the Place Pigalle. . . . Fred, his name was. . . . They only have regulars there, a good class of people, who wouldn't want to be seen just anywhere. . . . Businessmen from Roubaix and Tour-coing, you know the kind of thing. . . . There's dancing there in the evenings, and cabaret turns. . . . I started off there as a dancer three years ago . . .'

He would have liked to know her age, but dared not ask her.

'Waiter? Will you bring me a clean glass? I've let some cray-fish drop in it.'

While never losing the thread of her thoughts, she kept glancing at herself in the mirror, and she even seemed to be listening at the same time to the conversation between the lady in dia-monds and her two companions.

'What d'you suppose they are?' she suddenly demanded.

'I don't know. They surely can't be her sons.'

She burst out laughing. 'Gigolos, I'd say! And she's not known them long. Maybe nothing's happened yet, for they're glaring at one another and they don't know which of them is going to win. . . . Her, I mean. . . . Well, I bet she owns a food-store, a fishmonger's or a delicatessen, in some smart district where business is good. . . . She's treating herself to a fortnight in the Midi.'

The waiter brought Monsieur Monde his steak. 'The andouillette'll be ready in a minute. . . . It's coming along nicely . . .'

And the young woman went on: 'My real name is Julie. I called myself Daisy when I danced. The gentlemen used to drop in for apéritifs too, and that was the nicest time, because there weren't any tarts. We were all pals together. You may not believe me, but most of them behaved ever so properly with me. They just came there to get a change from their offices and homes, don't you see?

'One of them, the nicest of the lot, a big fattish chap rather like you are, was running after me for at least three months. . . . I knew what he was after but I wasn't in any hurry. . . . He came from Roubaix. . . . A well-known family, very wealthy. . . . He was scared stiff of being seen going into or out of the club and he always sent the pageboy to make sure nobody was passing in the street . . .

'He wanted me to give up dancing. He rented a nice flat for me in a quiet street with nothing but new houses. . . . And it'd all be going on still if it hadn't been for Jean. . . . When he came to see me he brought things to eat, the best he could find, crayfish ten times the size of these, pineapples, early strawberries in little boxes lined with cotton wool, champagne. . . . We had little supper-parties together . . .'

And suddenly, in an altered tone: 'What did I tell you?'

He failed to understand. She glanced meaningly at the neighbouring table and leaning forward, whispered:

'Talking to the waiter about fish, she's just told him that if she had the face to sell it at such a price. . . . I was right! She's a fishmonger! . . . As for the two kids, the chances are they'll be scratching one another's faces like a couple of cats before the day's out . . .'

'Where had I got to? It was so that you should understand that I'm not indebted to that Jean for anything. . . . On the contrary! From time to time I used to go back to the Boule Rouge, as a guest . . . because I'd got good friends there. . . . But I was respectable. . . . If I say so, you can believe me . . .

'That was where I met Jean. . . . He was just a clerk in a hardware store, but at first he tried to swank, to make believe he was something high-class. . . . Everything he earned went on his clothes and on drink. . . . You couldn't even call him good-looking.

'All the same I fell for him, and that was my misfortune. . . . I don't know how it happened. ... In the beginning he used to threaten to kill himself if I didn't do what he wanted and he was always making scenes.

'He was so jealous that I never dared go out. ... He even got jealous of my gentleman friend, and then life became impossible. ... "Never mind, we'll go away and I'll have you all to myself," he kept saying. But I knew that he only earned two thousand francs a month and had to give part of that to his mother.

'Well, he did what he'd said he'd do. ... One evening he turned up, looking white as a sheet. ... I was with my gentleman friend. ... He sent the ground-floor tenant up to fetch me ...

' "Mademoiselle Julie," she told me, "won't you come down for a moment?" She'd realized, from the way he looked, that it was something serious. ... He was standing there in the passage. ... I can still picture him, beside the coat rack, under the coloured light of the hall lamp.

' "Is *he* there?" he growled between his teeth.

' "What's the matter with you? Have you gone crazy?"

' "You've got to come at once. ... We're going to do a bolt."

' "What?"

' "Bring whatever you can. ... We're taking the midnight train. ..."And then he whispered – and his breath smelt of spirits: "I've taken the cash-box!"

'That was how it happened. What could I do? I told him to walk about on the pavement while he waited for me. I went upstairs and told my friend that I'd just heard that my sister was having a baby and wanted me to come right away ...

'He suspected nothing, poor man. ... He put on a woebegone look because, of course, he'd not had anything yet that evening ...

' "Well, I'll try and come tomorrow."

' "That's right. You come tomorrow."

'He went off. I lifted the blind and I saw Jean waiting for me under the gas lamp at the corner of the street. ... I stuffed some things into my case. ... I had only the one. ... I had to leave some perfectly good dresses behind, and three pairs of shoes.

... We took the night train. ... He was very frightened. ... He saw policemen everywhere. ... When we got to Paris he didn't feel safe there, he wouldn't even stop off at a hotel, for fear of being asked for his identity card, and we took the next train to Marseilles ...

'What could I have said to him? What's done is done ...

'We got here at night. ... We wandered about the streets with our luggage for at least an hour before he would bring himself to go into a hotel.'

She was devouring her andouillette, smeared with mustard, and from time to time nibbling a sour gherkin.

'He fell ill right away. ... I looked after him. At night he had nightmares and kept talking to himself, trying to get up; I had to hold him down, he struggled so ...

'It went on for a whole week. ... And d'you know how much he'd taken? Twenty-five thousand francs. ... With that, he was going to take a boat to South America. ... Only there weren't any in the port; all the ones on the list were sailing from Bordeaux ...

'Last night I felt stifled. I'd had enough of it, I needed air, and I told him I was going out for an hour. ... I ought to have guessed that, being as jealous as he was, he'd follow me. ... I may even have guessed it. ... But I couldn't help myself. ... Once outside I didn't even turn back. ... Two streets beyond this – I don't know the names of the streets – I saw a light like that of the Boule Rouge and I heard some music. ... I had such a longing to dance that nothing could have stopped me. ... I went in ...'

She turned round sharply as though, at that very moment, she had felt behind her the presence of the man she was thinking about, but it was only a young couple, so spruce and smiling that one could tell, at a glance, that they were on their honeymoon.

'I wonder where he can have gone. I know him, he's quite capable of having given himself up to the police. ... Otherwise, if he's still prowling round Marseilles, he's liable to play some nasty trick on me. ... Yes, indeed!

'I went dancing. ... A real gentleman, who was in the orange trade, offered to see me home. ... Just as I was leaving the dance hall with him I saw Jean standing on the edge of the pavement ...

'He didn't say a word to me. ... He started walking. ... I dropped the other chap, whom I'd hardly recognize if I saw him again, and I rushed after him, calling "Jean! Listen to me!"

'He went back to the hotel; his teeth were clenched and he was as white as his napkin. He began to pack his case. ... He called me all sorts of names ...

'And yet I give you my word I loved him. ... I even believe that if I were to see him again now ...'

The crowds were thinning out round the tables. Cigarette smoke began to fill the room, with the smell of spirits and liqueurs.

'Coffee, *messieurs-dames*?'

There was another scene which had often struck Monsieur Monde, a scene one can glimpse in the streets of Paris when one peers into a restaurant through the window: facing one another across a table from which the meal has been cleared, with a soiled tablecloth, coffee cups, glasses of brandy or liqueur, a middle-aged, stoutish man with a florid complexion and a happy, though somewhat anxious, look in his eyes, and a young woman holding her handbag up to her face and repainting the bow of her lips with the help of the mirror.

He had dreamed of that. He had envied them. Julie touched up her face, hunted in her handbag, called the waiter. 'Have you got cigarettes?'

And presently her lips stained the pallid tip of a cigarette with a vivid pink that was more sensuously feminine than a woman's blood.

She had said everything. She had finished. Drained now, she stared at herself in the mirror over her companion's shoulder, and little furrows in her forehead betrayed the return of her anxiety.

It was not a question of love, now, but of survival. What exactly was she thinking? Two or three times she scrutinized the man with swift little glances, weighing him up, gauging his possible usefulness.

And he, ill at ease and aware of the stupidity of his question, stammered out: 'What are you going to do?'

A curt shrug of the shoulders.

He had felt so envious of those who take no heed for the morrow and know none of the responsibilities with which other men burden themselves!

'Have you any money?'

Her eyes half closed because of the smoke she was exhaling, she picked up her bag and held it out to him.

He had already opened it the night before. He found it just as it was, with the cosmetics, a scrap of pencil, and a few crumpled notes, including a thousand-franc one.

She looked him sternly in the eyes, and then her lips formed a contemptuous, terribly contemptuous smile, as she said: 'That's not what's worrying me, for sure!'

It was late. They were almost alone, now, in the deserted dining-room, where the waiters were beginning to tidy up, and in one corner waitresses were already laying out cutlery for the evening meal.

'Waiter!'

'Coming, sir ...'

And the fluttering figures were snapped up by the purple pencil and set out in rows on a pad of paper, one sheet of which was pulled off and laid on the cloth in front of Monsieur Monde.

He had a great deal of money in his wallet. He had slipped in as many notes as it would hold, and it embarrassed him to open it; he did so with reluctance, in the furtive manner of a miser; he realized that Julie had noticed, that she had seen the bundle and was once more observing him with a suspicious eye.

They rose at the same time, visited the cloakrooms and then met again outside, in the sunshine, not knowing what to do, not knowing how to stay together nor how to part company.

They walked automatically to the quayside and mingled with the people watching small boys or old men angling.

In another hour's time Madame Monde was to alight from her car before the police station in the Rue La Rochefoucauld. He was not thinking of Madame Monde; he was not thinking of anything. He was conscious of moving restlessly in the midst of an outsize universe. His skin smelt springlike, because of the sunshine. His shoes were covered with fine dust. He was intensely aware of his companion's scent.

They had gone two hundred yards or so and were wandering aimlessly when she stopped.

'I don't feel like walking,' she decided.

Then they retraced their steps, past the three-storied restaurant with its wide windows where, now, only the bustling black-and-white figures of waiters could be seen. It seemed quite natural to walk up La Canebière and, in front of a brasserie whose striped awning was down, despite the time of year, Monsieur Monde suggested: 'Would you like to sit down?'

And then they were sitting beside the window, on either side of a small marble table; in front of him there was a glass of beer on a cardboard mat, and in front of her a cup of coffee which she was not drinking.

She was waiting. She said: 'I'm stopping you from going about your business.'

'I have no business.'

'That's true. You told me you had private means. Where d'you live?'

'I did live in Paris, but I've left.'

'Without your wife?'

'Yes.'

'On account of a bird?'

'No.'

Her eyes revealed bewilderment and, once again, suspicion.

'Why?'

'I don't know. . . . For no reason . . .'

'Haven't you any children?'

'Yes . . .'

'And you didn't mind leaving them?'

'They're grown up. . . . My daughter's married . . .'

Not far from them, people were playing bridge, important citizens and aware of their own importance, and two youths of Alain's age were playing billiards and looking at themselves in the glass.

'I don't want to sleep in that hotel again.'

He realized that she wanted to avoid unpleasant memories. He made no reply. And a long silence fell. They sat there, still and heavy, in the gathering darkness. Soon the lights would go on. The window, close beside them, shed a kind of frozen halo on their cheeks.

Julie was scanning the crowd that streamed by along the pavement, perhaps because she had nothing else to do, or to keep herself in countenance, or else perhaps in hope – or in fear – of recognizing Jean.

'I don't think I shall stay in Marseilles,' she said.

'Where will you go?'

'I don't know. . . . Further on. . . . Maybe to Nice? . . . Maybe to some small place by the sea where there won't be anybody. . . . I'm sick of men . . .'

They were free, at any moment, to get up and say good-bye to one another, to go their different ways and never meet again. It seemed almost as if they did not know how to set about it, and that was why they stayed there.

Monsieur Monde felt embarrassed at sitting so long over a single drink, and summoned the waiter to order another half-pint. She called him back to ask: 'When is there a train to Nice?'

'I'll bring you the time-table.'

She handed it over to Monsieur Monde, who looked up two trains, a fast train that left Marseilles at seven and another, at nine, that stopped all along the coast.

'Don't you find it gloomy here?'

The quietness was oppressive, the room seemed empty, there was too much unstirring air between the sparse customers, and every sound was detached, assumed importance: the exclamation of a card-player, the click of billiard balls, the snap of the lid of the soiled-linen bin as the waiter opened and closed it. The lights were switched on, but then, in the dusk, the slate-grey street proved a depressing sight, with its curious procession of men, women and children, walking fast or slowly, brushing up against or pushing past one another, all strangers to the rest, each going God knows where and perhaps nowhere, while obese buses bore past their full loads of tight-packed humanity.

'Excuse me.' The waiter, behind them, drew a heavy red curtain along its brass rod, and with a single gesture abolished the outside world.

Monsieur Monde sighed, gazing at his glass of beer. He noticed that his companion's fingers were clenched on her handbag. And he seemed to have to make a long journey through time and space to find the simple, commonplace words which he uttered at last, and which blended with the banality of the setting:

'Shall we take the nine o'clock train?'

She said nothing, but sat still; the fingers clutching the crocodile-skin bag relaxed. She lit a fresh cigarette, and it was later on, about seven o'clock, when the brasseries were full of customers drinking their apéritifs, that they went out, as grave and glum as a real married couple.

FIVE

From time to time he frowned. His pale eyes stared more intently. These were the only visible signs of his anguish, and yet at such moments he felt out of his depth and, if he had not retained a certain self-respect, would have been capable of tapping the shiny walls of the compartment to make sure they really existed.

He was in a train once more, a train which had the special smell of all night trains. Four of the compartments in the second-class carriage were dark, with drawn curtains, and when, a short while previously, looking for seats, he had opened doors at random, he had disturbed people sleeping.

He stood in the corridor, leaning against the wall which bore a number on an enamel plate. He had drawn up the blind in front of him, and the window was dark, cold and slimy; occasional lights could be seen in little stations along the coast; his carriage invariably happened to stop in front of the lamps marked 'Gentlemen' and 'Ladies'.

He was smoking a cigarette. He was conscious of smoking it, of holding it between his fingers, of blowing out the smoke, and this was what was so baffling, so bewildering; he was conscious of everything, he kept on seeing himself without the intermediary of a mirror, he would catch sight of one of his own gestures or attitudes and feel almost certain that he recognized it.

But he searched his memory in vain, he could not picture himself in any similar situation. Particularly not clean-shaven and wearing a ready-made suit that somebody else had worn!

Even that instinctive movement ... half-turning his head to glance at Julie, in the corner of the compartment, sometimes sitting with eyes closed as though asleep, and sometimes staring straight in front of her as though wrestling with some important problem.

But Julie herself formed part of his memories. He felt no surprise at seeing her there. He recognized her. Perplexed, he resisted the notion of some previous existence.

And yet, often, he was sure of it – he had always intended to note it down in the morning, but had never done so – three or four times at least, at any rate, he had dreamed the same dream, he had found himself repeatedly in a flat-bottomed boat with oars that were too long and too heavy to handle, in a landscape whose details he could recall even when awake and long after, a landscape he had never seen in real life, made up of greenish lagoons and hills of that purplish blue that one sees in the paintings of early Italian masters.

Each time he had had that particular dream he had recognized the place, he had experienced the satisfaction that one feels on returning to a familiar spot.

But this was clearly impossible in the case of this train journey with Julie. He was clear-headed, rational. This must be a scene which he had so often seen performed by other people, a scene which he had probably longed so violently to enact himself, that now ...

That glance back into the compartment, that air of satisfaction that must come over his face when he looked at his sleeping companion. ... And the woman's questioning gesture, that tilt of her chin when the train drew up noisily in a more important station and was invaded by a rush of new travellers; it meant: where are we?

As the glazed door was closed, he mouthed the name so that she could read it on his lips, separating the syllables: 'Toulon!' He repeated: 'Tou-lon ... Tou-lon ...'

Failing to understand, she beckoned him to come in, showed him the vacant seat beside her, and he went and sat down in it; his own voice had an unfamiliar ring.

'Toulon . . .'

She took a cigarette out of her bag. 'Give us a light . . .'

She called him '*tu*' for the first time, naturally, because for her, too, this was probably a moment of time that she had lived through before.

'Thanks. . . . I think we'd better go on to Nice . . .'

She was whispering. In the opposite corner an elderly man with white hair was asleep, and his wife, who was elderly too, was watching over him like a child. He must have been ill, for once before she had made him swallow a small greenish pill. She was watching Julie and Monsieur Monde. And he felt ashamed, because he guessed what she must be thinking about them. Moreover, although she dared not mention it, she probably resented Julie's smoking, which must upset the old man.

The train started off again.

'D'you know Nice?'

This time the '*tu*' came less naturally. Julie had had time to premeditate it. He felt convinced she was using it for the benefit of the lady opposite, and because it seemed more logical, conforming to a familiar situation.

'A little. . . . Not very well . . .'

He had been there several times, three winters running in fact, with his first wife after the birth of their daughter, who as a baby had suffered from bronchitis every year; in those days doctors still recommended the Riviera. They had stayed in a big middle-class hotel in the Promenade des Anglais.

'I don't know it myself . . .'

They fell silent. She finished her cigarette, which she had difficulty in crushing in the narrow brass ash-tray, then she crossed and uncrossed her legs, which gleamed palely in the bluish shadows; she tried out various positions, sank back against the padded upholstery and finally rested her head on her companion's shoulder.

This, too, was a memory that. . . . No, surely! It was an attitude in which he'd seen other people a dozen times, a hundred times. He had tried to imagine their feelings and now he was acting in the scene himself, it was he whom the young man standing in the corridor – he must have got on at Toulon – was watching, with his face glued to the window.

Then came the procession along the station platform, over the lines, the slow monotonous scuffle towards the exit, the search through his pockets for the tickets ...

'I tell you you put them in the left-hand pocket of your waistcoat ...'

She had reverted to '*vous*'. All round them, touts were calling out the names of hotels, but she did not listen to them. It was she who led the way. She walked straight ahead, threading her way much more swiftly than he could, and once they were through the gateway she remarked: 'We'd better leave our things in the left-luggage office.'

They had only one case each, but Julie's was heavy and particularly cumbersome.

Thus, once outside the station, they no longer looked like travellers. They made straight for the town centre; it was a fine light night, and there were still some cafés open. From afar they could see the lights of the Casino de la Jetée and their manifold reflections in the water of the bay.

Julie showed neither surprise nor admiration. Because she occasionally twisted one of her high heels, she clung to the man's arm, but it was she who led the way. She went forward without speaking a word, as calmly as an ant guided by its instinct.

'So this is the famous Promenade des Anglais?'

Branched lamps, stretching out to infinity. The vast sweep of the Promenade, all along the sea, with its little yellow paving stones and its deserted benches, and long lines of cars in front of casinos and grand hotels.

She was not dazzled by it all. She kept on walking, glanced down all the side streets and finally turned down one of them and went close to the window of a brasserie to peer through the gap between the curtains.

'We might try this one.'

'It's a café,' he objected.

But she pointed out, beyond the café and in the same building, a door bearing the word 'Hotel' in white letters. They went into the brightly-lit room, and she collapsed, somewhat wearily, on to a crimson seat; her next gesture, since there were people about, was to open her handbag, hold her mirror up to her face and redden her lips.

'Will you take supper?' the waiter asked.

She said to Monsieur Monde: 'D'you want to eat?'

They had not had dinner at Marseilles, because although they might have done so before the train left they'd not felt hungry then.

'What have you got?'

'Some excellent ravioli. . . . Onion soup to start with if you like. . . . Or a rare steak . . .'

Several tables were occupied by people having supper, and the waiter laid their places in front of them. In spite of the bright electric lights a certain grey weariness pervaded the air. The people present were speaking little and eating conscientiously, as at a regular meal.

'In the left-hand corner, look . . .' she whispered to him.

'Who is it?'

'Don't you recognize him? . . . It's Parsons, one of the three Parsons brothers, the flying-trapeze acrobats. . . . That's his wife with him. . . . She ought never to wear a suit, it makes her look like a teapot. . . . She's in their act now, in place of Lucien, the brother who had an accident in Amsterdam . . .'

They were very ordinary-looking people; the man, who was about thirty-five, might have been a well-dressed workman.

'They must be in a show here. . . . Oh, look! Three tables away . . .'

She brightened up, all her apathy had vanished, and to emphasize her remarks she kept laying her hand on her companion's wrist so as to compel his admiration.

'Jeanine Dor! The singer!'

This was a woman whose raven-black, oily hair hung down on either side of her cheeks; she had enormous, deeply ringed eyes in a pallid face, and her mouth was a crimson gash. Alone at a table, with a tragic disdainful air, her coat flung back behind her, she was eating spaghetti.

'She must be over fifty. . . . None the less she's still the only person who can hold an audience breathless for over an hour, just with her songs. .... I'll have to ask her for her auto-graph ...'

She rose suddenly and went up to the *patron*, who was standing by the cash desk. Monsieur Monde had no idea what she was going to do. Their food was brought, and he waited. He could see her talking self-confidently, then the *patron* turned to glance at him with apparent approval, and she returned.

'Give me the left-luggage ticket.'

She carried it off, and then came back.

'They've got a room with two beds. .... You don't mind, do you? For one thing they'd probably not have had two single rooms vacant. .... And then it wouldn't have looked natural! .... Oh, look! Those four girls to the right of the door. .... They're dancers ...'

She was eating with the same concentration as at Marseilles, but without missing anything that was going on around them.

'The *patron* tells me it's still early. .... The music-halls have closed but they won't start coming in from casinos and night-clubs till after three.... I wonder ...'

He did not understand at first. The girl wore an obstinate frown. She must be contemplating a job.

'The food's good here, and not too dear. I gather the rooms are clean.'

They were drinking their coffee when a boy came to tell them their luggage had come and been taken up into the bed-room. Julie, despite the previous night's ordeal, did not seem to be sleepy. She was watching Jeanine Dor going out, through a side-door, to the hotel staircase.

'They all stay here. .... In an hour's time there'll be some more of them ...'

But an hour was too long and dreary a wait. She smoked one more cigarette, and then rose with a yawn.

*

It was not until the third day that they made love. An incoher-ent three days. Their room, which overlooked a narrow court-yard, was furnished only with drab old things, a greyish threadbare carpet on the floor, a tapestry-covered armchair, wallpaper that was more brown than yellow and, in one corner, a screen hiding the washbasin and bidet.

The first night Julie had undressed behind the screen, emerging in blue-striped pyjamas. But finding the trousers uncomfortable, she had discarded them during the night.

He slept badly, in the next bed, separated from hers by a bedside table and a narrow mat. His supper was giving him indigestion. Several times, hearing sounds from the brasserie below, he had been tempted to go downstairs to beg for bicarbonate of soda.

He got up at eight, dressed noiselessly, without awakening his companion, who had flung back her bedclothes, for the radiator was boiling hot, the room overheated and airless. Perhaps that was why he had felt so uncomfortable during the night.

He went downstairs, leaving his suitcase clearly visible lest Julie should think he had gone for good. The coffee-room was empty. There was nobody to serve him and he went to have breakfast in a bar full of workmen and clerks, then walked along the seashore without thinking of that other sea by the edge of which he had dreamed of lying weeping.

Perhaps he needed to get used to things? The sky was a very pale, babyish blue, the sea too, like the sea in a schoolchild's watercolour, the gulls were chasing one another, white in the sunshine, and watercarts were tracing wet patterns on the tarmac.

When he got back, at about eleven, he felt compelled to knock at the door.

'Come in . . .'

She could not have known it was him. She was wearing only her briefs and her brassière. She had plugged an electric iron into the socket of the lamp and was pressing her black silk dress.

She asked him: 'Did you sleep all right?'

Her breakfast tray was on the bedside table.

'I'll be ready in half an hour, . . . What time is it? Eleven? Would you wait for me downstairs . . .'

He waited, reading a local paper. He was growing used to waiting. They lunched alone together again. Then they went out, and they had scarcely reached the Promenade des Anglais, up near the Casino de la Jetée, when she asked him to wait yet again and disappeared into the Casino.

Next she dragged him down a street in the town centre. 'Wait for me ...'

On an enamel plate there was a Greek name, followed by the word 'Impressario'.

She came back in a fury.

'He's a pig!' she announced, without further explanation. 'If you'd rather go off and walk by yourself ...'

'Where are you going?'

'I've two more addresses ...'

Grim and tight-lipped, she strode along the unfamiliar city streets, questioned policemen, climbed flights of stairs, and kept pulling scraps of paper with fresh addresses out of her bag.

'I know the place we must go for an apéritif ...'

This was the Cintra, the fashionable bar. She beautified herself afresh before going in. She put on a jaunty air. He understood that she was wishing he were better dressed. She was even wondering whether he would know how to behave in a place like this and it was she who gave the order with an air of authority, as she climbed on to a high stool and crossed her legs:

'Two pink gins, barman ...'

She nibbled some olives, ostentatiously. She stared boldly at men and women. It infuriated her to know nobody, to be merely a newcomer rating only a supercilious glance because of her cheap little dress and her shabby coat.

'Let's go and have dinner ...'

She knew where to go for dinner too. Afterwards, with a certain embarrassment, she began: 'Would you mind going back by yourself? ... Oh, it's not what you might think. ... After what I've been through, I can tell you I've had enough of men and you won't catch me at that again. ... But I don't want to be a burden on you. ... You've your own life to lead, haven't you? You've been very kind. ... I'm sure that backstage I shall meet people I know. ... At Lille I used to meet all the artistes on tour ...'

He did not go to bed, but walked about the streets alone. Then, at one point, because he was tired of walking, he went into a cinema. And this was another familiar image, drawn from the remote mysterious depths of his memory: an ageing man, all by himself, being guided by an attendant with an electric torch into a darkened room where a film has already begun, where voices boom and men larger than life gesticulate on the screen.

When he got back to Gerly's – that was the name of his hotel and of the brasserie – he caught sight of Julie sitting at a table in the café with the group of acrobats. She saw him go past. He realized that she was talking about him. He went upstairs, and she came to join him a quarter of an hour later, and this time she undressed in front of him.

'He's promised to put in a word for me. ... He's a decent sort. ... His father, who was Italian, was a bricklayer by trade, and he himself started off in the same way . . .'

Another day passed, and then another, and Monsieur Monde was getting used to things; he had even stopped thinking about them. After lunch, that third day, Julie decided: 'I'm going to have an hour's sleep. ... I got back late last night. ... Aren't you going to have a nap?'

He felt sleepy too, as a matter of fact. They went up one behind the other, and meanwhile he had a vision of other couples, hundreds of couples going up flights of stairs in the same way. And a slight flush rose to his cheeks.

The room had not been done. The two beds, unmade, revealed the livid whiteness of sheets, and there were traces of lipstick on Julie's pillow.

'Aren't you going to undress?'

Usually, when he took a siesta – and in Paris, in the course of his former life, he had done so from time to time – he would lie down fully dressed, with a newspaper spread out under his feet. He took off his jacket, then his waistcoat. Julie, with that snake-like movement which he was beginning to recognize, drew her dress up along her body and slipped it over her head.

She showed no surprise when he came up to her, with a rather shamefaced look. She was obviously expecting it.

'Draw the curtains.'

And she lay down, making room for him beside her. She was

thinking about something else. Every time he looked at her he saw that now familiar frown on her forehead.

On the whole, she was not sorry about it; things seemed more natural this way. But fresh problems occurred to her, and suddenly she lost all desire for sleep. Her head propped on her hand, her elbow on the pillow, she gazed at him with fresh interest as if from now on she had acquired the right to call him to account.

'What do you actually do?'

And as he failed to grasp the exact meaning of the question, she went on:

'You told me, the first day, that you had private means. ... People in your position don't go gallivanting about all by themselves. ... Or else surely they live in a different style. ... What did you do before?'

'Before what?'

'Before you went off?'

Thus she was making her way towards the truth as unfailingly as, landing in Nice in the middle of the night, she had made her way towards this hotel, where she was at home.

'You've got a wife. ... You told me you had children. ... How did you go off?'

'I just went!'

'Did you have a row with your wife?'

'No ...'

'Is she young?'

'About my age.'

'I understand ...'

'What d'you understand?'

'You just wanted to have a good time! ... And when you've spent all your money, or when you're tired ...'

'No.... It's not that ...'

'What happened, then?'

And he replied, with a sense of shame, chiefly because he felt he was spoiling everything by such stupid words, blurted out on that tumbled bed, in front of those bared breasts that no longer tempted him: 'I'd had enough of it.'

'Have it your own way!' she sighed.

She took this opportunity to slip behind the screen to wash, which she had been too lazy to do immediately after making love; from here she went on:

'You're a funny sort of chap, all the same!'

He put on his clothes again. He no longer felt sleepy. He was not unhappy. This squalid drabness was all part of what he had been seeking.

'Would you like to stop on at Nice?' she asked, emerging naked with a towel in her hand.

'I don't know ...'

'You're not fed up with me too? ... You know, you must tell me honestly. I keep wondering how we happen to have got hitched together. ... It's not really like me. ... Parsons has promised to look after me. ... He's well in with the man who runs the floor-shows at the "Pingouin". ... I shan't be long out of a job ...'

Why was she talking of leaving him? He did not want that. He tried to tell her so.

'It suits me all right like this ...'

She looked at him, as he tried to pull his braces over his shoulders, and she burst out laughing, the first time he had heard her laugh.

'You are a scream! Well. ... When you feel like clearing off, you just say so. ... If I may give you one piece of advice, it's to buy yourself another outfit. ... You're not miserly, by any chance?'

'No ...'

'Then you'd do better to dress decently. If you like, I'll go with you. Didn't your wife have any taste at all?'

She was lying down again, lighting a cigarette and sending the smoke up to the ceiling.

'Above all, if it's a question of money, don't be afraid to tell me ...'

'I've got money ...'

The bundle of notes, wrapped up in newspaper, was still in the suitcase, and he glanced at this instinctively. Since coming to Gerly's he had given up locking it, for fear of offending his companion. Under pretext of looking for something in it, he made sure the bundle was still there.

'Are you going out? Will you come back and collect me about five o'clock?'

That afternoon he spent sitting on a bench in the Promenade, his head bent, his eyes half closed in the sunshine, with the blue of the sea before him and the occasional flash of gulls' wings as they crossed his horizon.

He never stirred. Children played around him, and sometimes a hoop came to rest between his legs, or a ball was thrown at him. He seemed to be asleep. His face looked thicker and flabbier and his lips hung half open. Several times he gave a start, fancying he heard the voice of Monsieur Lorisse, his cashier. Not for one moment did he think of his wife or children, but it was the meticulous old clerk who appeared in his dream.

He remained heedless of time, and it was Julie who eventually came to look for him and remarked: 'I made sure I'd find you flopping on a seat.'

Why? This question bothered him for some little while.

'Let's go and buy you some clothes before the shops shut. . . . You see! I think of you and not of myself . . .'

'I must go and fetch some money from the hotel . . .'

'D'you leave your money in the bedroom? That's a mistake. . . . Specially if there's a lot of it . . .'

She waited for him below. He took a bundle of ten thousand francs, so as not to unfasten the pin. The maid was cleaning the passage, but she could not see him, for he had closed the door. Julie's words had made him anxious. He climbed on to a chair and pushed the parcel on top of the wardrobe.

She took him to an English firm where they sold smart ready-made clothes. She chose his outfit for him: grey flannel trousers and a navy blue double breasted jacket.

'With a cap, you'd pass for a yachtsman!'

She insisted on his buying summer shoes of brown and white leather.

'You look quite different. . . . I sometimes wonder . . .'

She said no more, but merely cast a furtive glance at him.

She must have already been to the Cintra on her own, for when they went in the barman made some imperceptible sign to her and a young man winked at her.

'You don't look exactly cheerful . . .'

They drank. They ate. They went to the Casino, where Julie stayed for a couple of hours and after winning two or three thousand francs ended by losing all that was left in her purse.

Vexed, she motioned to him: 'Let's go back.'

They had already formed the habit of walking side by side; when she was tired she clung to his arm. They slowed down automatically a few yards before their hotel, like people who are going home.

She did not want to go through the brasserie.

They closed their door. She bolted it, for it was always she who took this precaution.

'Where d'you hide your money?'

He pointed to the wardrobe.

'I'd take care if I were you . . .'

He climbed on to the same chair as that afternoon, passed his hand across the top of the wardrobe, but felt nothing but a thick layer of dust.

'Well, what's up?'

He stood there, aghast. She grew impatient.

'Have you turned into a statue?'

'The parcel's gone.'

'The money?'

Suspicious by nature, she refused to believe him.

'Let's see . . .'

She was not tall enough, even when she stood on the chair. She cleared the table and climbed up on that.

'How much was there?'

'About three hundred thousand francs, or a little less . . .'

'What did you say?'

He felt ashamed, now, of the vastness of the sum. 'Three hundred thousand . . .'

'We must tell the proprietor at once and send for the police. . . . Wait . . .'

He held her back. 'No. It's not possible.'

'Why not? Are you crazy?'

'We mustn't. . . . I'll explain why. . . . And in any case it doesn't matter, I'll manage somehow else. . . . I'll send for some more money . . .'

'Are you as rich as all that?'

She seemed resentful now, as though she were annoyed with him for having deceived her, and she lay down without a word, turning her back on him, and answered his good night with a mere grunt.

SIX

It was bitter and yet sweet, like the sort of pain that one cherishes and tends solicitously for fear of seeing it disappear. Monsieur Monde felt no anger, no resentment, no regret. About his fourteenth or fifteenth year, while he was at the Lycée, he had gone through a period of acute mysticism following a Lenten fast. He had devoted his days and part of his nights to spiritual exercises in search of perfection, and he had happened to keep a photograph of himself at that date – in a group, for he would have scorned to have his own likeness taken. He looked thinner and rather mournful, with a smile whose sweetness infuriated him later, when the reaction had set in.

Another time, much later, after his second marriage, his wife had given him to understand that she found a smoker's breath offensive. He had given up not only tobacco but any sort of spirits and even wine. He derived a savage satisfaction from this mortification of the flesh. This time again he had lost weight, so much so that after three weeks he'd had to go to the tailor's to have his suits altered.

It mattered little, now, whether they fitted him well or badly; but in the last two months he had lost weight far more drastically. He felt all the livelier for it. And although his once rosy complexion was now sallow, he would look with some complacency, when the occasion arose, at the reflection of a face that spoke not only of serenity but of a secret joy, an almost morbid delectation.

The hardest struggle was to keep awake. He had always been a big eater. Now, for instance, at four in the morning, he had to resort to various devices to stop himself falling asleep.

This was the moment, moreover, when general weariness pervaded the Monico like drifting dust. For the second time Monsieur René, who called himself Artistic Director, had come into the pantry, impeccably dressed in dinner jacket and immaculate white waistcoat, with his teeth gleaming aggressively.

Monsieur Monde could watch him coming through the room, for close to him at eye-level there was a minute round spy-hole which enabled him to keep watch, not so much on the guests as on the staff.

Monsieur René could not help smiling to right and left as he walked, like a prince distributing favours. He moved forward thus in the glowing light of the dance-hall, reached the folding doors, which were hung with red velvet on one side but shabby and squalid on the other, and at the precise moment when he pushed them open with an accustomed hand his smile disappeared, and there was no more sign of his splendid teeth; he was a quadroon from Martinique, whose hair was almost smooth, but whose bluish nails betrayed his mixed blood.

'What's the time, Désiré ?'

For the time is never publicly displayed in a place where so much art is used to make people forget time.

Désiré was Monsieur Monde, who had chosen the name himself. Désiré Clouet. It had first occurred to him at Marseilles, when he was sitting with Julie in a brasserie on La Canebière and the girl had asked his name. Caught off his guard, he had been incapable of inventing one. Across the street, over a cobbler's shop, he had read a name in yellow letters: 'Désiré Clouet, shoemaker.'

Now he was Désiré to some people, and Monsieur Désiré to the rank and file of the staff. The pantry was a long narrow room which had once been the kitchen of a private house. The green-painted walls were turning yellowish and, here and there, the colour of tobacco-juice. A door at the far end gave on to the back stairs. As this made it possible to leave the place by a different street from that in which the main entrance was situated, guests occasionally came through Monsieur Désiré's domain.

These were mainly the clients of the gaming tables, who were not offended by dirt and disorder. They did not mind seeing that the kitchens of the Monico consisted of a wretched gas stove whose red rubber tubing was forever coming apart, and which was merely used for warming up dishes fetched in from a nearby bistro. There was no sink. Greasy plates and cutlery were stacked in baskets. Only the glasses, marked with the letter M, were washed on the spot and put away in a cupboard. On the ground, under the table, bottles of champagne were waiting, and on that same table lay open tins of foie gras, ham, pieces of cold meat.

Désiré's place was in the corner, against the wall of the dance-hall, on a kind of platform where there was a desk. He replied: 'Four o'clock, Monsieur René.'

'Soon be through now!'

Apart from the hostesses there were scarcely half a dozen guests in the hall, and they had stopped dancing; the band took long rests between their numbers and Monsieur René was obliged to call them to order from afar, with a barely perceptible movement of his hands.

Monsieur René was eating. Almost every time he came into the pantry he ate something, a truffle which he'd pull out of the foie gras with his fingers, a piece of ham, a spoonful of caviar, or he would drain a bottle; if he felt like a square meal he would make himself a substantial sandwich and eat it slowly, his cuffs turned back, perched on a corner of the table which he had carefully wiped.

There were long intervals, like this, when Désiré had nothing to do. He had been given the title of steward. He was in charge of everything in the pantry: food and drink, cigarettes, accessories for the *cotillon*; he had to see that nothing left the room without being entered on a slip of paper, and then make sure through his spy-hole that the customer received that particular slip and no other, for waiters are up to all sorts of tricks; one night they'd had to strip one of them to find the money he denied having taken.

Julie was there in the orange-lighted dance-hall. Her customers had all gone. She was sitting at a table with Charlotte, a plump blonde; they were exchanging idle remarks, pretending to drink, and getting up to dance together every time Monsieur René came past and snapped his fingers.

It was Julie who had introduced Monsieur Désiré to the

Monico. The first evening, on discovering that his money had vanished, he had wanted to go away. Anywhere, he didn't care where. It was she who had been indignant to see him accept the situation so naturally, for she was incapable of understanding how such an event could come almost as a relief.

And yet this was so. It was bound to happen. He had made a mistake, in Paris, through maladroitness or through timidity perhaps, when he provided himself with so large a sum of money. In so doing he had not followed the rule, a rule which was unwritten but which existed none the less. When he had decided to go off he had felt no surprise or emotion, because he knew it had to happen. On the contrary, when he had gone to the bank to withdraw the three hundred thousand francs he had felt embarrassed and guilty.

On those other two occasions when he had dreamed of escaping, had he thought about money? No. He had to be quite destitute, out in the street.

And now this had happened at last.

'Wait a minute. I've something to say to the proprietor.'

Julie had gone downstairs. When she came back a few minutes later she announced: 'I was quite right. ... Where would you have gone? ... There's a little room free, up at the top. ... It's a servant's room, but Fred lets it by the month, quite cheap. ... I'll keep this room myself for a day or two and if I don't find anything I'll join you up on the sixth floor. ... I'm sure I'll find something!'

She had found herself a job first, as hostess at the Monico, and then a few days later she had found him the position that he had now held for nearly two months.

They had practically nothing in common now. Occasionally, when Julie was on her own, they would go off to their hotel together in the small hours. She would tell him stories about René or about the boss, Monsieur Dodevin, stories about her fellow-hostesses and her customers; he would listen patiently, nodding his head and smiling beatifically. So much so that she lost patience.

'What sort of man are you?'

'Why?'

'I don't know. ... You're always contented. ... You don't

mind how you're treated. . . . For one thing you never brought a complaint, and yet you're not afraid of the police. . . . I noticed that, you may be sure! . . . You say good morning to that bitch that stole your money, when you meet her on the stair . . .'

Julie was convinced – and he felt inclined to agree with her – that it was the chambermaid on their floor, an ugly girl with greasy hair and big slack breasts, who had taken the bundle of notes from the top of the wardrobe; for she was just the type to spy on guests in their bedrooms, being always on the prowl in passages with a duster or a broom in her hand as an excuse.

Julie had discovered that she had as a lover a musician from the Casino who treated her with harsh contempt.

'I bet you whatever you like that he's got the money now. He's too cunning to use it right away. He's waiting till the end of the season . . .'

It was quite possible. And what of it?

This, again, was something he had dreamed of. Perhaps indeed, it was just for this that he had left home? He often wondered about that. As a young man, when he passed a certain sort of woman in the darkness, particularly in sordid streets, he felt a great thrill of excitement. He would brush by them deliberately, but he never turned round; on the contrary, he would make his escape hurriedly as soon as they spoke a word to him.

Sometimes, especially in winter, he used to leave his office in the Rue Montorgueil and spend a quarter of an hour wandering, through drizzling rain, in the mean streets round the Halles, where certain lights seem redolent of mysterious debauchery.

Every time he had taken the train, alone or with his wife, every single time, he had felt a pang of envy, as he sat in his first-class carriage, of the people carrying shabby bundles and going off somewhere or other, careless of what awaited them elsewhere.

There was a night-watchman in the Rue Montorgueil, a former schoolmaster who had lost his job because of misconduct with his girl pupils. He was ill-dressed and unkempt. He would take up his post in the evening with a bottle of wine in his pocket and settle down in a small cubbyhole where he warmed up his supper over a spirit lamp.

On some mornings when Monsieur Monde arrived very early because of urgent business, he had surprised the man tidying things up, calm and unconcerned, doing a last round automatically to make sure that all was in order and then slipping off down the street in the bright early sunlight.

Where did he go like that? Nobody had ever discovered where he lived, in what corner he would go to ground, like an animal, during the daytime.

Monsieur Monde had actually envied him too.

And now Monsieur Désiré had begun to look like him.

'What d'you want, lad?'

The pageboy had just rushed into the pantry; he had come, needless to say, to speak to Monsieur René, who was still busy eating.

'Is the boss up there?'

'Why?'

'There's a dick coming up, a dick I don't know who wants to speak to him.'

Immediately, Monsieur René's thigh slid off the table, the sandwich vanished, he wiped his fingers, brushed his revers, as swiftly as though with a single movement, and he sped across the dance floor, with enough self-control not to break into a run but to go on smiling at his guests.

Just as he reached the main door, which led on to the marble staircase, it opened to let in a man who had refused to leave his overcoat in the cloakroom, and whom Monsieur René greeted solicitously.

Désiré watched them through the little spy-hole. Julie and her friend, at their table, had grasped what was happening. Monsieur René could be seen inviting the detective to sit down at a table at some distance from the dance-floor, but the policeman remained standing, shaking his head and speaking a few words; then Monsieur René disappeared through another door, the one that led to the gaming room. Other policemen, those who were on good terms with the establishment, had free access to this room, but it was wiser not to let a new man in.

He was a tall, strapping fellow of thirty-five. He waited, staring vaguely at the commonplace décor of the dance-hall. Then Monsieur René reappeared, accompanied by the boss,

Monsieur Dodevin, a former lawyer who had retained the outward dignity of his calling.

Once more the man was invited to sit down and have a bottle of champagne, but once more he refused. Then he was brought up to Désiré's den.

'Come in here,' Monsieur Dodevin said. 'We can talk better here. . . . René!'

'Yes, monsieur. . . .' And René, who had understood, looked out a good bottle of champagne among those that were left, and polished two glasses out of the cupboard.

'As you see, we're at close quarters here . . .'

And Monsieur Dodevin, who was invariably of a fine marble pallor, stepped into the dance-hall for a moment to fetch two chairs covered in red velvet.

'Do sit down. . . . Are you from the Nice squad? . . . No? . . . I thought I hadn't met you before . . .'

Désiré was not watching them. He was keeping his professional watch on the dance-hall, where everyone was impatiently waiting for the departure of the last guests, who lingered stubbornly, thus preventing twenty people from going off to bed.

Julie, who knew he was up there although she could not see his face, kept signalling to him from a distance: 'What's up? Something serious?'

He could not reply. It didn't matter. Julie felt the occasional need to make contact with him thus, pulling a face for instance when she was afflicted with a bad dancing-partner or a ludicrous companion.

He heard a whispered mention of the Empress, and he listened keenly.

'Really? Is she dead?' murmured the ex-lawyer in an appropriately solemn tone. 'Such an amazing woman. . . . And you say she died shortly after leaving here? Of course it's a sad misfortune, but I don't see how . . .'

Only the night before, the Empress had been there, barely five yards away from Désiré who, though himself unseen, could examine her at leisure.

Who had first called her the Empress? It was hard to say. Probably she had borne that nickname for a long time on the

Riviera. Some ten days earlier, Flip, the pageboy, had rushed in, just as he had done when the policeman arrived, and had then announced to Monsieur René: 'Good! Here comes the Empress!'

They had seen her come in, huge, obese, tallow-faced, a fur coat open on a bosom loaded with jewels. Under their puffy lids her eyes were so utterly lacking in expression that they seemd dead.

She was panting, from having climbed the stairs, for the Monico was on the first floor. She halted, like a queen waiting to be ceremoniously attended to. René hurried to welcome her, all smiles, bowing and scraping, pointing out one table and then another, finally leading her to a settee, while the Empress's companion, who carried a small pekinese dog, followed with the modest bearing of a lady-in-waiting.

Désiré had not flinched that evening. Perhaps he had smiled a little more bitterly.

The Empress's companion was his first wife. Thérèse, whom he had not seen for eighteen years. Much as she had altered, he recognized her, and he felt no hatred, no resentment, only a sort of extra burden laid on his shoulders, added to the heavy weight they already bore and which he no longer even attempted to shake off.

Thérèse must be about forty now, scarcely more, for she had been eighteen when he married her. She looked more than her age. Her features had become set. She still looked rosy, but there must be a layer of cosmetics on her face to give it that disturbing, masklike immobility.

When she smiled, however, and she happened to smile several times, it was almost the same smile as of old, a timid, ingenuous, delightfully childish smile, that smile which for years had misled Monsieur Monde about his wife's nature.

She had been modest, self-effacing, apt to droop her head a little and say, in an ideally gentle voice: 'Just as you please . . .'

Or else: 'You know I like whatever you do . . .'

A sudden movement would have shattered her, and yet she was the woman who had collected, in her desk, those obscene photographs that men thrust into strangers' hands on the

Grands Boulevards: who had annotated them, copying them carefully, exaggerating the size of the sexual organs: she, again – her husband had found out almost for certain, although he had not wished to pursue his inquiry any further – who had sought out their chauffeur in his attic bedroom and who, when he drove her into town, made him stop in front of dubious apartment-houses.

Afterwards she reassumed her pure smile as she bent over her children's cots!

Her eyelids were withered now, but had retained a certain charm, reminding one of those flower petals which, as they shrivel, assume an ethereal transparency.

The detective now accepted the champagne he was being offered, the Havana cigar which Désiré hastily entered on the expense account, since this was his responsibility and, by and by, he would have to get the boss himself to sign a chit for it.

'They were both living in the Plaza,' the policeman explained. 'A magnificent flat overlooking the Promenade. .... You can't imagine in what chaos and filth they lived. .... They wouldn't let the hotel staff clean up for them. They had a maid, a Czech or something of the sort, who brought up their meals on a tray and served them, usually in bed, for they often lay in bed for thirty hours at a time. ... When I got there with my colleague there were torn stockings in every corner, dirty linen all mixed up with jewellery and furs, money lying about on the furniture ...'

'What did she die of?' inquired Monsieur Dodevin.

And as Monsieur René was standing behind them, he motioned him to leave the room. The detective drew from his pocket a metal box, from which he took out a hypodermic syringe, dismantled, and showed it to Monsieur Dodevin, looking him in the eyes.

The ex-lawyer did not turn a hair, but merely shook his head, saying: 'No, never that ...'

'Indeed!'

'I give you my sacred word of honour that no morphine has ever come into this place, nor gone out of it. .... You know my business as well as I do. .... I don't claim to keep always strictly within the law, for that's impossible. Your colleagues on the

Gaming Squad, who often come to see me in quite a friendly way, will tell you I'm above-board. . . . I keep as close a watch on my staff as possible. . . . I've engaged a man specially . . .' (he indicated Désiré) '. . . specially to make sure that nothing illegal goes on in the hall. . . . Tell me, Monsieur Désiré, have you ever seen any morphine here?'

'No, monsieur.'

'Do you always watch the waiters, the pageboy and the flower-girls when they go up to the guests?'

'Yes, monsieur.'

'You see, Inspector, if you'd mentioned cocaine I might not have been so categorical. I play fair. I don't try to pretend what isn't true. With the sort of women we're obliged to accept here, it's inevitable that one day or another we get one who's hooked on snow. That soon becomes obvious. I nearly always notice it after a few days. It happened a couple of months ago, and I got rid of her immediately . . .'

The detective may have believed him, or may not. He was staring impassively at his surroundings, and cast an apparently casual eye over Désiré.

The latter was somewhat alarmed. Six days exactly after he left Paris, the day after his money had been stolen, his photograph had appeared in the newspapers, not on the front page, like those of wanted criminals, but on the third, sandwiched unobtrusively between two advertisements. It was a bad likeness.

Handsome reward offered for information as to the above person, who is probably suffering from loss of memory.

There followed the description of the clothes he had been wearing the day he disappeared and finally the address of a Paris solicitor, Madame Monde's own solicitor, who was looking after a lawsuit that she'd been carrying on for ten years about property in which she was co-heir with some cousins.

Nobody had recognized him. He had not reflected for one moment that, if they were trying to find him, it was because the key of the safe was useless without his presence, or at any rate his signature.

'Was she wealthy?'

They were talking about the Empress.

'She'd a fair amount left. . . . Only a few years ago she was worth tens of millions. . . . Actually she's an American, an American Jewess, daughter of a clothing magnate. She's been married four or five times. . . . She's lived all over the place. She's been the wife of a Russian prince among others, and that's why they call her the Empress . . .'

'And the other woman?'

Désiré averted his eyes and looked into the dance-hall, dreading the detective's watchful eye.

'A Frenchwoman, of a decent family. . . . Divorced. . . . She's done all sorts of things too. . . . When the Empress met her, she was a manicurist . . .'

'Have you arrested her?'

'What's the good? . . . There were men involved too. . . . The hotel staff aren't communicative. . . . They used to have people up to their bedrooms some evenings . . . nobody knows for sure . . . people they picked up goodness knows where . . . whom the staff were quite surprised to meet on the stairs of the hotel . . . and preferred not to see them, you understand?'

The ex-lawyer understood perfectly.

'Yesterday morning, about ten o'clock, the Czech maid went down to ask for a doctor's 'phone number. When the doctor got there the Empress was dead already, and the other woman, still under the influence of the drug, seemed quite unaware of what had happened. . . . Your good health!'

'And yours!'

'I was obliged to come here. . . . We're trying to find out where the morphine comes from. . . . This is the second case this winter . . .'

'I told you . . .'

'Of course. . . . Of course . . .'

'Another cigar? Take a handful; they're not bad . . .'

The detective did not demur; he slipped the cigars into the outside pocket of his jacket and picked up his hat.

'You can go out this way . . .'

The door of the back staircase creaked. The boss switched on the light and waited to turn it off till the policeman had reached the bottom of the stairs. Then he retraced his steps and put away the cigars in the box.

'Five, Désiré . . .'

'I've entered them, monsieur.' And Désiré handed him a pencil with which to sign the form in the counterfoil book.

'That's how one gets involved in things!'

He went off to join Monsieur René in the dance-hall. They stood near the door, arguing in low voices.

Julie was sitting with her legs crossed, swinging her left foot, to let Désiré know she was fed up. A waiter burst in and seized two empty champagne bottles from a basket under the table.

'I'm taking advantage of the least drunk of them having gone to the toilet!'

His customers were completely hoodwinked. Only the hostesses noticed the trick; the two bottles went to join those that the guests had drunk, and Désiré calmly put down two little crosses in his book.

He wondered what was going to become of his ex-wife. When she was a girl her parents had called her Baby because of her angelic look. The Empress was unlikely to have left her any money. Women of that sort never think of making a will.

He felt no resentment against her. Neither did he forgive her; it was unnecessary.

'No 9's bill!' called out a head waiter through the crack of the swing door.

When the guests at Table 9 had gone it would be the end. They were paying. The cloakroom attendant was waiting behind them with their things. She was quite young and fresh-looking, dressed in shiny black with a dark red ribbon in her hair. A doll. A play-thing. She was engaged to a pork-butcher's assistant, but Monsieur René made her sleep with him. Désiré suspected the boss of doing the same thing, but she was so secretive that one could never know the truth.

There was a scraping of chairs, noisy comings and goings, while the waiters, as they cleared the tables, drained the bottles and each ate something or other.

'A glass for me, Monsieur René!' Julie was thirsty, and he brought her one.

'It's been agony all evening! I was wearing my new shoes and

I couldn't stand on my feet. . . .' She pulled off her little gold slippers and put on her town shoes, which were standing beside the gas stove.

Désiré was finishing his accounts, and the gamblers could now be heard crossing the dance-hall on their way out. They were respectable citizens, all men, mostly tradespeople of Nice who, as such, were not allowed to visit the gambling rooms at the Casinos. They shook hands as they parted, like fellow-workers in an office.

'Are you coming, Désiré?'

Charlotte lived in the same hotel as themselves. Day had dawned, and the town was deserted. Out at sea they could see white fishing boats with green and red painted rims.

'Is it true that the Empress is dead?'

Désiré walked between the two of them. At one street corner they stopped automatically in front of a little bar that had just opened. A good smell rose from the percolator, which the *patron*, in a blue apron, was just polishing.

'Three coffees . . .'

They were blinking a little. They always had a peculiar after-taste in their mouths. And the smell of the nightclub still hung about the two women, who were wearing their evening dresses under their town coats. Theirs was a special sort of weariness, in their heads rather than in their limbs.

They started off again. At Gerly's, the door was left unlocked all night. The blinds of the brasserie were still down.

They went upstairs slowly. Julie's room was on the second floor and Charlotte's on the fourth. Désiré still slept up in the attic.

They stopped on the landing to say good night to one another. Julie, wholly unembarrassed by her friend's presence, glanced up at him. 'Coming in?'

He did so occasionally; but now he said no. He didn't feel like it. He went on upstairs.

'She's a nice girl,' Charlotte said. 'She's swell!'

He agreed.

'Good night . . .'

'Good night . . .'

He went on climbing, slowly. Once in his life, at home in the

226

Rue Ballu, he had climbed the stairs to his bedroom thus, one evening when he had been out alone and his wife, the second wife, was waiting for him. And involuntarily, unconsciously, under a sort of compulsion, he had stopped and sat down on a step, wearily, without a thought in his head; then, because of some creaking sound, made perhaps by a mouse in the wainscot, he had got up, feeling ashamed, and made his way upstairs.

Now he went up to the very top, opened the door with his key, and began to undress, looking out at the hundreds of red roofs spread out in tiers in the morning sunlight.

SEVEN

The bars of the iron bedstead were black, and the same shape as the backs of the chairs in the Champs-Elysées or the Bois de Boulogne. Désiré slept under a sloping attic roof. The skylight stood open. Birds were bickering along the ledge, and lorries from far afield were rattling past in the streets below, converging on the flower market; the sounds travelled so clearly through the thin air that one could almost smell the stacks of mimosa and carnations.

Désiré was almost immediately engulfed in sleep; he would first feel himself drop vertically, as though sucked down by an eddy, but it was not unpleasant, he felt no fear, he knew he would not touch bottom; like a cork, he rose up again, not quite surfacing but sinking and rising again, and almost always the same thing went on for hours, slow or sudden alternations between the glaucous emptiness of the depths and that invisible surface above which the world went on living.

The light was the same as that which pervades sheltered creeks of the Mediterranean; it was sunlight, he realized, but sunlight diluted, diffused, sometimes decomposed as though in a prism, suddenly violet for instance or green, the intense green of the legendary, elusive green ray.

Noises reached him as they must reach fishes through water, noises perceived not with the ear but with the whole of one's being, absorbed and assimilated until their meaning may perhaps be completely altered.

The hotel remained silent for a long time, because all those who lived there were nocturnal people; but there was a vicious creature over the way, a car that was taken out of a garage at the same time every morning and washed by the edge of the pavement under a spattering hose, after which the engine would be started up. This always required several attempts. He would wait tensely until the hoarse roar became a normal tone, and then for several minutes, he never knew how many, there was a sustained hum with a reek of petrol fumes that must be blue-tinged. And meanwhile, presumably, the chauffeur, in his peaked cap and dazzlingly white shirt sleeves, was calmly polishing the chromium while the creature warmed up.

There was a tram which always seemed to get out of hand and run into the kerb at exactly the same place, probably at a bend in the road.

When he sank deeper down the sounds became different, the images lost their clarity, even their separate identity; for instance, probably when a woman was washing herself in the attic next to his, at about eleven o'clock, he heard the splash of a fountain in the garden of his parents' country place at Le Vésinet, where, as a child, he had slept with the windows open during the holidays. He could clearly see the fountain, the wet dark stone, but there was something else he could not recall, the smell of the air; he tried to remember what the air of that holiday home was like – honeysuckle, maybe?

He would rise up, light as a bubble, and pause just before breaking the invisible surface; he knew none the less that the sunlight was cutting his hinged skylight in two, that it was just about to reach the foot of the bed, that he could dive down again, that the game was not up yet . . .

That morning, as on other mornings, his eyes were smarting, he had the raw sensitive skin common to those who do not sleep at nights, the lips particularly, which had the exquisite tenderness of a healing wound. He had gone to bed and let himself be caught up in the eddy, unresisting; he had sunk down, but had come up again immediately, he had surfaced, he had stared – so his eyes must have been open – at the white-washed wall against which his overcoat, hanging from a yellow wooden knob, formed a black patch.

Why did he let this Empress business worry him? He closed his eyes, he dived, he did his best, but his impetus was feeble, he could not recover the wonderfully elastic fluidity of his morning slumbers, and unconsciously he stared at his overcoat, thinking of that Empress whom he could clearly recall, with her black eyes and hair; he was searching for a likeness; it bothered him, there was a likeness, he knew, it was in the eyes; he made a violent effort and discovered that, surprisingly and improbably, the Empress reminded him of his second wife, from whom he had run away. The one was as lean as an umbrella and the other huge and flabby, but that was unimportant. It was in the eyes. That fixed stare. That unconscious, immense, haughty contempt, that apparent obliviousness to anything outside herself, anything unconnected with herself.

He turned over heavily on his hard bed that smelt of sweat. He had grown used to the smell of his own sweat again, just as when he had been a child. For too many years, for the greater part of his life, he had forgotten the smell of sweat, the smell of the sun, all those living smells of which people who go about their business are no longer conscious; and he wondered if that were not the reason why . . .

He was close to a truth, a discovery, he had begun to dive down again, then something brought him back to the surface and he thought: 'I won't go.'

What was the good? What could he do?

He remembered her look of distress, her childish 'oh!' when he took her for the first time, clumsily, because he felt ashamed. And each time after that, each time they had sex together, though he tried to be as gentle as possible, he knew she was wearing the same expression, he avoided seeing her face, and thus it happened that instead of being a pleasure the sexual act became an ordeal.

He found himself sitting up in bed again. He said no, tried to lie down again, and a few minutes later he had thrust his bare legs out of bed and was hunting for his limp socks on the floor.

He was quite surprised to see that it was ten o'clock already.

Because of this, the panorama of rosy roof-tops had an unfamiliar look. He started to shave. Then, as he let one of his shoes drop, somebody knocked against the wall: a call to order from his neighbour, a croupier at the Casino who had big blue-black moustaches.

He went downstairs. In the ground-floor passage he met the maid who had stolen his money and had looked at him with hostility ever since. He said good morning to her with exaggerated friendliness, to which she responded with a curt nod while she mopped the tiles with a damp cloth.

He walked on as far as the Plaza, but before going in, as his mouth felt dry, he went into a bar for a cup of coffee. The hotel was a creamy white building with a great many windows surrounded with ornaments, like a cake. He wondered whether the porter would let him in. Actually, the people who called at this time of day were chiefly tradesmen and workmen. The hall was vast and cool. He went up to the concierge's desk.

'I'm from the Monico,' he hurriedly said, as the other, who had a telephone receiver clamped to his ear, looked him up and down.

'Hullo? ... Yes. ... They're coming by road? ... About two o'clock? ... Good. ... Thank you. ...' Then, to Désiré: 'What is it?'

'The boss would like to know what's become of the lady who was with the Empress.'

A childish, ridiculous, useless lie.

'Madame Thérèse?'

So she hadn't changed her Christian name! She had become Madame Thérèse, just as he had become Monsieur Désiré. But his name was one picked up at random from a shop front.

'Is she still here?'

'No. ... I don't even know where you'll find her. ... They've been very mean to her ...'

'Who?'

'Not the police! ... The police realized that she was just someone who had to earn her living. ... Poor woman! She seemed so gentle. ... You must have seen her, at the Monico. ... I know the detective from Paris went there last night. ... Nothing, I suppose?'

'Nothing . . .'

'If I'd been here, I'd have rung you up to warn you, just in case. . . . When I heard about it I ticked off the night porter, who hadn't thought of doing so. . . . You never know . . .'

'Thank you very much. . . . I'll tell the boss. . . . And what about Madame Thérèse?'

'They questioned her for three hours at least. . . . Then they had some food sent up for her, for she was exhausted. . . . I don't know what the detective had decided to do about her. . . . He had informed the family . . . the Empress's family, I mean, for she's got a brother who's in the car business in Paris. . . . He's the French representative of an American make . . .'

The concierge greeted a slim Englishwoman in a tailor-made suit, who was walking brisky past behind Désiré.

'A letter for you, Miss . . .'

He watched her move away. The revolving door sent a patch of sunlight sliding down the wall.

'As I was saying, they let the brother know. . . . He immediately telephoned instructions to a local solicitor. . . . Less than an hour later, some legal people turned up and insisted on having seals affixed to everything. . . . The senior floor waiter, who'd been into the apartment several times to serve them drinks, told me it was a queer sight. . . . They were terrified of the least thing disappearing. . . . They'd pick up every little thing, stockings, handkerchiefs, an odd slipper, and put them all away in cupboards and seal them up . . .

'Apparently these people insisted on the police searching Madame Thérèse and they'd have sealed her up too if they could. It was all on account of the jewels, you see! . . . Seems they're all real. . . . There were such a lot of them I'd have sworn they were glass beads. . . . It'd have been a major disaster if Madame Thérèse had taken some little thing!

'Why, that telephone call, just as you came in, was to tell me the brother is coming here by car presently, with a solicitor. . . . They're on the road now, driving hell for leather . . .

'Hullo! . . . No, she's not here yet. . . . What's that? . . . Yes, she's still got her apartment, but she's not come in yet . . .'

Since he looked on Désiré as a colleague, he explained, though without specifying to whom he was referring: 'There's another queer customer for you! She never comes in before eleven in the morning and she stays in bed till ten at night. . . . You wanted to know what's become of Madame Thérèse? . . . I don't know. . . When they were through with their formalities they turned her out, there's no other word for it, without letting her take away anything, not even her personal possessions, which are all sealed up with the rest. . . . She had only her little handbag. . . . She'd been crying. . . . I can still picture her on the pavement. . . . You could see she didn't know where to go, and she was like a stray animal. . . . In the end she went off towards the Place Masséna. . . . If you're not anxious to meet the detective you'd better not hang around, for he's due here at eleven o'clock. . . . I don't know where they took the body. . . . It was taken away last night, but by the back entrance. . . . Apparently it's to be sent to America . . .'

Désiré too, lingered outside for a moment like a stray animal, and, as his first wife had done, he made his way towards the Place Masséna. He cast his eyes mechanically over the café terraces where, as yet, only a few people sat under the awnings, but he had little hope of seeing Thérèse there.

She must have taken refuge in a cheap lodging-house, in one of those squalid hotels in the old part of the town where the washing hangs across the street and where small girls with bare bottoms sit on the doorsteps.

He crossed the flower-market, where they were already sweeping up armfuls of flower-stalks and buds, withered petals whose scent reminded him of All Saints' Day.

Had he any chance of finding her again? He scarcely hoped to do so, and he didn't know if he wanted to. And yet one does meet people one has not expected to see, since on a narrow pavement he brushed up against the Inspector, who was hurrying along, presumably to keep his eleven o'clock appointment at the Plaza, and who turned back, trying to remember, then went on his way.

Had he, too, gone in search of Thérèse? Probably not. He must know where she was.

Désiré went on walking. Then at midday he found himself back in the Place Masséna, and he sat down on the terrace of a large café where most of the tables were crowded with people drinking apéritifs. Newsvendors were calling out the names of foreign papers. Coaches full of tourists in summer dresses stopped, then started off again, with rows of heads all turned the same way and all wearing the same smug expression of satisfied curiosity.

It was then that suddenly, amid the crowd, he caught sight of Thérèse. He almost lost her again, such was his astonishment. She was standing on the edge of the pavement, waiting for the policeman to halt the flow of traffic. He had to pay for his drink. The waiter, busy inside, was slow in coming. Monsieur Désiré knocked on the window with a coin. He was overcome with anguish, and yet he was incapable of leaving without paying.

The policeman lowered his truncheon. The waiter came along, bearing a small tray which he proceeded to unload at the neighbouring tables, pacifying his impatient customer with a 'Coming . . .'

The pedestrians poured across. The stream dwindled, there was only one stout man belatedly hurrying as the policeman raised his truncheon again.

'Haven't you any change?'

'It doesn't matter.'

Too late. He had to wait. He tried to see her in the shadow of the chestnut trees along the boulevard; once he caught a glimpse of her light grey figure.

When at last he was able to cross he dashed forward, jostling passers-by, almost breaking into a run, and at last, some fifty yards ahead, he saw her again, walking slowly along, like a person who is going nowhere in particular and pretending to look at the shop windows.

He slowed down. He had made no plan. He did not know what he wanted to do. He walked more and more slowly; they were only ten yards, then five yards, apart and she knew nothing about it, she seemed weary, maybe she was looking for somewhere to eat? The ridiculous thing was that finally she stopped in front of a window displaying pipes, and as he drew level with her, lacking the courage to go on his way with averted head, he called out automatically: 'Thérèse!'

She gave a start, and turned round, frowning. The expression was so characteristic of her and of nobody else that the years seemed to vanish and he recognized her completely, just as he had known her: a frail, defenceless little creature, petrified with fear at the slightest noise, aware of the impossibility of flight and standing motionless with head drawn back, watching with gentle, astonished eyes as the cruel world swoops down on it.

He recognized the whole thing so vividly that his throat felt constricted and for a moment his eyes were dimmed and he saw her less distinctly. The clarity of his vision was restored just as Thérèse, who had been feverishly searching her memory, discovered the truth at last and revealed her astonishment.

She could hardly believe, as yet, that this was not some fresh trap, and she seemed on the verge of flight; she stammered out: 'It's you!'

What did he say to her? He did not know. They were in the sunlit street; the shadows of the plane-tree leaves formed a quivering pattern on the tarmac. People were hurrying past. Cars glided by, a couple of yards from them. He looked at all the pipes in the window, and he spoke to her:

'I knew you were in Nice. ... Don't be afraid. ... I know all about it ...'

Amazement widened her mauve eyes. For they were really mauve. Monsieur Monde wondered whether they had always been that colour. True, the lids were coated with eye-shadow that left minute glittering particles. Under her chin the skin was streaked with fine wrinkles.

What could her thoughts be on seeing him again? Was she listening to what he was saying?

'I'll explain to you. ... We ought to go and sit down somewhere first. ... I bet you've had no lunch ...'

'No ...'

The 'no' did not refer to lunch; it was a protest, a feeble refusal of her whole being, with a shake of the head. Perhaps she thought it was not possible? Perhaps she was denying the reality of their meeting?

'Come along ...'

She followed him. He walked too fast. He had to wait for her. It had always been like that when they walked together. He seemed to be towing her along, and when she was exhausted she

234

would beg for mercy, or else she would stop without saying a word to get back her breath, and he would understand.

'I'm sorry ...'

Only, soon after, he was off again without realizing it.

At the corner of a street there was a little restaurant with a few tables outside; one of these, beside a green pot-plant, was free.

'Let's sit down here ...'

And he thought: 'Luckily we've got the street, the passers-by, the waiter coming to ask what we're going to eat and to straighten the glasses on the table. Luckily there's always something outside ourselves, we're never left face to face ...'

'Give us the menu ... anything will do ...'

'Will you take shellfish?'

'All right ...'

'There's *brandade de morue* ...'

He suddenly remembered that she disliked salt cod and he said no. She was looking at him, still in amazement, and had only just begun to see him as he really was. Their situations were dissimilar. He, for his part, had had the opportunity to watch her for hours through the spyhole at the Monico. She must have been surprised, above all, by the way he was dressed, for since becoming Monsieur Désiré he had resumed the ready-made suit he had bought in Paris.

'What do you do?'

'I'll explain. ... It's not important ...'

'Are you living in Nice?'

'Yes. ... I've been here some time ...'

It would take too long to tell, and it wasn't interesting. He was beginning to regret having shown himself to her. This was not what he had intended. He had only wanted to know where she was living, so as to send her a little money. For he had his earnings. And he still had some of what he'd had on him at the time of the theft.

She was even more ill at ease than he. She had almost addressed him as *vous*. The *tu* had sprung to her lips none the less, and they felt almost as if they were standing naked in front of one another.

'Here we are, *messieurs-dames*. ... And what wine?'

He was suddenly reminded of another restaurant, of that three-storied eating-place at Marseilles, by the rose-pink of the shrimps, the yellowish-grey of the clams and the aroma of the wine that was being set before them.

What a journey he had made since leaving Paris! He kept on touching the table to make contact with reality. And Thérèse, with her painted, ageing lips, asked hesitantly: 'Have you been very unhappy?'

'No. . . . I don't know. . . . I didn't understand . . .'

She seemed even more astonished, and her eyes, a little girl's eyes in an ageing woman's face with flaking skin, opened wider in ingenuous questioning.

Did he understand now? That was probably what she meant. It wasn't possible. And yet he was a different man. He, too, had faded. His cheeks had the flabby consistency due to a sudden loss of weight. His waistcoat hung loosely over his stomach.

'Eat up,' he said.

Did he know that she was hungry, that since last night she had been homeless and penniless? It was not obvious. Her light coat was uncrumpled. She must have gone in somewhere, perhaps to the Casino, where she was known, and maybe the barman had offered her something?

She went on eating. She was making an effort to eat slowly, with the tips of her lips. And then she said: 'If you knew how it distresses me to see you like this!'

So now she was sorry for him, she commiserated with him! Once again a tiny frown puckered her brow.

'How did it happen?'

He looked at her so intensely that he forgot to answer. She added, shyly – she was almost afraid of being heard:

'Was it because of me?'

'No, no. . . . It's nothing to worry about, I promise you. . . . I'm quite happy . . .'

'I thought you'd married again?'

'Yes . . .'

'Your wife?'

'It was I who left her. . . . It's of no importance . . .'

And the waiter laid before them a dish of tripe, succulent and strong-smelling. She was not struck by the contrast, because she was hungry, but Monsieur Monde found it hard to swallow a mouthful.

'I've just had a misfortune ...' she murmured as though to excuse her appetite.

'I know.'

'How did you know?' Then, with a sudden illumination: 'Are you something to do with the police?'

He did not laugh nor even smile at her mistake. It was true that in his drab clothes he looked rather like some humble auxiliary of the police.

'No. .... All the same I know about the whole business. ... I've been looking for you all morning ...'

'For me?'

'I called at the Plaza ...'

She shuddered

'They were so unkind ...' she admitted.

'Yes ...'

'They treated me like a thief ...'

'I know ...'

'They took away all that I'd got in my bag and only left me a twenty-franc note ...'

'Where did you sleep?'

'Nowhere ...'

He had made a mistake in speaking of that, for now distress was choking her and she could not eat.

'Have a drink!'

'I'm still wondering what you do here ...'

'I'm working. .... I was tired of living there ...'

'Poor Norbert ...'

He froze, suddenly. She should not have spoken so, in that foolishly pitying tone. He gave her a hard, resentful stare. They had barely been together a quarter of an hour, half an hour at most, and she had already degraded everything to the level of her own feminine mind.

'Eat up!' he ordered her.

Oh, he was well aware of her thoughts. Unconsciously she was, once more, putting herself at the hub of things. If she wore that guilty look, it was because she was convinced that she was responsible for everything.

And in her heart of hearts, for all her airs of distress, she must have been enjoying her triumph.

It was she, of course, who had caused him such pain when she left him! And although he had married again and sought to make a new home for himself, he had never found happiness again!

He would have liked to make her stop talking. He would have liked to go away now, leaving her the wherewithal to feed herself and keep going somehow.

'Was she unkind to you?'

There was unkindness in his own sharp retort: 'No!'

'How you said that!'

And a heavy silence fell between them, while she went on eating, without enjoyment or appetite.

'Waiter,' he called.

'Monsieur?'

'Bring me coffee, please.'

'No dessert?'

'For Madame, but not for me.'

It was as though she had sullied something. She was so conscious of this that she stammered out: 'Please forgive me . . .'

'For what?'

'I've said something silly, haven't I? You were always scolding me for saying silly things . . .'

'It doesn't matter . . .'

'If you knew what a shock it gave me just now! . . . To see you like this! . . . In my case it's my own fault. . . . And then I'm used to it after all these years. . . . It's not the first time I've been in this fix. . . . But you!'

'Stop talking about me.'

'I'm sorry!'

'I suppose the police are making you stay on in Nice?'

'How did you know? Yes, until they've finished their inquiry . . . and various formalities . . .'

He took his wallet out of his pocket, and felt himself blushing as he did so. Still, it couldn't be helped. He made sure that the waiter, stationed at the entrance of the restaurant, was not looking at them.

'You've got to find somewhere to stay . . .'

'Norbert . . .'

'Take it . . .'

Her lashes were wet with tears, but they were tears that did not flow, they rose to the surface but found no free outlet.

'You're making me unhappy . . .'

'No, no. . . . Careful, we're being seen . . .'

She gave two or three sniffs and, in a gesture with which he was becoming familiar, raised her open handbag to eye-level so as to repowder her face.

'Are you going to leave me already?'

He made no reply.

'Of course you've probably got your job. . . . I daren't even ask you what you do . . .'

'It doesn't matter. . . . Waiter!'

'Monsieur?'

'My bill . . .'

'Are you in a hurry?'

He was. His nerves were on edge. He felt that he might as easily be moved to anger as to pity. He needed to be alone again and above all not to have her in front of him, with her candid eyes, her wrinkled neck.

'Go and look for a room at once and get some rest.'

'Yes.'

'When do you have to appear before the police?'

'Not till tomorrow. . . . They're expecting the relatives . . .'

'I know . . .'

He rose. He had counted on her staying a little longer on the terrace, to finish drinking her coffee. That would give him time to get away. It would make things easier. But she rose too, and stood waiting beside him.

'Which direction are you going in?'

'Over there . . .'

Towards the Place Masséna. Towards his hotel. For some unknown reason he did not want her to know where he lived.

Once more she trailed along behind him. He was walking fast. In the end she understood that it was no good persisting and she slowed down, like a runner giving up a race, but she had time to whisper:

'I'll let you go off. . . . Please forgive me . . .'

Tactlessly, because he did not know how to set about it, he failed to say good-bye to her. His temples throbbed as he walked away in the sunshine. He was conscious of behaving cruelly.

'Please forgive me . . .'

This time, he felt sure, she intended no allusion to the past nor to all the things for which he might have reproached her. It was to the immediate present that she was referring, to their failure to make contact, to her own inability to behave as he would have liked her to.

He waited until he was far off before he turned round. She had only gone a few steps and then halted, to keep herself in countenance, in front of a leather-goods shop.

People who went past could not know. She was just a very ordinary woman. And he was just a man in a hurry, on his way to work like any other.

He reached Gerly's Hotel, and caught sight of Julie having lunch with Charlotte close to the open bay window. He could not get into the hotel without being seen and so he went through the brasserie.

'Been out already?' she asked without interrupting her meal.

The frown deepened on his forehead.

'Has something happened?'

He merely muttered: 'I'm going to have a sleep . . .'

'See you tonight?'

'Yes . . .'

Not until he was on his way up the dingy staircase did he grasp the meaning of her query. It disturbed him. Why had she asked him that? Was everything being called in question already?

He found the maid doing his room and he turned her out, almost rudely, contrary to his usual manner. He lay down and closed his eyes in a rage, but nothing was as it should be, neither the shadows nor the light, nor the sounds, nor even the twittering sparrows, and his whole being tossed impatiently in the drab limbo.

EIGHT

Gambling was these people's opium. Through his spyhole Désiré could see them arriving, one after the other. First the croupiers, the sleek black ministrants of the rite, the professionals, who dashed through the hall without glancing around them and made straight for the 'workshop'. They did not leave coats or hats in the cloakroom; they had their own cupboard in the holy of holies, their soap and towels and often a pair of clean cuffs as well.

Then came the clients, most of whom were important citizens. When they pushed open the door of the dance-hall they had already discarded their outdoor garments, so that they seemed to be quite at home. The waiters, instead of rushing forward to show them to a table, greeted them as old acquaintances. Almost all of them wandered about with the casual air of people who have not yet decided what they are going to do. They would go up and shake hands with Monsieur René, exchange a few words with him and smooth their hair with a careless gesture.

Monsieur Monde was well aware, by now, that they were inwardly in a ferment. He knew them all. The first to arrive that evening was a big orange-importer who, so it was said, had begun by selling newspapers in the street or shining shoes on the ramblas of Barcelona, and who, at the age of thirty-five, had millions to play with. He was as handsome and well-groomed as a woman. All the hostesses in the club looked at him with longing or envy. He would smile to them, showing fine gleaming teeth. Sometimes between two games he would take a turn round the dance-hall and order a few bottles of champagne for them, a sure sign that he had won; but he was not known to have any mistress.

There was also the mayor of a neighbouring town, who always hurried through for fear of being seen. He was a lean, tortured creature. At the gaming-table he had his own set of habits and superstitions.

There was only one woman, but she was regarded and treated

as respectfully as a man; a woman of about fifty, who ran a fashionable drapery store, and who never let a night pass without sitting down at the gaming-table.

Many of them, almost all of them, looked like Monsieur Monde's former self. Their bodies were well cared for, their skins rosy, their chins smooth-shaven, they were dressed in fine quality cloth and beautifully fitting shoes, and they were all mature enough to be people of importance, often indeed to be overburdened with responsibilities. They had offices, employees, workmen; or else they were lawyers or doctors with a wealthy and extensive clientele. All of them had homes, wives and families. And all of them, every night, at a certain almost mystic moment, were irresistibly drawn from their chairs, as though under a spell. Nothing could hold them back.

In all probability some of them told lies, inventing some fresh alibi for themselves every evening, some new professional or social engagement.

Others failed to avoid scenes and reproaches, the wrath and contempt of wives who could not understand them, and these would slink in with furrowed brows, ashamed of their presence here, ashamed of themselves.

None of them knew that behind a little round spy-hole a man like themselves was watching them.

There remained the suckers, the simpletons, the braggarts, the foreigners brought in by touts as though on a leading-string, who were made to drink at one of the tables before being gently propelled towards the 'workshop' for a game that was more or less rigged.

And finally those who did not gamble, for whom gambling held no attraction, who took the dance-hall and its crowd of women quite seriously and spent hours there in exasperated lust.

Monsieur Monde could see them, a hundred times in the course of an evening, leaning over towards their chance companion, Julie, Charlotte or another, and he knew exactly what they were saying: just a couple of words: 'Let's go . . .'

And the girls would answer, tirelessly and with unvarying innocence:

'Presently. . . . The boss wouldn't let me go out yet. . . . He's very strict. . . . We're under contract . . .'

They had to go on drinking. Bottles of champagne succeeded one another, flowers, boxes of chocolates, fruit. The whole thing was rigged. And when the time came at last, when dawn was near, sometimes when the sun had risen, the man, dead drunk, was thrust outside; very occasionally, the woman would accompany him to his hotel, where because he had drunk too much he was unable to satisfy his lust.

Monsieur Monde, that evening, was thinking about them and about himself, meanwhile making a note of the bottles that left the pantry. He was thinking, too, about Thérèse. He had slept badly that afternoon. Afterwards he had gone back to the restaurant where they had lunched together. Since they had made no plan to meet again, this was the only place where he might possibly find her. It had struck him that she might come back there, following the same line of argument as himself. He had questioned the waiter, who however had already forgotten her.

'A lady in a white hat, wasn't it?'

It was no such thing. It didn't matter. Besides, did he really want to see her again?

He felt tired. He felt old.

Monsieur René was, as usual, propped up on one corner of the table eating something. The pageboy pushed open the swing-door. He made no announcement, merely summoned the dance-floor superintendent with a jerk of his head.

Monsieur René drew himself up at once and darted, quite unruffled, into the hall. The pageboy hurried him to the main entrance. Just as he reached it, the door opened; and Monsieur Monde saw Thérèse herself appear. And Thérèse was quite obviously no longer welcome in the Monico. Monsieur René without appearing to do so, was blocking her way. She was talking to him. She looked humble. He was shaking his head. What could she be asking him?

Monsieur René was moving forward gradually to make her retrace her steps through the door, but she outwitted his manoeuvre. The hostesses, who had understood that something was happening and who perhaps guessed what it was, were all looking curiously in that direction.

Thérèse went on imploring; then she changed her tone, uttered threats, insisted on coming in, wanted to speak to somebody else.

This time the man from Martinique laid a hand on her shoulder. She shook him off, and Désiré pressed his face closer to the spyhole.

What could she be shouting at him with such vehemence? And why did the waiters, of their own accord, move forward strategically in support of their boss? How could they have guessed what was going to happen?

Suddenly, in fact, just as Monsieur René was slowly pushing her away with both hands, Thérèse drew herself up and began to scream, her body tense, her face unrecognizable, presumably hurling coarse insults or threats at him.

Désiré could not tell how it had happened, but there she was on the ground, literally writhing in a wild fit of hysterics; the others, the *maîtres d'hôtel* in black and the waiters in their white aprons, bent down quite unmoved, picked her up and carried her out, while the music went on imperturbably.

Monsieur Monde looked at Julie and saw that she was unconcerned. A waiter, whom he had not heard come into the pantry, sighed philosophically:

'She may as well go and have her fit on the pavement. She's bound to finish the night in the police-station . . '

'What fit?'

'She's run out of morphine . . .'

Then he slid off his high stool, abandoned his so-called desk and made his way to the squalid back-stairs. Half-way down he began to hurry, for he had to go a roundabout way to reach the main entrance. From a distance, in the darkness, he could see two or three of the Monico staff in the doorway, watching a retreating figure that kept stopping and turning round to shake a fist at them and hurl fresh insults.

He took his former wife by the arm. She gave a start, not recognizing him at first, and tried to struggle. Then she saw his face and burst into dreadful laughter.

'What do *you* want? . . . So you followed me, did you? . . . You're even more of a bastard than the rest!'

'Be quiet, Thérèse!'

He could see figures at the corner of the street. People were coming towards them. They might be policemen.

'Of course! I've got to keep quiet. ... You paid for my lunch! ... I ought to be grateful to you! ... And you gave me some money. ... Say it, why don't you? You gave me some money! ... But you took care to leave me stranded in the street. ... You couldn't care less about anything else ...'

He held on to her arm, and was surprised to find such strength in it. She kept on struggling, escaping from him, starting to run, and he would catch her up, and she would turn on him and spit in his face.

'Leave me alone, I tell you! ... I'll find some. ... I've got to find some. ... Or else ...'

'Thérèse!'

'You beast!'

'Thérèse!'

Her face was distorted, her eyes wild. He saw her collapse on the sidewalk at his feet, scrabbling at the pavement with her nails.

'Listen, Thérèse, I know what you want. ... Come along ...'

She did not hear him. The people who had come round the corner passed close by them and stopped for a moment. A woman was muttering: 'It's shocking!'

Another, rather older, woman was saying to the two men who were with them: 'Come on ...' And they went, regretfully.

'Get up. ... Follow me. ... I promise you ...'

'Have you got some?'

'I haven't, but I'll find some ...'

'You're lying!'

'I swear to you ...'

She was laughing hysterically and looking at him wide-eyed, torn between mistrust and hope.

'What'll you give me?'

'Morphine.'

'Who told you?'

She struggled to her feet, unconsciously using her hands like a child. She was swaying and weeping.

'Where are you going to take me?'

'To my place.'

'Where's that? ... Are you sure you're not going to take me to hospital? They did that to me once before. ... I'd be capable of ...'

'No, no. ... Come along ...'

'Is it far? ... Let's go and find some morphine together.'

'No. ... When you're calmer. ... I give you my word of honour I'll bring you some ...'

It was grotesque, tragic and ugly: at times the scene would lose some of its intensity, as Thérèse grew calmer, and they would walk a little way past the houses, like ordinary passers-by; then she would stop again as though she was drunk, forgetting what he had just told her and clinging to him. Once her weight nearly dragged him to the ground.

'Come along ...'

They made a little headway. And they both ended by uttering incoherent words.

'I went everywhere. ... I went to the doctor that *she* got it from ...'

'Yes, of course. ... Come along ...'

'They gave *her* as much as she wanted, because of her money ...'

'Yes, yes ...'

Twice he was on the point of leaving her there and walking off. The journey seemed interminable. At last they saw the lights of Gerly's Hotel, and then there was a fresh scene when he tried to make her go in.

'I want to wait for you in the café ...'

'No. ... Come up to my room.'

He managed it, by dint of patience. He had never imagined life could be so tedious. He went up behind her, pushing her. She was in his room at last, but her suspicions revived, and he realized that she would try to escape; he went out swiftly and locked the door behind him.

Pressing his ear to it, he spoke to her under his breath.

'Stay quiet. ... Don't make a noise. ... In less than a quarter of an hour I'll be back and I'll bring you some ...'

Was she exhausted? He heard her collapse on to the bed, where she lay moaning like an animal.

Then he went down. In the brasserie he went straight to the *patron* and spoke to him in low tones. But the *patron* shook his head. No. He hadn't got any. They didn't go in for that sort of thing. It was dangerous. You had to be very careful.

'Where, then?'

He didn't know that either. Cocaine and heroin were easier to get. He had heard tell of a doctor, but he didn't know his name or address.

Monsieur Monde was determined to leave no stone unturned. He didn't care what people might think of him. There was one doctor who came to the Monico almost every evening, played for high stakes and often left again looking pale and distraught. He, perhaps, might understand.

The hardest part, for one who was only a member of the staff, would be to make his way into the 'workshop' and get close to the gaming-table. Still, it couldn't be helped; he would go.

Then the *patron* of the brasserie raised his head. 'Listen!'

In spite of the six floors that separated them from the attic, they could hear a noise. It came down the stairs. The two men hurried up. The higher they went, the more clearly they could hear someone banging on a door, screams, the voices of a maid and of a lodger who happened to be at home and who was questioning the frantic woman.

'You shouldn't have brought her here,' the *patron* sighed.

What could Monsieur Monde do? He was at his wits' end.

'Call a doctor, will you? ... Any doctor will do. ... We can't let this go on ...'

'Would you like me to?'

He nodded, thrust aside the maid and the lodger and fitted his key into the lock. They wanted to come in with him, but he disliked the thought of anyone else witnessing the scene, and slipped into his attic, closing the door behind him.

The quarter of an hour which he then spent, alone with the woman who had once had such innocent eyes and who had borne him two children, was something about which he never spoke afterwards, and of which perhaps he managed to stop thinking.

The lodger, a jazz musician who had been confined to his room for a few days with pleurisy, had gone back to bed. Only the maid lingered on the landing. She was relieved when at last she heard the doctor's footsteps on the stair.

When the latter opened the door, Thérèse was lying across the bed with her legs hanging down. Désiré was stretched half across her, pinning her down with his weight and holding her mouth shut with his hand, from which the blood was streaming.

He was in such a dazed condition that for a moment he could not understand what the doctor had come for, and stayed there in his strange position.

Then he got up, rubbed his hand over his eyes and swayed. For fear of fainting, he went to lean against the wall, and the whitewash left marks all over one side of his suit.

*

The doctor had offered to take her into hospital, but he had refused. The others could not understand why. One injection had quietened her. She lay with her eyes wide open. But she was so calm, with such a vacant look, that she seemed to be sleeping.

On the landing he had had a whispered conversation with the doctor.

And now the two of them were alone together. He had sat down on a chair. Sometimes he felt a great hammering inside his head and at other times a dizziness, as though a sort of vacuum were sucking him down and preventing him from thinking. Now and then he would say mechanically, as though speaking were a relief to him: 'Go to sleep . . .'

He had switched off the electric lamp, but the moonbeams were streaming in through the open skylight and it was in that cold light that he saw her, transfigured; he tried to avert his eyes, because she looked like a dead woman, with the same pinched nostrils that the dead have, the same unsubstantial quality.

Once when he glanced towards the bed a shudder ran through

him, because he seemed to see there not Thérèse but his son Alain, who had almost the same features, and in any case the same pale eyes and waxen complexion.

People were returning to the hotel. Their footsteps almost always stopped on the lower floors. He automatically counted the landings. Four. . . . Five. . . . This time they came on, up to the sixth floor. A woman's. There was a knock on the door.

He realized that it was Julie.

'Come in . . .'

She was taken aback by the darkness, the strange look of those two creatures, the woman prostrate and open-eyed, the man sitting on a chair and holding his head in his hands. She began, in an undertone: 'Is she . . .'

She dared not finish.

'Is she dead?'

He shook his head, and rose wearily. Now he'd have to explain things. Good Lord, How complicated it all was!

He drew her to the door and on to the landing.

'Who is she? Did you know her? I heard, at the Monico. . . . The boss is furious . . .'

He disregarded this.

'You knew her, didn't you?'

He nodded. And she promptly guessed something further.

'Your wife?'

'My first wife . . .'

She showed no surprise, rather the reverse. It looked as if she had always suspected something of the sort.

'What are you going to do?'

'I don't know . . .'

'Tomorrow you'll have to start all over again. . . . We know her sort . . .'

'Yes.'

'Who gave you some?'

'The doctor . . .'

'When the time comes she'll want some more . . .'

'I know. . . . He's left me an ampoule.'

It was extraordinary. Words, phrases, even facts themselves – realities, in short – had lost all importance for him now. He was lucid and he was aware of it, he knew he was giving rational answers to all her questions, and behaving like a normal man. At the same time he felt very far away, or rather very high up; he could see Julie in her evening dress, on the landing, under the dusty electric lamp, he could see himself with ruffled hair and open-necked shirt.

'You're bleeding ...'

'It's nothing ...'

'She did it, didn't she?'

Yes, of course! All this was unimportant. In the last few hours, perhaps in the last few minutes, for he didn't know quite when it had happened, he had taken such a prodigious leap that he could look down with cold lucidity on the man and woman whispering, on a hotel landing, a little before daybreak.

He was certainly not a disembodied spirit. He was still Monsieur Monde, or Désiré, more likely Désiré.... No! it didn't matter. ... He was a man who, for a long time, had endured man's estate without being conscious of it, as others endure an illness of which they are unaware. He had always been a man living among other men and like them he had struggled, jostling amid the crowd, now feebly and now resolutely, without knowing whither he was going.

And now, in the moonlight, he suddenly saw life differently, as though with the aid of some miraculous X-ray.

Everything that had counted previously, the whole integument and flesh and the outward appearance of it all had ceased to exist, and what there was in their place ...

But there! It wasn't worth talking about it to Julie or to anyone else. And in any case it wasn't possible. The thing was *incommunicable*.

'Is there anything you need?' she was asking. 'Wouldn't you like me to have some coffee sent up?'

No.... Yes.... He did not care. On the whole, no, so that he could be left in peace.

'You'll let me know how things are going?'

He promised. She only half believed him. Perhaps she expected to discover, when she woke at midday, that he had gone away with the woman now lying on the iron bedstead?

'Well, cheer up!'

She went off, regretfully. She would have liked to communicate something to him herself, to tell him ... what, exactly? That she had realized from the start that it wasn't for ever. That she was just a common girl but that she could guess how things were; that ...

He saw her, at the bend in the staircase, looking up at him again. He went back into the bedroom and closed the door; he had a shock on hearing a voice mumble faintly: 'Who was that?'

'A girl I know ...'

'She's your ...'

'No ... just a friend ...'

Thérèse reverted to staring at the sloping ceiling. He sat down on his chair again. From time to time he raised his handkerchief to wipe the blood from his lip, which she had bitten deeply.

'Did he leave you any more?' she asked again without moving, speaking in the blank voice of a sleepwalker.

'Yes.'

'How much?'

'One.'

'Give it me now ...'

'Not yet ...'

She resigned herself, like a little girl. And in her present state she seemed far more childish and yet far older than when he had seen her in town the day before. His own face, too, when he lingered for a quarter of an hour in front of his mirror, shaving, often seemed to him like that of a child grown old. Is a man ever anything more than that? One talks of the years as though they existed. Then you notice that between the moment when you still went to school, even between the moment when your mother tucked you up in bed, and the moment you're living through now ...

The moon was still shining faintly in the sky when the dark blue of night yielded to the light blue of the morning, and the bedroom walls assumed a less vivid, less inhuman whiteness.

'You're not asleep?' she asked again.

'Not now.'

'I do so want to sleep!'

Her poor weary eyelids were fluttering, she was clearly on the verge of tears; she was far thinner than she used to be, an old woman with barely anything left of her body.

'Listen, Norbert . . .'

He got up and went to splash his face with water, making a noise on purpose to prevent her from speaking. It was better so.

'Won't you listen to me?'

'What's the use?'

'Are you angry with me?'

'No. . . . Try to sleep . . .'

'If you'd give me the second ampoule . . .'

'No. . . . Not before nine o'clock.'

'What time is it now?'

He looked for his watch, which he had laid down somewhere, and was some little time finding it.

'Half past five . . .'

'All right . . .'

She waited, resignedly. He did not know what to do or where to go. He tried to distract himself by listening to the familiar sounds of the hotel, where he knew nearly all the lodgers. He could tell who had come in, he recognized voices that only reached him as faint murmurs.

'It would be better to let me die . . .'

The doctor had warned him. A short while before, while the doctor was still there, she had played the same trick on them, but then it had been on an impulse; at the height of her hysteria she had seized a pair of scissors that were lying about and tried to cut her wrists.

Now she was trying it out again, deliberately, and he was unmoved. She persisted: 'Why won't you let me die?'

'Go to sleep!'

'You know I can't sleep like this.'

There was nothing to be done about it! He went with a sigh to lean against the attic window, from which he could see his red roofs once again and hear the noises from the flower market starting up. This was the moment when his night watchman in the Rue Montorgueil, in his little cubbyhole, would be warming up his morning coffee in a small blue enamel coffee-pot and drinking it out of a rustic bowl with a pattern of big flowers. The Halles would be in full swing now.

And for years, a little later than this, in a double bed in the Rue Ballu, he had woken of his own accord, invariably at the same time, and slipped noiselessly out of the bed, leaving a lean, hard-featured woman lying there. While he washed and dressed with meticulous care, as he did everything else, an alarm clock would sound over his head and the tall youth who was his son would yawn and get up, with his hair on end and a sour taste in his mouth.

Had his daughter made it up with her mother-in-law, now that he was no longer there? Probably not. And when she was short of money she had no one to turn to. It was strange. She had two children. Presumably she loved them, as all mothers do – or was that all a fairy tale? – and yet she lived without bothering about them, often staying out late at night with her husband.

It was the first time since his escape that he had thought about them so clearly. Indeed, he could hardly be said to have thought of them at all.

He felt no pity for them. . . . He was quite cold. He saw them one and all as they really were. He saw them far better than before, when he used to meet them almost every day.

He had ceased to feel indignant.

'What are you thinking about?'

'Nothing . . .'

'I'm thirsty . . .'

'Shall I get you some coffee?'

'If you would . . .'

He went downstairs, in his slippers, with his shirt still unfastened over his chest. The brasserie was closed. He had to go outside. At the end of the street he caught a glimpse of the sea. He made his way to a small bar.

'Would you give me a small pot of coffee and a cup? I'll bring them back presently.'

'Is it for Gerly's?'

They were used to this in the neighbourhood. People from Gerly's were always fetching things at the most unexpected time of day.

253

On the counter there were some hot croissants in a basket, and he ate one, and drank a cup of coffee, gazing vaguely into the street, and finally carried off, for Thérèse, the small pot, a cup, two pieces of sugar in his pocket and some croissants.

Early-morning people met him and turned back to stare at one who was so obviously a nocturnal creature. A tram passed.

He climbed up to his attic again and guessed that Thérèse had been up. Perhaps she had hurriedly got back into bed on hearing his step on the stair?

She was no longer quite the same. She had a fresher look, perhaps because she had powdered her face, touched up the delicate pink of her cheeks and painted her thin lips afresh. She was sitting up in bed with a pillow behind her back.

She gave him a wan, grateful smile and he promptly understood. He laid the coffee and croissants on the chair, within her reach.

'How kind you are' . . . she said.

He was not kind. She followed him with her gaze. They were both thinking of the same thing. She was scared. He opened the drawer of the bedside table and, as he expected, the ampoule was not to be seen. The syringe was there, fitted up and still wet.

With a pleading look, she stammered out: 'Don't be cross with me . . .'

He was not cross with her. He was not *even* cross with her. And a few minutes later, as she was drinking her coffee, he caught sight of the empty ampoule gleaming on the sloping roof, just below the attic window.

NINE

Leaving Nice proved as simple as leaving Paris. There was no conflict, there was practically no decision to be taken.

About ten o'clock Monsieur Monde closed his door quietly and went down four flights to knock gently on Julie's door. He had to knock several times. A sleepy voice asked sulkily: 'Who's there?'

'It's me.'

He heard her coming, bare-footed, to open the door. Then, without even a glance at him, her eyelids half glued together, she hurried back to the warmth of her bed. But though almost asleep again, she asked him (and her face reflected her effort to keep on the surface): 'What did you want?'

'I'd have liked you to stay up there for a while. I have to go out.'

Julie, struggling against sleep, breathed good-naturedly: 'Wait a minute . . .'

This was the last time, he knew, that he would be in her room, breathing its intimate atmosphere, its cheap pungent scents. The bed was warm. As usual, her underclothes lay in a heap on the rug.

'Pass me a glass of water . . .'

The tooth glass would do. She sat up, asking as though in a dream:

'Anything wrong?'

'It's all right. She's asleep. Only I think it'd be better not to leave her alone.'

'Just as you like. Should I get dressed?'

'It doesn't matter.'

She put on no underclothes, no stockings or panties. She merely slipped a brief woollen dress over her body, and thrust her bare feet into high-heeled shoes. On the other hand she peered into the mirror to powder her shiny face and put on some rouge, and passed a comb through her hair.

'What am I to tell her if she wakes?'

'That I'm coming back.'

She went up the stairs, docile and indolent, while he went down and entered the brasserie. This morning he was not wearing his drab, night-worker's suit, but the more elegant outfit, the flannel trousers and double-breasted blue jacket that Julie had made him buy on the first day.

He had a call put through to Paris and went to wait for it in the brasserie where the proprietor was doing his accounts.

'Are you leaving?'

It seemed self-evident to him, as it had to Julie.

The telephone conversation was a long one. At the end of the line Doctor Boucard uttered profuse and interminable exclamations. Monsieur Monde, who knew that he was rather scatterbrained, repeated each of his injunctions several times.

Then he made his way to the shop where he had bought the suit he was now wearing. He found another, more formal, more suitable for Monsieur Monde, and they promised to alter it by the afternoon.

When he returned to the hotel he found the two women sitting amicably on the bed together. They fell silent as he came in. Curiously enough Julie's expression had now become more respectful and more subdued.

'Am I to get dressed?' Thérèse asked almost gaily. And she added, pouting: 'Couldn't we all three have lunch together?'

It was all of little consequence now. He accepted all their whims, including the choice of a somewhat luxurious restaurant and a somewhat over-splendid menu. From time to time Thérèse's eyes betrayed anxiety and her features grew tense. At last she asked him, tremblingly:

'Could you get any?'

He had some in his pocket and, with their coffee, he slipped her an ampoule; she knew what he held in his closed hand, took her bag and rushed off to the toilet.

Julie gazed after her and stated with conviction: 'She's lucky!'

'Oh?'

'If you knew how happy she is! The things she said about you this morning . . .'

He neither smiled nor frowned. At Gerly's Hotel a money order, telegraphed by Boucard, awaited him. Leaving the two women together again, he went back to the tailor's and then to the station to reserve his seats. The train left at eight o'clock. Julie, at the station, was torn between laughter and tears.

'Funny how it makes me feel,' she said. 'Will you think of me from time to time?'

Monsieur Monde and Thérèse got on to the train, had a meal in the dining-car and then went off to their compartment in the sleeping-car.

'You'll give me another tonight, won't you?'

He went out into the corridor so as not to see the gesture that he anticipated, the sharp, almost professional jab of the needle into the thigh. He still mistrusted her, and gave her the top berth. He himself slept very little, and kept waking with a start.

He was very calm and clear-headed. He had thought of everything. He had even informed the Detective-Inspector, before he left, that he was taking Thérèse to Paris.

At the station a new morning, a new town awaited them and Doctor Boucard was waving to them from the end of the platform.

Monsieur Monde and Thérèse walked the length of the train, jostled by other travellers. She dared not cling to his arm. She was surprised to see that someone had come to meet them.

'Will you excuse me for a moment?'

He watched her out of the corner of his eye while he exchanged a few words with his friend, who could not conceal his amazement.

'Come here, Thérèse. Let me introduce one of my very good friends, Doctor Boucard.'

She looked suspicious.

'Let's get out of this crowd first . . .'

Once outside he sought a taxi and made her get in; the doctor followed.

'I'll see you presently. You can trust him. He's not taking you where you might suppose.'

The taxi moved away just as Thérèse began to struggle, protesting loudly at her betrayal.

'Don't be afraid,' Boucard said with some embarrassment. 'Norbert telephoned me to rent a comfortable flat for you. I was lucky enough to find one right away, in Passy. You'll be at home; you'll be quite free. I think you'll have *everything* you want . . .'

Thérèse's pointed features expressed surprise mingled with a kind of fury.

'Had he promised you anything different?'

'No . . .'

'What had he told you?'

'Nothing. . . . I don't know . . .'

She bit her lips, vexed with herself for having been so stupid.

Only a short while before, in the train, when the smell of Paris was already in the air, she had laid a hand on Monde's arm and had been on the point of bursting into tears, perhaps of prostrating herself in gratitude. They had been standing in the corridor and only the arrival of a fellow-traveller had prevented her from doing so.

'I'm just a fool!' she spat out in a tone of contempt.

For she had believed that it was for her sake that he was coming back!

*

At ten o'clock Monsieur Monde, before making his way to the Rue Ballu, got out of his taxi near the Halles and walked the short distance to the Rue Montorgueil. The weather was dull this morning. Perhaps it had been dull in Paris all the time he had been in the South? The absence of sunlight only made things sharper and clearer. Their outlines showed up starkly.

A lorry came out of the porch, and he stepped back to let it pass. He went into the covered courtyard, turned left and entered the office which he used to share with Monsieur Lorisse. The latter, overcome with emotion, began trembling and repeating in an excited stutter: 'Monsieur Norbert! ... Monsieur Norbert! ...' Then, suddenly embarrassed, he introduced a personage whom Monsieur Monde had not noticed and who was sitting at his own desk.

'Monsieur Dubourdieu. ... An administrator whom the Bank ...'

'I understand.'

'If you knew in what a fix ...'

He listened. He looked. The whole thing, including Lorisse, including the administrator in his funereal black, made him think of a stiffly posed photograph. He went out of the room in the middle of their conversation, leaving the astonished Lorisse with his sentence unfinished, and made his way to the other offices.

When he reached the last of the row, he looked through the glazed door and saw his son. The boy happened to look up, saw him too, opened his mouth and sprang up.

As he opened the door Monsieur Monde saw him turn pale,

sway and topple over. By the time he stood at his son's side, the boy was stretched out on the dusty floor and they were slapping his hands to revive him.

Later on, in the lunch break, two clerks who had witnessed the scene discussed it with a warehouseman, and one of them asserted, almost indignantly:

'He didn't turn a hair. He was completely unmoved. He just looked him up and down and waited for him to come to. You'd almost have said he was annoyed about it. When the kid opened his eyes and stood up at last, in fear and trembling, the boss merely gave him a kiss on the forehead and said: "Good morning, son!" A man that everyone had believed dead for the past three months and more!'

However, when Monsieur Monde went for lunch to his usual restaurant in the Halles, his son was his sole companion. He had not telephoned to the Rue Ballu, and had forbidden Monsieur Lorisse to do so.

'So you really believed I'd never come back? . . . How's your sister?'

'I see her from time to time, secretly. Things are going very badly. They're up to their ears in debt and they're suing Mother.'

Alain seemed reluctant to meet his eyes, yet Monsieur Monde had the feeling that in time he would succeed in making friends with his son. At one point he involuntarily fixed his gaze on the lace-edged handkerchief, and the lad noticed this and blushed. A few minutes later he left the room to visit the toilet, and when he returned the handkerchief had disappeared.

'I don't know very much about it, but I think all the trouble was about the safe . . .'

'Your mother had the key . . .'

'Apparently that's not enough . . .'

Monsieur Monde wasted no time. By three o'clock he was with his bank manager. At five, and not before, he stepped out of a taxi in front of the house in the Rue Ballu. The concierge gave vent to exclamations. Monsieur Monde, however, was simply coming home, not even like a returning traveller, since he had no luggage; he just rang and went in, as he had done every day for years and years.

'Is Madame up there?'

'She's just gone out with the car. I heard her giving Joseph the address of her solicitor.'

Nothing had changed. On the staircase he met the maid – his wife's personal maid – who gave such a start that she nearly dropped the tray she was carrying.

'Look here, Rosalie . . .'

'Yes, monsieur?'

'I don't want you to telephone to Madame.'

'But, Monsieur . . .'

'I tell you I don't want you to telephone to Madame. That's all!'

'Has Monsieur had a good journey?'

'Very good.'

'Madame's going to be . . .'

He did not listen to any more, but went up into his own room, where with evident satisfaction he put on his own clothes again. Then he went down into his study, the old study with the coloured glass windows which had been his father's and his grandfather's.

Nothing was obviously changed there, and yet he knit his brows. He tried to find out what was wrong. Then he saw that the ash-tray was missing from the desk, as were the two pipes which he only smoked in private, in this room. In their place he saw a pair of spectacles, his wife's, and on the blotter a file of unfamiliar business papers.

He rang, and handed the lot to Rosalie.

'Take these up to Madame's room.'

'Yes, monsieur.'

'Do you know where my pipes are?'

'I think they've been put away in the bottom of the cupboard.'

'Thank you.'

He was trying out the room, as one might try out a new suit of clothes, or rather as one tries oneself out a suit one has not worn for a long time. Not once did he look at himself in the glass. On the other hand, he went to press his face against the window pane, in his usual place, and beheld once again the same bit of pavement below him, the same windows over the way. At one of these, on the third floor, a little old woman who hadn't left her room for many years was staring at him through her curtains.

He had just lit a pipe, and the smoke was drifting cosily through the room, when he recognized the sound of his own car drawing up in front of the house, and the creak of the door as Joseph opened it.

At the same moment the telephone bell rang and he lifted the receiver.

'Hullo! Yes, speaking. . . . What? . . . Did it go all right? . . . Poor woman! I expected that . . .'

Steps on the stair. The door opened. He saw his wife framed in the doorway. But he went on listening to Boucard.

'Yes, yes, she'll get used to it. . . . No, I won't go. . . . What's that? . . . What's the use? . . . So long as she's got what she needs . . .'

Madame Monde stood there motionless. He looked at her calmly and saw her little black eyes lose some of their hardness, and betray, possibly for the first time, a certain confusion.

'Right. . . . Tomorrow. . . . See you tomorrow, Paul. . . . Thanks. . . . Yes, yes. . . . Thank you!'

He hung up, quite calmly. His wife came forward. Her throat was so constricted that she could scarcely speak.

'You've come back,' she said.

'As you see.'

'If you knew how I've suffered . . .'

She was sniffling, and wondering whether she ought to fling herself into his arms. He merely brushed her forehead with his lips and clasped both her wrists for a second, in an affectionate gesture.

She had noticed everything, he was well aware: the pipes and the ash-tray, the absence of the spectacles and the file. She felt impelled to remark: 'You haven't changed.'

He replied, with that composure which he had brought back with him, and under which could be glimpsed a terrifying abyss: 'Yes, I have.'

That was all. He was relaxed. He was part of life, as flexible and fluid as life itself.

Without irony, he went on to say: 'I know you had some

trouble about the safe. I'm very sorry. I never thought for one moment about that formula which I've signed so many times: "*I certify that my spouse . . .*" '

'Don't say it!' she begged.

'Why not? I'm alive, as you see. I shall presumably have to go and make a statement to that effect before the police, whom you must have notified of my disappearance . . .'

He spoke of it without a trace of embarrassment or shame. He said no more, however, gave no explanation.

Every week, or almost, Julie would write to him on headed notepaper from Gerly's or Le Monico. She told him news of Monsieur René, of Charlotte, of all his acquaintances. And he would answer her.

Boucard, meanwhile, talked to him every evening at the Cintra about Thérèse, who longed to see him again.

'You ought to go there once, at least.'

'What's the use?'

'Just imagine, she believed that it was for her sake that you . . .'

Monsieur Monde looked him quite calmly in the eyes. 'And so?'

'She was dreadfully disappointed.'

'Oh!'

And Boucard desisted, probably because like everyone else he was deeply impressed by this man who had laid all ghosts, who had lost all shadows, and who stared you in the eyes with cold serenity.

MORE ABOUT PENGUINS, PELICANS,
PEREGRINES AND PUFFINS

For further information about books available from Penguins please write to Dept EP, Penguin Books Ltd, Harmondsworth, Middlesex UB7 0DA.

In the U.S.A.: For a complete list of books available from Penguins in the United States write to Dept DG, Penguin Books, 299 Murray Hill Parkway, East Rutherford, New Jersey 07073.

In Canada: For a complete list of books available from Penguins in Canada write to Penguin Books Canada Ltd, 2801 John Street, Markham, Ontario L3R 1B4.

In Australia: For a complete list of books available from Penguins in Australia write to the Marketing Department, Penguin Books Australia Ltd, P.O. Box 257, Ringwood, Victoria 3134.

In New Zealand: For a complete list of books available from Penguins in New Zealand write to the Marketing Department, Penguin Books (N.Z.) Ltd, Private Bag, Takapuna, Auckland 9.

In India: For a complete list of books available from Penguins in India write to Penguin Overseas Ltd, 706 Eros Apartments, 56 Nehru Place, New Delhi 110019.

Simenon in Penguin

MAIGRET'S PIPE

MAIGRET loses his favourite briar pipe, and finds himself investigating a much more mysterious disappearance ...

A MAN lies slumped in a first-class compartment on the train from Berlin, a needle pierced through his heart ...

DIGITALIS mixed with bicarbonate of soda produces a nasty accident – or murder?

In these and fifteen more intriguing cases Maigret applies wit and intuition, his genius for detection and a certain *je ne sais quoi* ...

MAIGRET AND THE GHOST

Three stories by the writer who blends, *par excellence*, the light and the shadow, cynicism and compassion ...

Maigret and the Hotel Majestic finds Superintendent Maigret investigating the murder of a woman whose strangled body was found in a hotel basement. There are several suspects ...

Three Beds in Manhattan is the poignant story of two lonely people who meet in a bar in Greenwich Village. Unable to part, they drift from one sordid bar to another as they talk over their past lives and muse on the future.

In *Maigret and the Ghost* a plain-clothes detective is shot and the young woman with whom he had been spending the night vanishes. Maigret's investigations lead him into the world of art-collecting as the story draws to a dramatic close.

and

MAIGRET AT THE CROSSROADS

MAIGRET IN EXILE

MAIGRET MEETS A MILORD

MAIGRET'S RIVAL

ACT OF PASSION

THE IRON STAIRCASE/THE TRAIN

THE MAN WHO WATCHED THE TRAINS GO BY/
THE BRETON SISTERS

A CHOICE OF PENGUINS

☐ *Further Chronicles of Fairacre* **'Miss Read'** £3.95

Full of humour, warmth and charm, these four novels – *Miss Clare Remembers, Over the Gate, The Fairacre Festival* and *Emily Davis* – make up an unforgettable picture of English village life.

☐ *Callanish* **William Horwood** £1.95

From the acclaimed author of *Duncton Wood*, this is the haunting story of Creggan, the captured golden eagle, and his struggle to be free.

☐ *Act of Darkness* **Francis King** £2.50

Anglo-India in the 1930s, where a peculiarly vicious murder triggers 'A terrific mystery story . . . a darkly luminous parable about innocence and evil' – *The New York Times*. 'Brilliantly successful' – *Daily Mail*. 'Unputdownable' – *Standard*

☐ *Death in Cyprus* **M. M. Kaye** £1.95

Holidaying on Aphrodite's beautiful island, Amanda finds herself caught up in a murder mystery in which no one, not even the attractive painter Steven Howard, is quite what they seem . . .

☐ *Lace* **Shirley Conran** £2.95

Lace is, quite simply, a publishing sensation: the story of Judy, Kate, Pagan and Maxine; the bestselling novel that teaches men about women, and women about themselves. 'Riches, bitches, sex and jetsetters' locations – they're all there' – *Sunday Express*

A CHOICE OF PENGUINS

☐ *West of Sunset* **Dirk Bogarde** £1.95

'His virtues as a writer are precisely those which make him the most compelling screen actor of his generation,' is what *The Times* said about Bogarde's savage, funny, romantic novel set in the gaudy wastes of Los Angeles.

☐ *The Riverside Villas Murder* **Kingsley Amis** £1.95

Marital duplicity, sexual discovery and murder with a thirties backcloth: 'Amis in top form' – *The Times*. 'Delectable from page to page . . . effortlessly witty' – C. P. Snow in the *Financial Times*

☐ *A Dark and Distant Shore* **Reay Tannahill** £3.50

Vilia is the unforgettable heroine, Kinveil Castle is her destiny, in this full-blooded saga spanning a century of Victoriana, empire, hatreds and love affairs. 'A marvellous blend of *Gone with the Wind* and *The Thorn Birds*. You will enjoy every page' – *Daily Mirror*

☐ *Kingsley's Touch* **John Collee** £1.95

'Gripping . . . I recommend this chilling and elegantly written medical thriller' – *Daily Express*. 'An absolutely outstanding storyteller' – *Daily Telegraph*

☐ *The Far Pavilions* **M. M. Kaye** £4.95

Holding all the romance and high adventure of nineteenth-century India, M. M. Kaye's magnificent, now famous, novel has at its heart the passionate love of an Englishman for Juli, his Indian princess. 'Wildly exciting' – *Daily Telegraph*

A CHOICE OF PENGUINS

☐ *Small World* **David Lodge** £2.50

A jet-propelled academic romance, sequel to *Changing Places.* 'A new comic débâcle on every page' – *The Times.* 'Here is everything one expects from Lodge but three times as entertaining as anything he has written before' – *Sunday Telegraph*

☐ *The Neverending Story* **Michael Ende** £3.50

The international bestseller, now a major film: 'A tale of magical adventure, pursuit and delay, danger, suspense, triumph' – *The Times Literary Supplement*

☐ *The Sword of Honour Trilogy* **Evelyn Waugh** £3.95

Containing *Men at Arms, Officers and Gentlemen* and *Unconditional Surrender*, the trilogy described by Cyril Connolly as 'unquestionably the finest novels to have come out of the war'.

☐ *The Honorary Consul* **Graham Greene** £1.95

In a provincial Argentinian town, a group of revolutionaries kidnap the wrong man . . . 'The tension never relaxes and one reads hungrily from page to page, dreading the moment it will all end' – Auberon Waugh in the *Evening Standard*

☐ *The First Rumpole Omnibus* **John Mortimer** £4.95

Containing *Rumpole of the Bailey*, *The Trials of Rumpole* and *Rumpole's Return*. 'A fruity, foxy masterpiece, defender of our wilting faith in mankind' – *Sunday Times*

☐ *Scandal* **A. N. Wilson** £2.25

Sexual peccadillos, treason and blackmail are all ingredients on the boil in A. N. Wilson's new, *cordon noir* comedy. 'Drily witty, deliciously nasty' – *Sunday Telegraph*

A CHOICE OF PENGUINS

☐ **Stanley and the Women** Kingsley Amis   £2.50

'Very good, very powerful . . . beautifully written . . . This is Amis *père* at his best' – Anthony Burgess in the *Observer*. 'Everybody should read it' – *Daily Mail*

☐ **The Mysterious Mr Ripley** Patricia Highsmith   £4.95

Containing *The Talented Mr Ripley, Ripley Underground* and *Ripley's Game*. 'Patricia Highsmith is the poet of apprehension' – Graham Greene. 'The Ripley books are marvellously, insanely readable' – *The Times*

☐ **Earthly Powers** Anthony Burgess   £4.95

'Crowded, crammed, bursting with manic erudition, garlicky puns, omnilingual jokes . . . (a novel) which meshes the real and personalized history of the twentieth century' – Martin Amis

☐ **Life & Times of Michael K** J. M. Coetzee   £2.95

The Booker Prize-winning novel: 'It is hard to convey . . . just what Coetzee's special quality is. His writing gives off whiffs of Conrad, of Nabokov, of Golding, of the Paul Theroux of *The Mosquito Coast*. But he is none of these, he is a harsh, compelling new voice' – Victoria Glendinning

☐ **The Stories of William Trevor**   £5.95

'Trevor packs into each separate five or six thousand words more richness, more laughter, more ache, more multifarious human-ness than many good writers manage to get into a whole novel' – *Punch*

☐ **The Book of Laughter and Forgetting**
Milan Kundera   £3.95

'A whirling dance of a book . . . a masterpiece full of angels, terror, ostriches and love . . . No question about it. The most important novel published in Britain this year' – Salman Rushdie

PENGUIN OMNIBUSES

☐ *Victorian Villainies*   £4.95

Fraud, murder, political intrigue and horror are the ingredients of these four Victorian thrillers, selected by Hugh Greene and Graham Greene.

☐ *The Balkan Trilogy* **Olivia Manning**   £5.95

This acclaimed trilogy – *The Great Fortune, The Spoilt City* and *Friends and Heroes* – is the portrait of a marriage, and an exciting recreation of civilian life in the Second World War. 'It amuses, it diverts, and it informs' – Frederick Raphael

☐ *The Penguin Collected Stories of*
   Isaac Bashevis Singer   £4.95

Forty-seven marvellous tales of Jewish magic, faith and exile. 'Never was the Nobel Prize more deserved . . . He belongs with the giants' – *Sunday Times*

☐ *The Penguin Essays of George Orwell*   £4.95

Famous pieces on 'The Decline of the English Murder', 'Shooting an Elephant', political issues and P. G. Wodehouse feature in this edition of forty-one essays, criticism and sketches – all classics of English prose.

☐ *Further Chronicles of Fairacre* **'Miss Read'**   £3.95

Full of humour, warmth and charm, these four novels – *Miss Clare Remembers, Over the Gate, The Fairacre Festival* and *Emily Davis* – make up an unforgettable picture of English village life.

☐ *The Penguin Complete Sherlock Holmes*
   Sir Arthur Conan Doyle   £5.95

With the fifty-six classic short stories, plus *A Study in Scarlet, The Sign of Four, The Hound of the Baskervilles* and *The Valley of Fear*, this volume contains the remarkable career of Baker Street's most famous resident.

PENGUIN OMNIBUSES

☐ *Life with Jeeves* **P. G. Wodehouse** £3.50

Containing *Right Ho, Jeeves, The Inimitable Jeeves* and *Very Good, Jeeves!* in which Wodehouse lures us, once again, into the evergreen world of Bertie Wooster, his terrifying Aunt Agatha, his man Jeeves and other eggs, good and bad.

☐ *The Penguin Book of Ghost Stories* £4.95

An anthology to set the spine tingling, including stories by Zola, Kleist, Sir Walter Scott, M. R. James, Elizabeth Bowen and A. S. Byatt.

☐ *The Penguin Book of Horror Stories* £4.95

Including stories by Maupassant, Poe, Gautier, Conan Doyle, L. P. Hartley and Ray Bradbury, in a selection of the most horrifying horror from the eighteenth century to the present day.

☐ *The Penguin Complete Novels of Jane Austen* £5.95

Containing the seven great novels: *Sense and Sensibility, Pride and Prejudice, Mansfield Park, Emma, Northanger Abbey, Persuasion* and *Lady Susan*.

☐ *Perfick, Perfick!* **H. E. Bates** £3.95

The adventures of the irrepressible Larkin family, in four novels: *The Darling Buds of May, A Breath of French Air, When the Green Woods Laugh* and *Oh! To Be in England*.

☐ *Famous Trials*
   Harry Hodge and James H. Hodge £3.95

From Madeleine Smith to Dr Crippen and Lord Haw-Haw, this volume contains the most sensational murder and treason trials, selected by John Mortimer from the classic Penguin Famous Trials series.

PENGUIN OMNIBUSES